VISIONS FROM TWO CONTINENTS

The Life of Australian/ American Artist Sheila Buchanan Buell

REVISED

PATSY BUELL STIERNA

CONTENTS

Author's Note...v

CHAPTER 1: Australia Equals Home 1

CHAPTER 2: The First War 17

CHAPTER 3: Drought..28

CHAPTER 4: 1920-1921 33

CHAPTER 5: The Decision...39

CHAPTER 6: The Journey 46

CHAPTER 7: St. Cloud, Minnesota..58

CHAPTER 8: St. Paul, Minnesota...68

CHAPTER 9: Joy to Grief..78

CHAPTER 10: What Now? 87

CHAPTER 11: Driving 96

CHAPTER 12: Back to St. Paul...105

CHAPTER 13: Losing 119

CHAPTER 14: Married 130

CHAPTER 15: Changing Times 138

CHAPTER 16: The Decade of Disconsolation 146

CHAPTER 17: On My Own 157

CHAPTER 18: Unity 168

CHAPTER 19: Dexter 181

CHAPTER 20: Pregnant? 195

CHAPTER 21: The War Ends and 207

CHAPTER 22: A New Life 219

CHAPTER 23: A New Addition 229

CHAPTER 24: The Organic Farm 243

CHAPTER 25: Painting and Farming 251

CHAPTER 26: Everything Changes 262

CHAPTER 27: Aftermath 269

CHAPTER 28: Two Years Later 279

CHAPTER 29 : Afterword: Patsy's Voice 286

Bibliography 287

AUTHOR'S NOTE

This book is a re-creation of the stories my mother, Sheila Buchanan Buell, told me and other members of the family. Like many adults left orphaned when the last parent dies, my brothers and I were overwhelmed when she passed. She left us her paintings, photos and the letters she and her sisters had saved over the years. Just as she would not sell her paintings because they were her life, we could not throw these away.

She always said, "I don't need to watch soap operas. I lived one. Soap operas are for people who haven't lived."

I tried to write this as a biography to go with her pictures. It was a disaster, a series of tragedies, and did not show her strength and resilience or the joy she radiated almost every day. It did not tell her story as she would have told it.

So this is written in her voice, with footnotes indicating what is real and what I have extrapolated from facts learned during my research.

I want to thank my family in the United States, Canada, England and Australia, both living and deceased, for helping me research and write this story. An extra shout-out to my writing groups in Austin, Texas, and Door County, Wisconsin, for reading my worst drafts and helping me rewrite, and rewrite again.

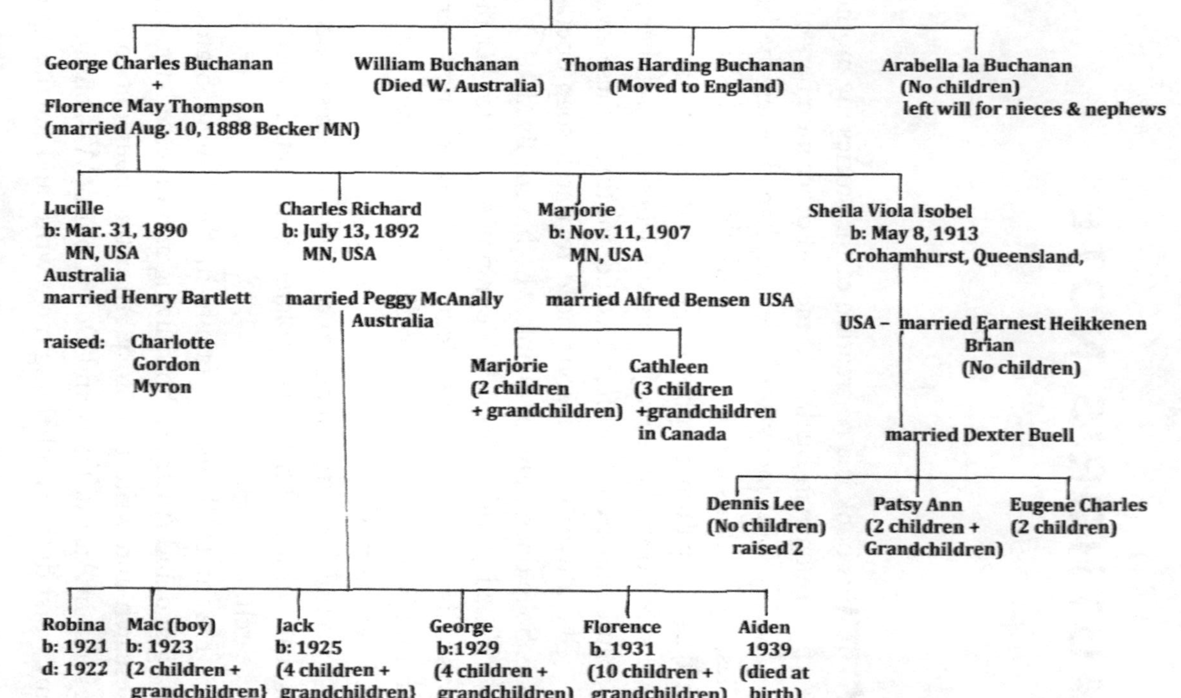

Sheila's Family Chart

Charles Todd Buchanan b: 1831 Dublin, Ireland

married Arabella Harding Going

George Charles Buchanan
+
Florence May Thompson
(married Aug. 10, 1888 Becker MN)

William Buchanan
(Died W. Australia)

Thomas Harding Buchanan
(Moved to England)

Arabella la Buchanan
(No children)
left will for nieces & nephews

Lucille
b: Mar. 31, 1890
MN, USA
Australia
married Henry Bartlett

raised: Charlotte
Gordon
Myron

Charles Richard
b: July 13, 1892
MN, USA

married Peggy McAnally
Australia

Marjorie
b: Nov. 11, 1907
MN, USA

married Alfred Bensen USA

Marjorie
(2 children
+ grandchildren)

Cathleen
(3 children
+grandchildren
in Canada

Sheila Viola Isobel
b: May 8, 1913
Crohamhurst, Queensland,

USA – married Earnest Heikkenen
Brian
(No children)

married Dexter Buell

Dennis Lee
(No children)
raised 2

Patsy Ann
(2 children +
Grandchildren)

Eugene Charles
(2 children)

Robina
b: 1921
d: 1922

Mac (boy)
b: 1923
(2 children +
grandchildren}

Jack
b: 1925
(4 children +
grandchildren}

George
b:1929
(4 children +
grandchildren)

Florence
b. 1931
(10 children +
grandchildren)

Aiden
1939
(died at
birth)

AUSTRALIA EQUALS HOME

I always dreamed of going home. My sisters, all older than me, never talked about Australia. They were born in Minnesota so North America was their home.

I was born Sheila Buchanan on May 8, 1913, in Crohamhurst, Queensland, Australia. On my birth certificate[1] from the District of Cabolture in the State of Queensland, it said that my father, George Charles Buchanan, was 55 years old. His profession was farmer, and he was born in Dublin, Ireland.

Dr. George C. Buchanan,
my father

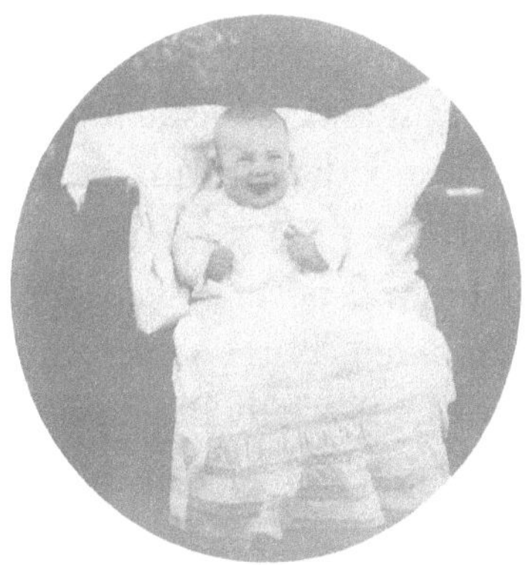

Sheila at Christening

---

1. Copy of birth certificate dated from May 10, 1922. On file. The birth certificate has colony crossed out, showing how recently Queensland had become a country not a colony.

The birth certificate listed Mother as Florence Mary (it was actually May), formerly Thompson, and said she was 40 years old,[2] born in St. Cloud, Minnesota, United States of America. It also listed my sister Lucille age 22, my brother Charles 20, and my sister Marjorie, 6 years old on the day I was born.

Thinking of my childhood I remembered every detail of the large hill that was called Candle Mountain. Our home was at the base of Candle Mountain. As I created this pastel painting I was home again, heading up the path. Once again I walked up to the top of it. I sat where the aborigines had made signal fires and looked out into the distance at Moreton Bay and the sailboats floating there.[3] My sister Marjorie first saw this painting when it hung in a show at Northrup Auditorium on the University of Minnesota campus. Marjorie stared at it and then she looked at me in amazement.

Florence May Buchanan, my mother.

"Why I didn't think you remembered. That's exactly how it looked."

Marjorie never talked about living in Australia. I know she remembered, but I never thought she cared. She liked North America, especially Beamsville, Ontario, Canada, where she lived as a little girl. She never talked about Papa either.

---

2. Mother's age is not correct on this document. She was actually 45 years old when I was born.

3. This is paraphrased directly from a story Sheila wrote for her high school English class. She said nobody really cared much about listening to stories about her home. Original on file with the author.

"Candle Mountain." Sheila Buchanan Buell c. 1950. To see painting visit blog: Visionsfromtwocontinents.blog

Mother told me that she cried the whole first year we were in Australia. I was born during that first year. She arrived in Brisbane in May, 1912, and I was born the following May, conceived on the Australian continent. Like a baby chick that imprints on its mother when it hatches from the egg, I imprinted on my Papa. At naptime I curled up in my Papa's arms. He napped too, in utter contentment. When I walked I followed him all over the place, taking multiple steps to keep pace with him. When I began to speak, I did not talk like my American sisters or my mother, but rather it was Papa's Oxford accent that came out of my mouth. I heard every word that came out from under the mustache and above the beard. My questions were never ending.

"Ha, ha, ha, ha," laughter screamed from the trees.

"Papa wahts' dat?" I would ask just learning how to talk.

"That is a kookaburra telling you that life is to be laughed at."

I heard a loud screeching sound.

Eggs in the tall grass, red brown snake by the tree in the left corner. Watercolor by SV Buell circa 1950. To see painting visit blog: Visionsfromtwocontinents.blog

"Papa wahts' dat?"

"Why, that's a sulphur-crested cockatoo scolding you: 'Don't come close, this is my tree,'" he answered.

"Papa wahts' dat?"

"Shh stay still! Do not move." At first I saw nothing, but then following his pointed finger, I saw it. A large red-brown snake was slithering in the underbrush. We stood totally still, watching. A proud mother hen with her newly hatched chicks came marching by. She had hidden in the bush and hatched her eggs.

I wanted to scream, "Watch out," but I already knew better. The eastern brown snake is one of many deadly poisonous snakes in Queensland. If we startled him he might strike us.

The snake turned back towards the hen. I'm sure I heard him say, "Do not worry mother hen, I'm full today." Then he slithered away into the bush.[4]

---

4. Watercolor 1950's belongs to Sheila's granddaughter, Amanda Stierna Hovis. Sheila always told the story of the painting with the snake telling the hen not to worry.

My mouth stayed open as I watched the drama unfold before my eyes. I wished I could be that white bird in the tree watching all that goes on, warning the creatures on the ground. The cockatoo was not warning about us; he was warning the hen about the snake.

Papa spent time with me in a way he was never able to with my brother and sisters. My eldest sister Lucille was born in 1890, when Papa was a practicing physician in Little Falls, Minnesota, in the United States. Two years later, my brother Charles, was born. Papa practiced medicine in that small town of Little Falls for 15 years.

In 1907, the year my sister Marjorie was born, Marjorie said that Papa lost his medical license because he had a nervous breakdown.

Someone (perhaps the railroad magnet James J. Hill) told Papa where the Canadian Railroad planned to build, and where he should buy land in Ontario. He bought an orchard there along the publically unknown, upcoming, railroad corridor. He moved his family to Beamsville, Ontario, Canada, and he actively farmed for five years, even starting a fruit-growers co-operative.

My mother and sisters must have really loved that place, because they were always telling me about it. My sister Marjorie described that place in her autobiography written in 1936:

> *My memories of that Ontario home are very pleasant. I remember most plainly my pet pigeons, Jack and Jill, the families of kittens in the hayloft, the rides on my sled with old Rover pulling me, the walks in the woods and the excitement when the fruit was ripe and the pickers came. I think I loved everything about that place, and I cried bitterly when my father told me that we were going to a place where there would be no snow. Even the promise of a pony of my own to ride did not console me. I hid under the table as if that would postpone the inevitable.*[5]

---

5. Marjorie Buchanan 1936 essay. On file with author.

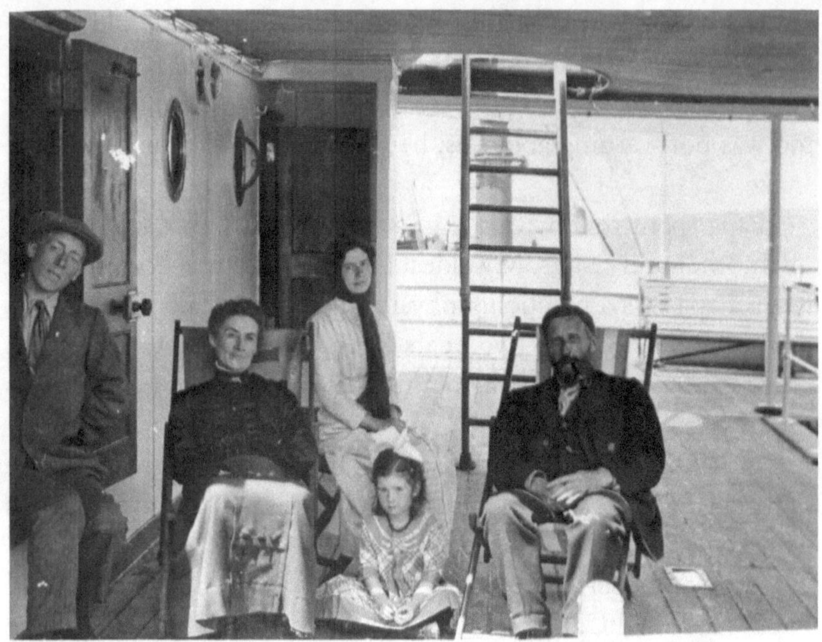

On the boat to Australia. Brother Charlie far left, Mama, sister Lucille, Marjorie sitting and then Papa.

Eventually Papa sold the land to the railroad for a very good profit. In 1912, he used that profit to move his family to Australia. Queensland, Australia, had elected the first labor government in the world in 1899, and he was certain that Australia was the place to create a society for the working man, a society different from what he had experienced growing up in Ireland, or again in the United States in the economic collapse of 1907. Plus there would be no snow, no endless winter. My mother was very opposed to this idea; Canada was fine, but Australia? What insanity!

He packed up everything he thought would be useful in this new life: his tools, all his books and his medical supplies. Although he was no longer practicing medicine, he would always help anyone in need. Mother dutifully packed the family linens, the dishes, and even the furniture for the move. Marjorie never forgot her grief when Papa made her leave her China doll behind.

Waimate, 1912

They traveled by train from Toronto to St. John, New Brunswick. On March 22, at 1:00 p.m., they sailed for Sydney on the freighter steamship the Waimate of the New Zealand Shipping Company. My sister Lucille kept a diary of the trip. I spent many hours reading and rereading it. Maybe someday I would take a ship to America. Here are my favorite parts of the diary:

> *The Waimate is a boat of eight thousand tons with a speed of ten knots. She has accommodations for twelve passengers but is not a regular passenger steamer and we made the run to Sydney without calling at any port and for 52 days never saw land. We went by the Cape of Good Hope.*[6]
>
> *I think we saw 8 ships on our voyage to Australia and steamers in the ports from all parts of the world. The "Waimate's" cargo was paper, farm machinery (Massey & Harris) motor cars, organs, (It was some from Guelph) and lumber. Marjorie and I were ill a little the first night and after that we were good sailors. The rest of the family can boast of never being seasick. The next day was spent getting my sea legs as the saying is so I could exercise on deck when the ship was rolling and making the acquaintance of Captain Ryley*

---

6. Quoted from diary of Lucille Buchanan.

and his officers. The Captain and officers (five) who are English gentlemen are our associates as we are the only passengers. We sit at a long table in the dining saloon with the Captain at the head of the table and we call him Father. Captain Ryley is an Oxford man, and all the crew are young unmarried men so we had jolly times. There is a piano, gramophone and two mandolins on board so we have plenty of music. The time is spent reading, playing cards (mostly bridge) chess, quoito, sewing and skipping for exercise, and the sailors put up a swing for Marjorie. Marjorie is happy as a lark playing hide and seek with the Captain. All have such enormous appetites. I fear the ship will run short of provisions.

Saturday Mar. 30

Captain inspects the boat every Saturday morning, and the stewards hear some sharp words if everything is not in perfect order. Boat drill in afternoon after afternoon tea 4:00, and the same every Saturday when weather permits. As soon as the alarm rings the officers and crew, except those on duty rush to the boat deck, just as they are and swing the life boats (six in number) out as quickly as possible, ready to lower.

Sunday Mar 31.

We are fifty miles from Bermuda and it is just like summer. The sun is so warm. It is my birthday. I had no idea the officers knew of it and to my great surprise they all came in the saloon to breakfast at 9 o'clock and wished me many happy returns of the day. Everyone was in white and the effect was very nice. Just before we finished lunch (12:30) the Steward placed a huge cake 1 foot across and six inches deep in front of me. Captain Ryley ordered it to be made and imagine the expression on my face when I saw it. After lunch Captain Ryley took us to his cabin where my health was drunk. In the afternoon saw a Portuguese man of war and spoke to a passenger boat from New Orleans. In the evening there was partial eclipse of the moon

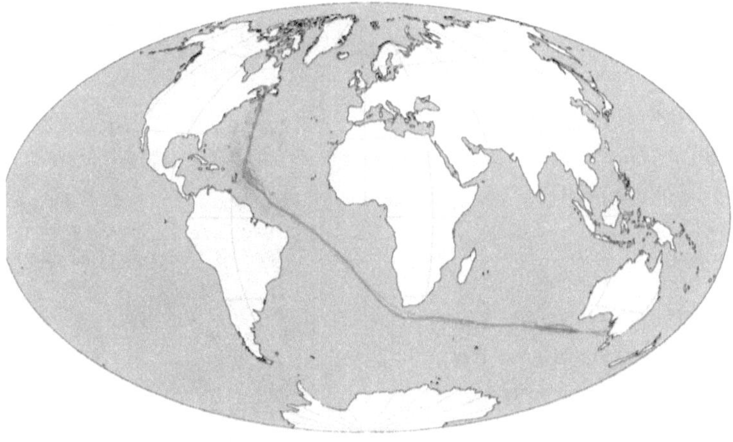

Path of the Waimate, based on Lucille's description.[7]

Good Friday April 5, sat in deck chair and watched others getting hot. We are in the tropics and it certainly is <u>hot</u>.

Easter Sunday April 7:

A beautiful day. The engines broke down early in morning & we were a drift for four hours. I woke up as soon as the engines stopped but the sea was so smooth that is was not unpleasant.

Monday April 8:

There was a perfect rainbow & it was beautiful to see it on the water. The Southern Cross, a group of stars in the shape of a cross, which is not seen in Canada, was very brilliant. Saw porpoises today. They are very large fish which run races with ships & jump many feet up in the air. There were hundreds of birds following us through the topics the chief ones were, ice birds, little white birds which look like butterflies on the water. Albatross, a beautiful black

---

7. www.freeworldmaps.net/printable/briesemeisterpdf. Path hand drawn by author.

bird with white spots on back and wings tipped with white, they glide through the air & sometimes touch the water with the tip of one wing & sometimes just touch the water with their feet when looking for fish. They measure fifteen feet across with wings spread & I never saw them flap their wings once. When the cook throws food overboard it is a grand sight to see three hundred birds riding on top of one wave & disappearing behind another. Murray Hawk, brown bird about the size of an albatross. Mother Cary's chickens, small black birds spotted with white,

Lucille in her twenties

Cape Hens, small brown birds, and Sea Hawks. Saw several whales spouting but none of them very near.

April 24

Steward calls me every morning at 6:15 when I have a salt water bath & go on deck to watch the birds & flying fish. I am always the first one of the family up & Papa told the Captain he thought I went on the bridge at four with the chief officers whom I was friendly with. But that was against the rules & the Skipper would laugh because he knew I wouldn't do anything like that.

April 25

Passed "Arawa" from England with emigrants for Australia. We talked to her with flags & learned that coal strike was over, the first news we learned after leaving Canada.

April 26

First real storm. Saw a sailor waving farewell to his cap which the wind blew over board. The ship rolls so you are first going down hill & then climbing up hill, if you try to walk about. The fiddles (thin pieces of wood to keep things on the table) have been on for sometime as there was quite a swell for a few days. When a big swell comes along we all have to stop eating & hang on to our plates & tea & very often come near sliding out of our chairs.

Sunday April 28

The storm increased during the night and my trunk slid across the cabin to my bunk & I fell out of my bunk on top of it. Papa came to see what the trouble was but I crawled into bed as quickly as possible & pretended I was asleep. During the day Charlie & I spent most of the time on deck watching the waves which were forty & forty-five feet high. We had to hang on & run the risk of a shower bath when we shipped a sea, but we hung on.

Friday May 3

The event of the day was a fight between a pantry boy & a steward. The steward had his face all cut up & Papa assisted in sewing up the wound; for punishment the boy was put in the coalhole to shovel coal. Soon after we left the tropics Captain Ryley gave me permission to visit the engine room. The chief engineer put me in charge of one of the young engineers & when we arrived down below where the principal machinery is another young chap was on watch & the two nearly had a fight because both wanted the honour of showing me around and I made peace by asking them both to take me. They took me in the bunkers where I put a shovelful of coal on the fire for luck & I oiled the engines. It was certainly hot work & we went in the tunnel (twenty feet below deck) to cool off & the chief engineer turned the lights off for a joke.

Monday May 12

Cape Otway in sight at 8 a.m. Our first glimpse of Australia & the first sight of land since leaving Canada. A pilot boat met us outside Port Phillip Heads entrance to Melbourne harbor to take us safely through the heads as it is dangerous for ships.

May 13

Moored at Victoria dock, Melbourne up the Yarsa river at 9:30 a.m.

One evening while in Melbourne two of the offices took me to see "Kismet" a play taken from the Arabian Nights. The players were all London artists & Lily Brayton who was born in Melbourne was the leading lady, she is the most beautiful woman I have seen, & her husband Oscar Ashe (leading actor) is ugly. We had dinner after the play & arrved at the ship just before twelve. They all joined in giving Charlie & I a good time & made us feel at home in a strange land. We visited the Botanic Gardens & saw a willow taken from Napoleon's grave, but if I try to tell everything this time I shall never have my letters ready from the next mail' I am taking notes from my diary.

Saturday May 18

We sailed again for Sydney, no pen can describe the beauty of that harbor. Left Sydney on Tuesday May 21 on the steamer "arawata" I arrived in Brisbane the capital of Queensland May 23. I forgot to mention that when we were coming out of Melbourne something went wrong with the steering gear & we were within ten minutes of being dashed to pieces on the rocks. However things were righted in time. We remained in Brisbane a few days & then came here a suburb of Brisbane. We are in a little cottage by the sea until Papa selects the land he wants & has a house. When you are at Grimsby Beach think of us at Manly by the sea. We could have come to Australia in three weeks via Vancouver B.C. or San Francisco but it is very expensive & we decided we had a far nicer time of the "Waimate", here we had the best of everything, & comfort. The boats from Vancouver heading for Australia are very crowded this year. Captain Ryley said we had a wonderful voyage. Only one bad storm & where bad weather was expected it was beautiful. It is winter in Australia from May to September & the weather is like June weather in Canada.

Queensland is semi tropical. Everything grows the year round & how you can raise every fruit (except peach) and vegetable you can think of. At Christmas everyone is trying to keep cool in place of having sleigh rides. The trees shed their bark in the fall & never loose their leaves.[8]

When they got to Australia in April of 1912, Papa left my mother and sisters in Manly, a suburb of Brisbane, while he and my brother Charles searched for our new home.[9] I have a letter he wrote in November, six months later, when he is still looking for the right place. "*The land is a long way short of pasture capabilities vouched for by the surveyors and rangers, also considerable short of the food arable land. This then makes me stop to tell you that I am not quite done thinking.*"[10] The land was very stony, which any Minnesota

---

8. The diary no longer survives; these are excerpts from a letter written June 24, 1912, to Mrs. Crain in Canada. In her letter Lucille quotes extensively from her diary. Letter is on file with the author.

9. *The Rockhampton Morning Bulletin.* Friday, June 8, 1912. Found at the Australian newspaper website. http://trove.nla.gov.au/ndp/del/article/53266462.

10. Letter on file with author.

farm girl like my mother would think was not very suitable farmland. He goes on to describe building a house and damming the creek to make pasture. "*We have marked our road into the building spot. It seems as if we could likely get some crop in. We can put corn in up to February, other things at all times.*" The letter continues on trying to show some concerns for Mother, "*I hope you are not feeling in any way bad. Certainly I am anxious about it. The problem of having you with proper comforts here when you come is bothering me a great deal. You must hang on to our money and keep it to spend after one sees what is needed here. Buy nothing but what must be bought.*"

This makes me think he did not really know Mother. I cannot remember Mother ever not hanging on to money. Perhaps he was talking about himself.

He goes on to describe native flora and fauna: "*I met with a monster Goanna (Australian lizard) 8 feet long at least and maybe 10 feet. Legs as big as ours, he made a noise on the ground like a horse galloping. He looked just like a small crocodile. I enclose some fronds from a small fern very plentiful on the mountain. . . . The survey men have just brought up a carpet snake that measured 9 feet exactly. . . .*" I can just imagine Mother's reaction to the snake. Mother was terrified of snakes. She may have screamed just reading it.

Papa finally came to his senses and realized that Mother was not up to totally untamed bush, especially since she was pregnant with me. He purchased a well-built home in Crohamhurst, Queensland, "*on Block 52V Parish Durundur from Mrs. Coburn the second owner. Mrs. Coburn was described as being 'landed gentry' employing others to do the work. Mrs. Coburn would dress up complete with gloves and parasol to inspect employees' work for the day*"[11] It was a day's buggy drive from Brisbane (60 miles). Landed gentry were the lords and ladies that Father despised, because they had the peasants do all their work. Our family did most of the work on the farm ourselves.

---

11. *Peachester Pioneers,* p. 32.

I am the baby held by my mother on the far side of this picture, my sister Marjorie is in the second row.

When we first moved to Crohamhurst Mother and Father enrolled Marjorie in Crohamhurst School. The first school in that isolated pioneer community, it had just been built on land donated by our neighbor, Owen Jones. The school was a long walk, or a short pony ride, down the mountain from our home. I was just a baby in my mother's arms when Marjorie started school there.[12]

My sister Marjorie wrote about this school in her autobiography:

I knew how to read before I went to school and was dreadfully bored at having to stand in a semi-circle and repeat in unison with the rest of the class c-a-t, cat; r-a-t, rat; m-a-t, mat. Our arithmetic was mainly a study of the complicated English monetary system of pounds, shillings, and Pence, with guineas, florin,

12. Picture from *Peachester Pioneers*, school days.

crowns, half-crown, half sovereigns, halfpence, and farthings mixed in for variety. My father did not approve of this school, because no algebra, French or Latin was taught. I think he almost welcomed the chance to teach me himself when, at ten years of age, I developed a heart weakness as the result of an attack of diphtheria and was unable to attend school.[13]

Marjorie was ten, and I was four, when school started at home. I don't remember it as well as she did. She said our Father taught, *"Latin, French, Gaelic, geography, Irish history, physiology, geometry, Bible history, and the catechism. He allowed me a holiday on every saint's day which I remembered."*

I learned how to write. I was left-handed and Father taught me how to write with my left hand. This was very progressive at the time as people who were left-handed were discriminated against. Mother worried about my being left-handed so when Father was not looking she had me switch hands and write with my right hand. I became ambidextrous and able to use both hands.

I was very little, but I remember Papa pacing up and down on the verandah, a long porch that surrounded our Queenslander home. He would walk back and forth and back and forth again and again. I knew he was worried about something, I just did not understand what on earth it could be.

---

13. Marjorie Buchanan, 1936 essay. On file.

CHAPTER 2

THE FIRST WAR

Bells were ringing across Australia in 1914, not for peace, but for war. I was too young in 1914 to remember the excitement, as Australia rushed to join World War One.

Father arrived in Australia just after Australia had elected the first labor government in the world. He was excited to be part of creating a new society where everyone had equal rights. Father had no love for the British Empire which he believed had enslaved Ireland, his home.

The argument for the war was that Australia should be involved not only for the love of the Empire, but to make Australia safe from German ambition, and German warships in the Pacific and Indian Oceans. The popular belief was that the Germans thought their destiny was to dominate Britain and seize all its colonies.[14] Father felt all of this was just so much nonsense and he wanted no part of this war.

My brother Charlie loved Australia. He wanted to volunteer in 1914, but he was not yet 21, and Father refused to give him permission. Lots of Australians were worried that the war would be over before they could fight and show their dedication to the Empire.

Charlie was always near home, helping on the farm and milking the cows. When he was older he went to work for a neighbor,

---

14. Keneally, *Australians: From Eureka to the Diggers.*

International Bell Dog. To see painting visit blog: Visionsfromtwo continents.blog

but came home often. I remember him striding across the pad-dock in long strides, a smile always dominating his face. He would whisk me up into his arms as he spoke to my sister Marjorie.

"Marjorie, what are you up to now."

"Why I'm reading *Robinson Crusoe*,"[15] she would answer in her all-knowing way.

---

15. *Robinson Crusoe*, a novel by Daniel Defoe, was first published in 1719.

Marjorie was always reading or writing and he would listen closely to her projects, teasing her about her red hair. It seemed he'd never get to me; then he tousled my blond curls sticking out every which way, and asked, "How is the wee one?" tossing me up into the air.

Suddenly Charlie did not come home anymore. I didn't know it, but on May 18, 1916, Charlie had enlisted in the 1st Australian Imperial Force in Brisbane with his friend, Frank Nicklin. Frank ater became Premier of Queensland. Charlie had not come home to say good-bye. He knew Father would not approve.

Charlie stated on his enlistment:

(1) He was born in Ontario, Canada. (Not true he was born in Little Falls, MN, USA.)

(2) He was 22 and 10/12 years of age, and

(3) His next-of-kin was his Mother, Mrs. Florence Buchanan, of Crohamhurst via Beerwah, Queensland.[16] (Not even mentioning his Father.)

Shortly after Charlie disappeared Father kept going off to Brisbane on business. One day when he was home our neighbor, Inigo Jones, came over. I remember their conversation and how it started with their usual polite exchanges.

"Good day, my dear sir."

"Good day to you. How are your weather observations going?" Father was always interested in Inigo's theories about the weather.

"Well, we may be in for a bit of a wet spell, but that is not what brings me here," said Inigo.

"What might I help you with?"

"Well I understand that you are involved in the campaign against conscription."

"What concern is that of yours?" Father asked.

"I should think the concern should be yours. You have a very brave son fighting for Australia. Your son needs reinforcements, and conscription would help your son."

---

16. From document sent from the Central Army Records Office, dated 1986, addressed to Rosalyn Buchanan.

"My son chose to go over there against my advice. I will not have anyone's son forced to fight for the Empire."

"This is not for the Empire, this is for Australia. Are you mad? Are you against Australia?"

"I am not against Australia. This war might be good for profits and capital, but it is the workers and their sons who are left to rot on the battlefields. Just because my son is there, I am going to do everything in my power to keep other sons from having to go."

"Empire, workers, what nonsense are you talking about? Australia has more at stake in the war even than England. Do you want the Huns over here raping our women?"

"They are not here. I'm not against Australia. I am against this bloody war, and sending our boys to fight in it!" yelled Father.

"You should be proud of your son Charles. He is a real Queenslander, that young chap!" Indigo yelled back.

"Don't tell me what I should think!" retorted Father.

I did not understand this yelling.[17] Never in my life had I heard him yell, and say "bloody." Why we did not talk like that. We did not even say pee and poop, we said number one and number two. I was young but I knew proper language. What had Charlie done to make Father so angry?

Mother just moped around the house, often starring out into space. Charlie did not come home to visit. I wondered where he had gone.

---

17. Dramatization from Sheila's memory of an argument her father had with Inigo Jones. Sheila told stories about how angry her Father was at Inigo Jones, and at Charlie's joining the fight.

One day Marjorie came running down the lane.

"Sheila, come quick. It's Charlie!"

I came running, looking for Charlie, looking for him to throw me up in the air. He was nowhere around. Where was he?

Marjorie laughed, "No he's not actually here, but he sent us a card. Look here is his picture."

I took the postcard in my hand and stared at it. Yes that was my brother Charlie, looking very fine indeed.

Father was often gone, traveling around Queensland campaigning against something called conscription, or the draft. Father was "a very vigorous opponent of conscription and did much good work fighting that menace to freedom in both the 1916 and 1917 campaigns."[18] In Australia there was a ballot and people got to vote for or against the draft. Just after Good Friday in 1917, Father wrote this poem.

Against or for Australia
For or against– it is a truth you say
An Empire red in lurid smoke of fire,
Love words half said breath that on pale lips expire
And crimson streams from nerveless veins astray?
The child footsteps on the street today,
For the new flowers fruit of old desire
For homes for homeless lifted from the mire
And free Australia, radiant on her way?

Against or for? And is the voice now dumb
"Do unto others"? life is but its sum
Spirit of this life's cloud, shade, and light
The measure of all years, all rules long span
Choose ye the way! Tis yet not day nor night,
Against or for the freed white soul of man[19]

---

18. *Peachester News.* Article from 1921 issue. On file.

19. Transcribed from original unpublished poem signed GCB, Good Friday, 1917.

Unknown to his father, Charlie also was writing poetry. In his diary entry of Thursday, May 24, 1917, Charlie wrote a poem about being in the trenches. The trenches had planks in them that the troops called Duck Boards:

Duck Boards[20]

Up and Down the Duck Boards
Up and down the duck boards, up and down again
Blinkin' at the star shells falling in the rain,
Thinking of the rations, if they're getting wet,
Thinking if there's any rum, and how much we will get,
Thinking if a bullet hurts, if there's any pain.
Yow! Here comes a bleeding bomb, up and down again

Up and down the duck boards, screaming at the moon,
.... On the bully strafe we got this afternoon,
Thinking how explosives make you jump and shake and sweat,
Thinking how you duck and run and hug the parapet,
Thinking of the next one - if it's joy or pain,
Hell it's getting hotter, duck and off again!

Up and down the duck boards, good and bad and norm,
From "stand to" in the evening, till "carry on" at morn,
Thinking all the blooming things you never thought before,
Thinking of the stunt last night and feeling pretty sore,
Thinking you chuck thinking up before you turn insane,
Two whiz-bangs, a nine-two-eight, then you think again.

Often it seemed like we were just waiting for a letter from Charlie or writing to him. I didn't like having to write to Charlie;

----

20. This poem was not written by Charlie, it was widely circulated among the troops.

it was all right writing to my big sister Lucille, but not Charlie. I wanted Charlie home. Lucille was away at the convent, studying and praying the war would end and that Charlie would come home.

It was late October, 1917, when the telegram arrived addressed to Mrs. Florence Buchanan. I remember it. It was all white with black edges all around it.

I was in the front garden doing my job, picking flowers to fill the bouquets Mother set out in each room. I heard her scream and scream, holding the envelope out like it contained the devil itself. I ran in, looked at the envelope and ran to get Father.

He came and held Mother in his arms, trying to calm her. He took the telegram and read it.

"Look my dearest. You must look. He is not dead, he is just in hospital. He will come home one day."

Mother stayed in his arms, sobbing.

So many others received the same telegram saying their son had died. We were lucky, my brother was still alive. For us that envelope was not a death notice.

Mustard gas shells at Ypres wounded Charlie on Oct. 16, 1917, on the western front. Mustard gas was a terrible weapon:

"Mustard gas burned all membranes. It burned the eyes, the face, the mucus membranes and the walls of the lung. . . . It created a pain in the head like acid laced water was invading the nasal passages, giving a sense of drowning."[21]

Charlie was in the hospital for many months and then in rehabilitation. Finally he got to work in the Army Post Office. We still did not hear much until finally we got this long letter January 10, 1918:

---

21. As described in Keneally, *The Daughters of Mars*, p. 388.

Dear Marjorie and Sheila,

I don't know how long it is since you wrote; I know I should have written long ago, but what one should do and what one does are generally different in the army. It is like standing on one's head compared to civilian life. . . .

Last spring before the battle of Messines, near Armentieres in Belgium in a part of the line then very quiet, I heard a curious thing. There is an invention we use called the microphone; it is placed underground, and through it you can hear every move-ment of the enemy, even what he is saying, and our side have extra good ones; of course much information is gained that way. But this night I happened to be the man on duty inside. In that pillbox over there, there is a woman putting children to bed, and I listened and heard her singing to them. It sounds very weird I can tell you, but no one bothered her. The German women often come in the line though and some have been captured fighting. You will be wondering what "pillboxes" are. They are cement blockhouses the Germans built when our armies were a considerable way back; old Hindenburg little dreaming that some day we would not only capture them but find them useful for shelter; their walls and roof are about nine feet thick, bound around with iron rods, but our shells have made holes in many of them; incidentally they were made of English cement imported via Holland. The weird-est night I remember though was at Ypres after the big advance in October I was on guard at midnight, the machine gun loaded ready for any unlucky German; it was very quiet, unusual for such a place of horror as Ypres, but it was a beast of night, cold, wet, suddenly in the still air a bloodhound bayed. The Germans use them for sentry, no one knew where the Germans were that night but I felt very nervous I can tell you, especially being ill with that dose of gas, but there were only two of us left to man the guns and it was a case of stick it out."[22]

---

22. From a letter dated January 10, 1918, written on Red Cross stationery. Original on file.

On October 22, 1918, he wrote from the field post office:

Dear Marjorie and Sheila,

Thank you both very much indeed for your lovely letter written of Aug 1. You are getting to be a very nice writer Marjorie, and so is Sheila for such a wee girl, but goodness me you won't be very wee when I come home again.

It is nice that a priest comes round occasionally; it makes you feel a bit more civilized. It's a good while since I have been at church for we have to work here on Sunday mornings. There are very big mails going out to Australia for the Christmas mail closes this week. . . .

I don't know when I am coming home, Marjorie, not until this job is finished. If I have anything to say in the matter, if the war lasts another year I will just about to be due a furlough at home, but I really expect that the war will end next spring, though of course, it is likely to be a year after that before I come home, that will be one happy day.

Sister Vaughan who took care of me when I was in the hospital in Plymouth came down here to see me this weekend, to see why I wasn't better, she is planning a trip to Australia to see the wives of Australian soldiers. If she comes as far as Brisbane she will come and see you all and tell you all about your soldier brother, a lot of things she ought not tell you I suppose, she is a very nice woman

There is an awful lot of sickness here now, and an awful lot of our poor boys have died. It is an epidemic of influenza,[23] and

---

23. The influenza pandemic of 1918-1919 killed more people than the Great War, known today as World War I (WWI), somewhere between 20 and 40 million people. It has been cited as the most devastating epidemic in recorded world history. More people died of influenza in a single year than in four years of the Black Death Bubonic Plague from 1347 to 1351. virus.stanford.edu. First paragraph.

it catches chaps who have just arrived from Australia before they get acclimated as per usual there have been no proper precautions taken until it was too late.

Mother says you do all the milking, Marjorie, that is very good for you Marjorie, and I am glad to hear it. Don't the cows ever get frightened of your hair?

I hope Peggy has been back to see you. She sent some lovely snapshots of herself, especially one taken with a pet lamb that was awfully good. You ask her for one, I hope you write to her.

Well dear sisters I must finish now. I hope you have a very merry Xmas and a happy new year, and that next Xmas we will be all together again for a real Xmas. Fondest love to you & Dad & Mum & Lucille & be sure to write for this is a lonely country unless you have tons of money then people look at you, such as they are.

Your very loving brother,
Charlie[24]

We read and reread that letter. It was a sad Christmas without Charlie tossing me into the air and laughing at my jokes. No one else seemed to be able to play with me like my brother. I hoped and prayed he would come home soon, before the next Christmas.

---

24. From copy of letter written October 22, 1918, from Field Post Office.

AUSTRALIAN

RED CROSS.

Hurdcott, England.

Jan 10, 1918

Dear Marjorie & Sheila

I don't know how long it is since you wrote, know I [...] but what one should do and what one does are generally different in the army, it's like standing on your head compared to civilian life.

I had a letter today from a Beamsville girl. She said our place was much the

First page of red cross letter

CHAPTER 3

DROUGHT

Company arriving via Beerwah-Crohamhurst mailcoach

harlie was right; the war did end by the next year. In fact, it ended November 11, 1918. From 1914-1918, of the 416,809 Australians who volunteered to fight overseas, 60,000 were killed, and 156,000 were wounded, gassed or taken prisoner.[25] This was a casualty rate of over 50%. Charlie was one of

25. First World War 1914-18 / The Australian War Memorial. https://www
.awm.gov.au/articles/atwar/first-world-war.

the many soldiers who were gassed. He returned to Australia from France on the hired transport "DELTA" on March 4, 1919, and was discharged from the Australian Imperial Force in Queensland on April 23, 1919.[26]

"Charlie, Charlie," I yelled, running down the lane to greet my lost brother.

Charlie looked gaunt, thin as a rail and so pale, not the same as I remembered him. But then he smiled.

"Sheila, my wee little one." He gave me a big hug. Mother and my sisters hugged Charlie.

Father shook his hand, holding it tightly, man-to-man. "Welcome home, son." I could see tears in the corners of Father's eyes.

I was so overjoyed I could not stand still. I jumped up and down, not at all ladylike, but so happy.

With Charlie home it looked like everything would be back to normal. The drought that had gripped our little valley since the floods of January,1917, appeared to relax its grip in March with some fall rains. March is in the Australian autumn so September, October and November are in the spring. After that rain the drought returned with a vengeance. Winter was dry and by September, when Australian spring began, even the Melbourne paper was writing about the drought in southern Queensland.[27] If it did not rain in the next month all the cows would die. The streams had dried up, the gilgais (water holes) dried up. The grass in the paddocks was brown and shriveled. All the leaves drooped, like the cows with their tongues hanging out. Even the birds were quiet as if they were holding on to their voices to preserve moisture. Our water tanks were empty, and Father was boiling water out of a mud puddle for us to drink.

We were desperate for water. Father went out and found a dowsing rod, a tool used by the ancients to find water. I followed

---

26. From document sent by the Central Army Records Office dated 1986, addressed to Rosalyn Buchanan.

27. *The Argus*. September 27, 1919. From online archives.

him as he silently walked through the bush and the paddock holding this Y-shaped stick out in front. He held it by the two ends of
the Y. The bottom of the Y dipped and pointed to a certain spot
and this was where we dug for water. Father, Charlie, the help, and
the neighbors all dug and dug and they did find water! There was
enough water that our neighbors were able to bring their cows for
a drink. Even Inigo Jones brought his cows over. What politics
tears apart the reality of weather brings together.

It was not until the wet season in January,1920, that this
drought was finally over. I remember the joy of that time. Every
creature was celebrating the rain.

The little joeys and I ran out into the rain. Of course, unlike in
the painting, I had on my clothes. Every drop of rain soaked into
my skin through my clothes, and freed my soul of the dust and
death of the drought.

Mother and Father stayed inside, like the parent kangaroos
huddled under the tree branches, but the joeys and I, we danced
in the rain.

When the wet season finally came it hung on ever so long.
Everything became wet; even my sheets at night were wet. When
it got wet enough the leeches climbed up into the bushes, waiting
to latch on when I walked by. I hated the leeches sucking my
blood.

My sister Marjorie disliked the Australian climate most of all.
In her autobiography she wrote:

> *Interspersed with droughts when our cattle died of starvation,*
> *were floods when we were shut in from the rest of the world for*
> *days at a time, and two bush fires in which we almost lost our*
> *home.*[28]

I loved everything about Australia. To me the floods and the
droughts were just things that happened. We survived, and I was

---

28. Marge Benson, autobiography, 1936. On file.

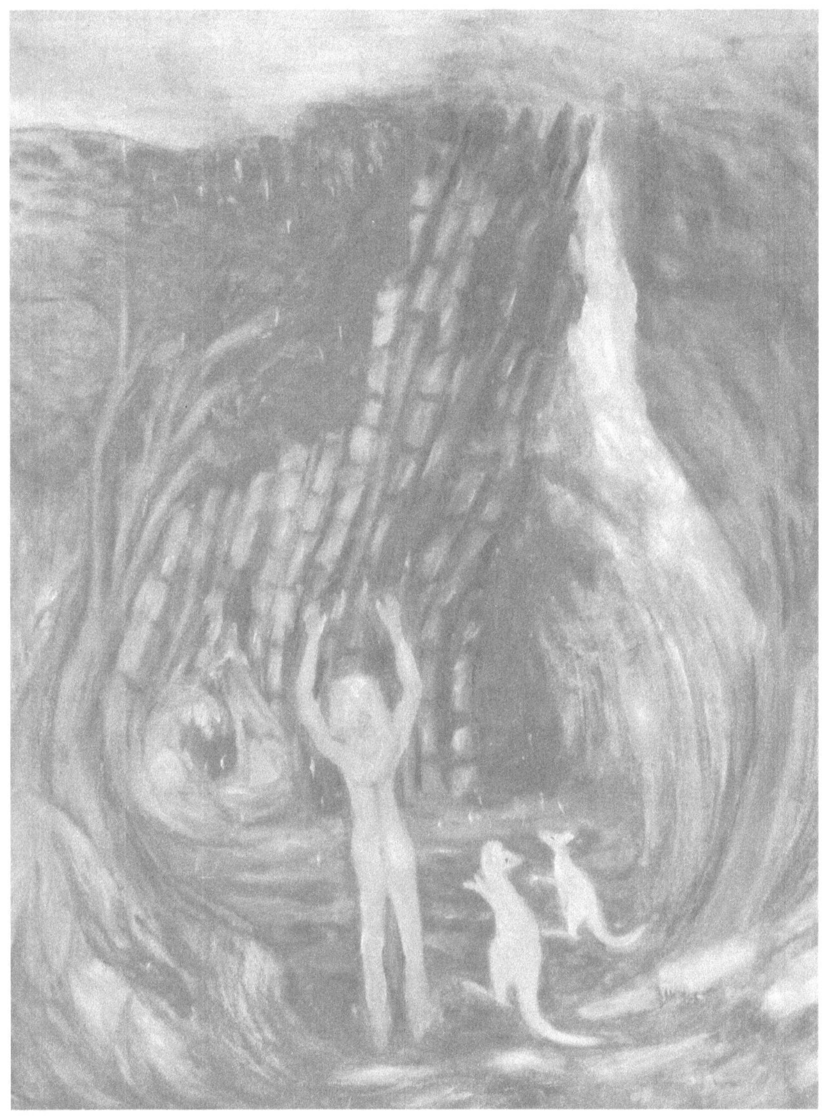

Sheila Buchanan Buell, oil c. 1950. "When the Rains Came." To see painting visit blog: Visionsfromtwocontinents.blog

happy every day. Mother survived too. She worked in the gardens around our home, and grew all of our vegetables, except lettuce and green peas. In Queensland it is easy to grow tomatoes and green peppers, but lettuce likes cool weather. The lettuce grown in that heat tastes bitter, and the peas bolt and turn brown before you can eat them.

One day when Mother and I were in the garden, I saw a little elf in the bush, just outside the garden. I pointed to the elf, "Mother, look there, can you see there is a little elf sitting on a leaf."

Mother turned her head and looked, smiling to herself. She shaded her eyes looking into the bush. Then she turned to me and said, "Little girls can see elves in the bush, grown ups just can not see them."

I was shocked! I never realized that if I grew up, I would lose the ability to see the elves. I thought, *If that is what it means to be grown up, I don't ever want to grow up.*

Of course I did grow up. But that part of me, the imagination that saw little elves in the bush, or forest, that part never grew up.[29]

---

29. Quoted directly from a video of Sheila describing one of her paintings.

CHAPTER 4

1920-1921

The Queensland wet season is in January and February. The year 1920 was wet, and by winter the bush was again green and lush. Christmas comes in the summer. My older sister Lucille wrote a lovely description of our Christmas celebration in the Australian summer:

Such a hustle ensued to get away from work that you might have thought that we were preparing for a rare event – and in truth it was a rare event, having a Christmas tree in Australia. A Christmas tree there however is a species of pine not unlike the American spruce. With hatchet and saw we started out on a hot midsummer morning to hunt for a tree. The locusts buzzed in the roadside trees. The heat made waves in the air. Leaving the main road we pierced into the forest where the leaves on the trees brushed our cheeks. Little streams lazily wended their way. Like garlands of blue in and out among the green. The sun shone with such intense heat that even the birds were quietly resting in the trees. Now and then we stumbled over fallen timber and the jovial Kookaburra would glance at us from his perch in a gum tree and break into hilarious laughter, ha! ha! ho! ho! hi! hi! hi! hi! Truly we had to laugh with him. After skirmishing around among the palms and pines the chosen tree was felled. Then we proceeded to cut down a palm tree in order to have the branches and red berries that grow at the top for decoration. When I was cutting down the tree one of the girls suddenly shouted run!, run! My young sister[30] was standing in the path of the falling tree and narrowly escaped injury. Pitter pat, Pitter, pat sang the rain drops in the leaves. A tropical thunderstorm was upon us. Like rats we scurried into nearby hollow trees to keep dry. The storm soon ceasing we emerged from our hiding places. What a trans-formation! Each one stood and looked at the other and grinned, for from head to foot we were black. The trees we hid in had been burned over by a previous fire. The trees and the decorations were dragged home through the wet.[31]

Santa Claus stopped by our home on Christmas Eve, and we opened presents. Father did not believe we should spend the night worrying if we'd been good or bad. Christmas 1920 was a Christmas like no other. Santa gave me a lovely porcelain doll that came all the way from England. I totally believed in Santa Claus, and because I was the youngest no one wanted to tell me anything different.

After Christmas, the New Year began. It was 1921, and Father finally answered my pleas to let me go to school. I knew the neighbors, the Bretons, went to school and I wanted to go so badly. I remember that morning well. We got up early, and Father walked Marjorie and me to school. It was hot and sticky, even in the early morning. We left the horses in the paddock. Some kids rode ponies to school, but we were close enough to walk. We walked down the lane through the bamboo, which creaked, "ee, ee," as we went by, with a slight breeze.

---

30. Probably Sheila or her sister Marjorie.

31. Original essay labeled Lucille Buchanan, no date. Since she used her maiden name it likely was written shortly after coming to the USA. On file.

Bamboo Path, oil, painted in the 1950s.[32] To see painting visit blog: Visions-fromtwocontinents.blog

The school was built up on posts to let the air flow under it, and so they could treat the poles for termites. Father, Marjorie and I walked up the steep stairs to the school and he opened the door. He called the teacher over to us and said to her, "This is my daughter Sheila. She wants to come to school. But you must not ever lay a hand on her. You may never hit her. If there are any problems you come to me." Then he left. He didn't say anything about Marjorie; he knew Marjorie always behaved perfectly.

I was scared. I didn't know they hit kids at school. No one had ever hit me. The boy next to me giggled and smiled at me. The teacher said, "Bob Briton, come up here."[33]

---

32. Oil, Sheila Buchanan Buell.

33. Sheila visited Bob Breton years later and he showed her scars from that time. Each time he was hit it was written up in the teacher's records. Bob Briton's description of this was also written up in the Peachester Historical

My neighbor Bob hung his head down and meekly walked to the front of the room.

I watched the teacher take out a switch; she bent it and swished it back and forth. Then "whack," I heard it crack across Bob's legs. He stood quietly, then came and sat down. While knowing she could not hurt me, I worried that I had caused this. Despite this scare, I enjoyed being in this little school with the other children.

In March we received wonderful news from Charlie. On March 2, 1921, he married his sweetheart, Peggy MacIntyre. She waited for him all through the war, and then, after he was home, she waited until he had a good job. Charlie got a job working for the State Forestry Department at Imbil, Queensland. There he could work outside, which was better for his lungs which had been damaged when he was gassed during the war.

Things seemed to be going well, but then Father got sick. Sometime during the Australian winter, I think around July, I snuck in Father's room and lay down with him. He did not teach us anymore or go for walks in the bush, he just stayed in bed. He did seem to perk up when I was there. After that I crawled into Father's arms at night. Mother saw that my presence cheered him up. I felt his heart beating next to mine and listened to every breath. I prayed he would get better soon. It was October, then November. A doctor came from Caboolture and said he would operate on him as soon as he got better.[34] Mother told me later that he was ill from lead which lodged near his heart from some troubles in Ireland, long, long ago.

In December, the weather was stifling hot. My eldest sister Lucille was home for Christmas. On December 22 she sent me away to my own room. She said, "Sheila you must sleep in your own bed, I'll watch after Father."

Father groaned, "Sheila, go to your own bed." Slowly I walked

---

Society's publication.

34. A visit was written up in the *Peachester News*.

Lucille Buchanan por-
trait age 30.

away, wandering around the house, finally falling asleep on my favorite pillow in the living room.

Early in the morning on the December 23, I heard people crying. Mother was sobbing. After I left that night Father had directed Lucille to give him some morphine for his pain. As always, Lucille followed his directions, but it was too much. Father died shortly after the injection. Lucille believed that she had killed him.[35]

They buried Father the next day. It was hot and there was no

35. Lucille's stepdaughter, Charlotte, recalled that years later Lucille was hospitalized for depression and received insulin shock treatments. Doctors felt the depression was due to this repressed guilt. Thus was created a deep dark family secret.

refrigeration to slow down the decomposition. The doctor filled in the Death Certificate. It said Father died of heart failure. The priest came and they laid him in a coffin right away. I remember him laid out, pale and thin, still and cold, not like Father at all.

That was December 24, 1921. It was Christmas Eve. No one remembered that I still believed in Santa Claus. All the neighbors came over. Guests came and went. They hugged Mother and my sisters, and patted me on the head.

I waited quietly. I listened for the jingle of Santa's sleigh bells. The sun sank quickly down in the bush and the huge fruit bats flapped together swishing into the orchard for their nightly feast. The insects buzzed, but Santa never came.

Grave of Dr. G.C. Buchanan.

CHAPTER 5

THE DECISION

D r. George Charles Buchanan's obituary appeared in *The Worker*, published in Brisbane on Thursday, January 5, 1922, and in *The Catholic Press*, Thursday, January 12, 1922.

A FINE LABORITE PASSES

Death of Dr. G. C. Buchanan

Dr. G. C. Buchanan, whose death was reported as having taken place at Peachester on December 23, after an illness lasting about six months, was a warm friend of the "Worker" and was well known in the surrounding districts and in Brisbane as a staunch Laborite. He was born in Round Town, Dublin, 64 years ago, and he spent his boyhood in Fermanagh a»d Tipperary. Subsequently Dr. Buchanan went to the United States, and for many years he was a practicing physician in Minnesota. Later he went to Canada and engaged in fruit farming in Ontario. For some time he was President of the Ontario Co-operative Fruit Company. About 10 years ago Dr. Buchanan came to Queensland, and eventually he settled at Peachester and engaged in dairy farming. He has since done much good work in the matter of propaganda among farmers. He was a very vigorous opponent of conscription, and did much good work in fighting that menace to freedom in both the 1916 and 1917 campaigns. Dr. Buchanan was a facile writer and contributed widely to different newspapers both in prose and verse. Prior to his health breaking down, Dr. Buchanan was developing a plan for organizing a farmers' industrial Union. The widow, a son, and three daughters survive. The son, Charles Buchanan, who is a returned soldier, is engaged in the State Forestry Department at Imbil. One who knew the late Dr. Buchanan intimately well describes him as "a -sterling supporter of the people's cause, a great and true Irishman, and a heart-whole Sinn Feiner."[36]

After the funeral, everyone left and we were alone, without Father. Mother just sat and stared into space. She was paralyzed by grief. I tried to comfort her, to bring her flowers. Sometimes I would just run up to her and touch her gently on the arm. She would look up at me with just a faint light of recognition in her eyes.

It was about two days after the funeral. Lucille just stayed off alone, silently sobbing, or perhaps praying. I walked by Mother and Father's room and smelled a familiar smell. It was the sweet-sick smell of chloroform. I remembered that was what Father used to put sick animals to sleep, never to wake up again. I walked up and opened the door. Mother sat on the edge of the bed, holding a handkerchief soaked in chloroform up to her nose and mouth. Father's bottle of chloroform sat on the end table next to the bed.

I hurried over beside her, "No, Mother, No!" I said quietly but forcefully. I took the handkerchief and the bottle, and ran out of the house. Mother stayed on the bed, sobbing into her closed fists, her strong body rocking back and forth in grief.

I poured the bottle out in the garden and buried the handkerchief Mother had used. I sobbed silently to myself. I did not tell anyone. Years later, after my sister Marjorie had died, I told her daughter, and my niece Cathleen about it.[37]

My brother Charlie did not make it home for the funeral. On

---

36. Found in Trove: http://trove.nla.gov.au/ndp/del/printArticleJpg/71056389/3?print=y.

37. Sheila told this story to her niece, Cathleen Benson, in Canada, many years later.

December 21, 1921, his first child "Bobbie" was born, the first Buchanan grandchild. On December 22, Peggy was just recovering from the birth when Charlie got word that his father had died. It was a total shock, as everyone thought he was getting better.

I finally got to meet my nephew Bobbie a few weeks later. He was a lovely baby, a tiny little angel. Mother seemed to recover when she met her first grandchild. She held that little baby and smiled for the first time since Father died.

Although he lived in Imbil, some distance away, Charlie tried to help Mother. He found people to work on the farm. He came over as often as possible, bringing Bobbie and Peggy if he could.

We seemed to be struggling through each day. Then Bobbie got sick and seemed to get weaker, instead of stronger. I remember that sad little thing, so weak he hardly cried. In October, Bobbie died.

This time, Mother did not become paralyzed or cry. She was just angry. "There is nothing here, just drought and death, floods and snakes, it is time to go back home. I never wanted to come here. All I see is death."

Charlie did not pay too much attention. Charlie had his work and his grief, and did not think his Mother meant it.

Mother proceeded to make a plan. She wrote to her sister, my Aunt Lil, in St. Cloud, Minnesota. In those days, the law stated that when a woman married a foreigner and left the United States, she lost her American citizenship.

My brother Charlie tried to reason with her. "Why are you going? There is nothing there. Our home is here now."

"Perhaps your home is here. I never wanted to come here. There aren't any good schools for the girls. There will be many more opportunities in America," Mother responded.

"What opportunities? Father left in 1907 because there weren't any opportunities. Don't you remember the booms and the busts?[38] In 1907, there wasn't any work for anyone. People

---

38. Before there was a Federal Reserve the American economy went through a continuous series of booms, when business was booming, and busts, when everything stopped, like in the Great Depression of the 1930s.

could hardly get food to eat. Here, we have each other. What are you going to do there?" Charlie argued, but it was useless. Mother was determined to leave.

She started working to get her papers in order.

In April, 1922, her sister in America, Lil McClintick, sent a signed affidavit stating that my mother, Florence Buchanan, was born in St. Cloud, in the State of Minnesota on July 15, 1867.[39] Mother used this statement to apply for her visa to return to the United States.

In order to finance this trip Mother sold the farm, its animals and all the household furnishings. The family china that had come all the way from Canada was sold. My favorite pillow that I slept on the night Father died was sold.

Mother's and Lucille's horses were sold.

My sister Marjorie was 14-years-old. She knew what was going on; she had been through this when they left Canada. She clearly remembered the doll they made her leave behind in Canada.

My favorite corner

We went to Brisbane. I was shocked to see all the people. The smell from the cars burned my nose. I had never seen a car before. The noise from the street-cars rattling down their wires and buzzing hurt my ears. I missed my home, the bush, and I missed Father.

Mother enrolled me in school in Brisbane and I hated it. We were seated by how we did our work. I was seated at the front of the class because Father had taught me everything, and I knew the answers to all the questions. I did not understand why I was

___

39. Affidavit, notarized by Thomas H. Howard, on April 7, 1922. On file.

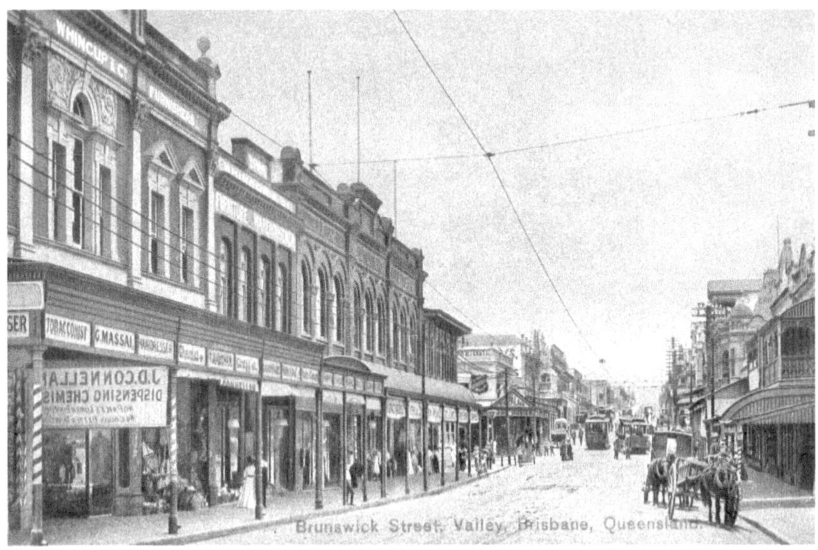

Postcard of Brisbane, collected by the family. On file.

at the front, and the other children teased me about it. I had never even been in a class where everyone was the same age, nor with such a large number of children.

At every opportunity Marjorie said "Mother, be sure Sheila gets to take her doll." I kept my doll, and in America Marjorie kept it safe for me. Mother kept some of the money and sent the rest to Father's brother, Thomas Buchanan, in England to invest. It was Thomas who had helped when they purchased the orchard in Ontario in 1907. He was a very successful stockbroker in London. The farm had been sold, but Mother still had neither a passport nor a visa to go to America. We were in Brisbane to wait for papers. She thought this would take just a little while, but we ended up staying for months.

Finally on May 15, 1923, my mother, Florence Buchanan, was issued a passport by the Australian government. I was listed on Mother's passport.

The American Consulate in Newcastle, New South Wales, Australia, issued a visa for her to go the United States on May 29, 1923.

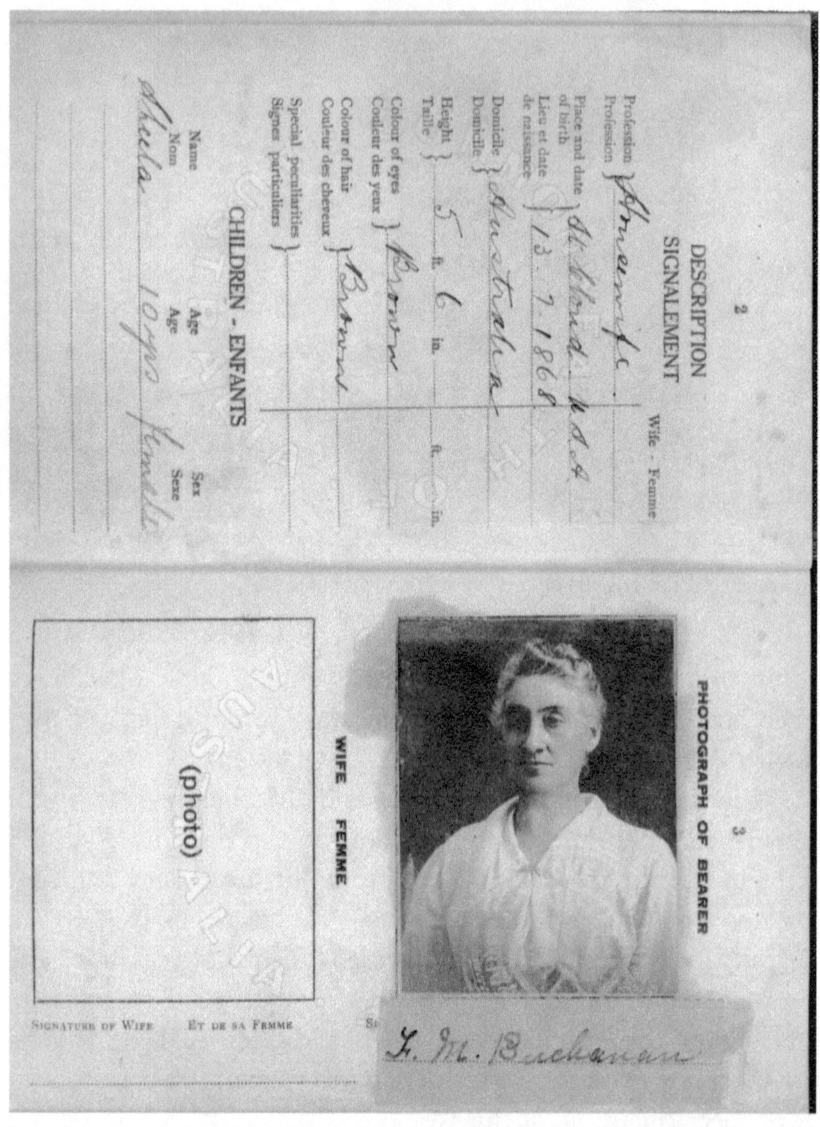

By this time I was excited and happy to be leaving. We were going on a steamship just like Father, Mother, Lucille, Marjorie and Charlie had gone on when they came to Australia. Mother told me wonderful stories about America, how I would meet my Aunt Lil, and how beautiful snow was. She said there were lovely lakes everywhere.

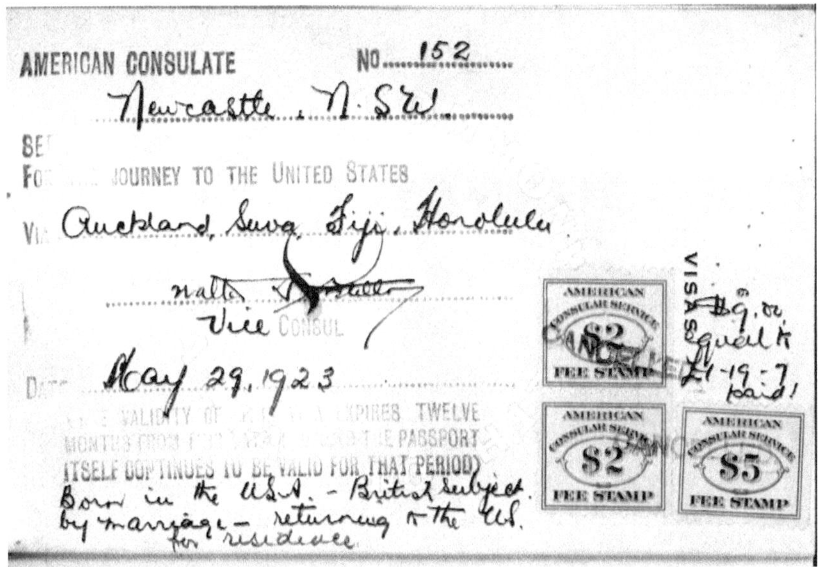

She said, "Sheila, I will take you on the streetcar to Lake Minnetonka, and there you can get on a streetcar boat that will take you to an amusement park on Big Island." By then I had seen streetcars in Brisbane, but a streetcar boat, that sounded wonderful. Lakes. What were lakes? I had never seen a lake.

CHAPTER 6

THE JOURNEY

apers-in-hand we boarded a small steamship in Brisbane to take us to Sydney, where we transferred to the R.M.S. Makura. It was a lovely ship, much larger than the steamship Father and Mother had taken when they came to Australia in 1912. The Makura was built in Glasgow in 1908, and had been remodeled in 1920. Its coal boilers were converted to oil; it was a clean modern ship.

Mother was not interested in high society socializing and she wanted to save money. We had two second class cabins next to each other. Mother and I were in one cabin and Lucille and Marjorie were in the other. The cabin was small and cramped. A sink with drawers underneath dominated the space. A bunk bed with two berths was on one side, and a couch for sitting lined the other wall. I got the top bunk. I loved climbing up and hanging my head over to smile at Mother underneath me.

Second class cabin aboard the Makura steamship[40]

40. Used with permission from Rare Books & Special Collections http://www.library.ubc.ca/spcoll/. Chung Collection id 21834
From website: http://digitalcollections.library.ubc.ca/cdm/ref/collection/chung/id/21834

Before we left Sydney my sister Marjorie wrote to our brother Charlie about how she was looking forward to getting to America. Charlie wrote back,

I don't know what some people must say when they arrive at their destination in heaven or hell and they won't be able to wish they are, where they aren't. But you reserve your opinion about the U.S.A. until after next winter, anyway you will find it is much like all countries, no gold lying about the streets and plenty of people wanting a share before you get any and singing God save the almighty dollar instead of God save the King.[41]

He included some exciting news about the Makura steamship.

I see you have Australia's champion tennis players on the Makura too, would be nice if you could see them playing for the Davis cup, but you will not have an opportunity.[42]

As soon as I discovered that there were places to go on the ship I begged Mother to get out of that cramped cabin. "Mother, can I please go out to the game room?" I would ask.

"Not until you are properly dressed." She dressed me in lovely pastel dresses, with large bows, long white stockings with patent leather shoes on my feet. She brushed my curly hair into ringlets, twisting the hair around her fingers.

In the game room I met Andrew, the only other child traveling in Second Class. Everyone else got motion sickness and lay in their beds groaning. Our Mothers were too busy minding their stomachs to watch Andrew and me as we wandered around the ship.

---

41. Charlie Buchanan, letter dated October 6, 1923.
42. Ibid.

We bounced up the stairs to First Class. We slowed down and smiled at the ladies and gentlemen promenading on deck. They smiled back; no one complained. We were cute, a joyous sight to all the adults confined on board. We got braver and descended down stairs to Third Class, and then down further to the boiler room. The seamen looked at us in surprise and then smiled. They showed us how the oil fed the engines and made steam to turn the turbines that moved the ship.

When I returned to our cabin I was dirty. Mother woke from her misery, and asked, "Where on earth have you been?"

"Andrew and I went exploring," I replied.

"Well, I hope you stayed on the Second Class deck."

"Yes Ma'am." She didn't ask, she just hoped. I would never lie to Mother. I was merely agreeing with her hopes.

That evening when Mother started to comb out my hair she screamed, "Lice, you have lice! Where did you get them?"

"What are lice?" I asked.

She did not answer. She said very sternly, "Sheila, you stay here. Do not leave this cabin!"

She went out and returned with kerosene. She bent my head over the small sink in our cabin and poured kerosene all over my head. My scalp burned, fumes filled up that little space and I felt tears well up in my eyes. She made me stay sitting with my hair covered in kerosene forever. Finally, she rinsed my hair, but did not let me leave the cabin for two days. She kept combing my hair with a fine comb, removing any lice eggs, called nits that might be there.[43]

We had been at sea for some time, traveling first to Auckland, New Zealand, where we stopped long enough to get this postcard.

---

43. These scenes are recreated directly from stories Sheila told to her children.

KINGSLAND NEAR AUCKLAND N. Z.   Protected Aug. 1st 1906 by Muir & Moodie, Dunedin, N. Z.

Hawaii. To see color version visit blog: Visionsfromtwocontinents.blog

Moonlight in Honolulu. To see color version visit blog: Visionsfromtwocontinents.
blog

Then we went on to Suva, Fiji, and Honolulu, Hawaii. Hawaii was beautiful, with people in brightly colored clothes gathering to greet the ship.

When the sun set over the ocean and the moon came up in Honolulu Harbor, it was like a blanket of peace had spread over everyone. We all gathered on deck staring at the sunset.

We began the longest part of our journey across the vast expanse of the Pacific Ocean to San Francisco. By the time we arrived, Andrew and I had become very close friends. I never dreamed that when we stepped off the ship, I would never see him again.

Mother held my hand as we stood in line at customs in San Francisco. My sisters held their passports with their American birthplace written on them. My sisters went first. The customs official looked at them, looked at their picture, smiled and stamped their passports. Mother and I came up to the customs officer. He looked at Mother's passport, with me listed as her child, and at the visa the American Consulate had given Mother. He frowned and asked, "Was your daughter born in Australia?"

"Yes," my mother replied quietly. "She is listed on my passport."

"Where is your daughter's visa?" he asked.

"The American Consulate in Australia did not think I needed one. She is just a child."

"We can't let her in the United States of America. She was not born here. You will have to apply for a visa for her, before she is allowed into the country."

Mother stood there in shock. She did not know what to do.

"You will have to take the girl back on the ship, Ma'am," the customs officer said.

Lucille walked back to Mother and asked, "What is the matter?"

"I ... I don't have a visa for Sheila. They won't let her in the country!" Mother whispered in a terrified voice.[44]

We all got back on the Makura. The ship's captain volunteered to take Mother and me to Vancouver to wait for my visa.

Lucille said, "I will take Marjorie on the train to Minnesota."

All the Canadians still on board waiting to go on to Vancouver were shocked to see Mother and me get back on the ship. She was such a proper lady, why was she being denied entry into the United States? When they found out why, I heard them quietly whispering, "What's wrong with those Americans? They won't even let a poor widow bring her daughter home?"

---

44. Sheila often told this story. She always said that it was because her Mother had married a foreigner and left the country that she lost her citizenship. But another reason was probably the Immigration Quota Act of 1921, which strictly limited the number of non-American-born people entering the country. Now, any child born of an American citizen, even outside the country, is a citizen: http://library.uwb.edu/guides/USimmigration/1921_emergency_quota_law.html.

Mother reassured me, "Don't worry, Sheila, we'll get to see Lucille and Marjorie in Minnesota." I had no idea where Minnesota was. I thought perhaps that meant tomorrow.

Lucille and Marjorie boarded the train in San Francisco. They had a comfortable sleeping car and were whisked across the Rocky Mountains, through the Great Plains to the oak woods of St. Cloud, Minnesota. Lucille wrote to her brother Charlie describing this beautiful ride. Charlie was not impressed. He wrote back,

Lucille evidently the Yank trains are some trains, but you know this is only a young country and the people manage to run along quite well without God's help if that is what makes the Yankee trains so wonderful? You never traveled on the best trains in Australia, as on a trans-continental train here. [45]

Charlie's letter continued on about the vegetables that were at the Imbil farm show in Queensland.

The vegetables were the best I have ever seen and if the banks of Mississippi can beat them I'll admit the Yanks 'can beat all creation'. The carrots weighed six pounds each, cabbages were as big as stylish hats, and all the vegetables and fruit were luscious enough to tempt any Eve.

Mother and I left for Vancouver on the Makura the next morning, and arrived in Vancouver in the afternoon. Vancouver seemed to be a magical place; it was so green, a different green than in Australia, even in the wet season. There was water everywhere but without it being a flood. Mother took me at once to the American Consulate to apply for my visa. They were very sorry

---

45. Letter dated September 10, 1923, in response to two letters of July 27, 1923. On file.

about the confusion. "I am sure madam, you must not have told them about your daughter at the Consulate in Australia," they said. Mother did not answer; she just looked at them.

"We will try to get this visa as quickly as possible, but it will be at least a week."

Mother decided to make the most of this expensive detour to Vancouver. We went sightseeing.

"Oh, Mother look. Can we please go there?" I asked handing her a brochure. The brochure pictured the Capilano Suspension Bridge. It gave directions on how to take the streetcar to the park. So far we had only done things that did not cost money. On that day we packed a picnic lunch and took the streetcar to Stanley Park. Stanley Park was lovely with its manicured lawns, ponds, and wild geese, but it did not have the wild look of the Capilano River. I longed to see the bush, maybe the tall green pine trees shown in the brochure would be like the bush.

Mother carefully read the brochure, and said, "Yes, let's see about doing that tomorrow."

The next morning we arose early and got on the streetcar heading to North Vancouver. It was a perfect day, with a slight breeze wafting off the ocean. The streetcar buzzed along, its wire clanging, up steeper and steeper hills, until we reached the entrance to the park. There it stopped.

We stepped off the streetcar and Mother got in line to pay our entrance fee. I stood still. My nose filled with the rapturous perfume of pine and cedar trees. I listened to the sound of water cascading over the rocks, somewhere far down below.

We walked slowly towards the bridge. Mother stopped. The bridge swung back and forth as other tourists walked across. "Are you sure you want to cross that Sheila?" she asked.

"Yes. Mother, I do. See everyone else is going across."

"Are you sure about this?" she asked again.

I was sure, but I was worried maybe she wasn't sure. "You can stay on this side Mother, and I'll just run across if you would prefer."

"Oh, no, I am going with you."

With that statement she lifted her long skirts and carefully stepped on the bridge, holding tightly to my arm. The bridge trembled with each step on its cedar planks. I thought my arm would fall off, she held on so tightly, as we slowly made our way across the bridge. The bridge had a rope railing which swayed back and forth, with the whole bridge moving under our feet. Mother had to take extra care since she still wore long skirts.

I loved that little trip. I was so happy when, years later, I was able to share this joyous experience with my children. But the bridge was not the same. It had been rebuilt in 1956.

My visa arrived. Our waiting time was over. Mother decided that rather than go back and take the American train to Minnesota, we would go on the Canadian Pacific Railway (CPR) through Canada to Minnesota. Many years ago Father had sold our Orchard in Beamsville to the CPR, which had given Father the means to move to Australia, so it was only fitting that the CPR should take Mother home to Minnesota. The trip over the Canadian Rocky Mountains was breathtaking. I remember stopping at the Banff Springs Hotel, built along a turquoise glacial lake at the foot of a mountain. I thought *if I climbed that mountain I'd surely come upon Grandpa's cottage like Heidi in the Swiss Alps,*[46] *and I could stay here forever.* Then I remembered, *thank goodness I'm not an orphan, I'm with my mother.* Then we were whisked across the plains. Flat lands that seemed to go on forever passed by my window. In Winnipeg, Canada, we transferred to the train that would take us to St. Cloud, Minnesota. Mother said, "It won't be long now. Soon you will see your sisters, and meet Aunt Lil."

The new train continued to travel across miles and miles of flat land through waving fields of wheat. It stopped in the middle of this flat land, and a man with a uniform got on. He moved quickly down the aisles of the train, talking to each passenger. When he got to our seats he said to Mother, "Papers, please."

Mother nervously handed him her passport, with her visa, and a certificate of admission for me.

---

46. *Heidi,* a children's classic by Johanna Spyri originally published in 1881, has been made into numerous movies and television shows.

The man carefully looked over our papers. I wondered if he was going to send us back to Canada.

He looked at Mother, smiled, and said, "Welcome home." He turned to me and said, "Welcome to America." He was much friendlier than that man in San Francisco.

I looked excitedly out the window. Was this really America? It did not look any different than the Canadian prairie we had been traveling past for ages.

CHAPTER 7

ST. CLOUD, MINNESOTA

Slowly the scenery outside my window changed. There were more houses in the towns. The farms seemed closer together. The land stayed flat for a long time, then it got just slightly hilly. After a while there were pine trees like those I saw in Vancouver, but not as big. Then the pine trees thinned out, until we saw just a few pines and lots of large trees with big trunks and loads of leaves.

"Mother what are those big trees?" I asked.

"What trees?"

"See, look, there they are all grouped together. The cows are standing under them. They don't look like gum trees or any trees at home, but they aren't pine trees either."

"Oh, that's an oak woods. Those are oak trees. St. Cloud is part of an oak forest."

"What is a woods? What is a forest? At home wild areas were called bush."

"I forgot we called the woods and the forest bush in Australia," mumbled Mother.

Mother was home now. She understood this foreign place. She forgot that I did not even know what so many of the words meant.

The train stopped in so many little towns, so I was surprised when mother stood up and said, "This is the place. This is St. Cloud." We grabbed our handbags and the porter took our luggage out to the platform.

I looked for my sisters. Mother had said we would see them in Saint Cloud when we parted in San Francisco, so long ago. I didn't see them anywhere.

"Flo, it is so wonderful to see you," said a strange tall lady. She walked totally upright, straight as an arrow.

"Oh Lil, it has been such a long time. I thought I'd never get here. That business in San Francisco; it has been a very long journey."

"Marge and Lucille arrived almost two weeks ago. Whatever did you do all this time?" asked Lil. "Never you mind, I'm sure we will have plenty of time to talk later. Let us get your luggage and get you home to see those girls."

"Where are they?"

"There is not enough room in the motorcar for everyone, so they are waiting on our farm."

Mother turned to me and said, "Sheila, this is your Aunt Lil."

Tall Aunt Lil in front ,
Mother in striped dress.

I bowed my head, and tried to curtsy or smile, but I just wanted to hide. I knew I was too big to hide behind Mother's skirts.

"Oh, never mind, she's just shy," said Aunt Lil, and I felt relieved. "I have someone I want you to meet. He is shy too."

Just then I noticed a smaller, very thin man standing in the background, leaning against a motorcar.

Aunt Lil walked to the motorcar and brought over the thin man. "This is my husband, Cass McClintick. He is your Uncle Cass, Sheila."

Uncle Cass just stood there smiling. He did not say a word, but he smiled at me, his eyes twinkling. He walked over and picked

Uncle Cass checking his tobacco plants.

up the heavy luggage tossing it in the back of the motorcar. That luggage was almost as big as Uncle Cass, but he didn't have any trouble loading it in the Model T. He walked around to the front of the car and turned the crank once. The motor started up with a roar. He opened the car door and motioned politely for us to get in. He still had not said anything. Yes, he was shy too.

When we arrived on the farm, I was so tired I could hardly greet my sisters. The next day I awoke to a busy Minnesota farm day. It was harvest season, and Uncle Cass was out harvesting tobacco, his cash crop. Five acres of tobacco could give a farmer as much profit as ten dairy cows or raising 50 hogs.[47] But it was a lot of work. Uncle Cass had soaked the seeds and started the plants in a greenhouse in the spring. He planted each hairy little tobacco plant by hand, and tended them all summer, turning the soil between the rows with a cultivator pulled by horses, and weeding by hand between the plants. He picked the grubs off by hand and trimmed the leaves. By the time we arrived, they were ready to harvest.

---

47. Sauk Center Herald. January, 1928.

Marjorie and the dog in front of tobacco plants.

He laid the leaves down on the ground to wilt in the sun; then he came by with the wagon and strung each leaf up on hooks in the wagon. They were taken to a special shed to finish drying.

Marjorie was very impressed by the tobacco plants. She sent pictures and a description to my brother Charlie in Australia.

Charlie wrote back, "*I am surprised at such good people growing tobacco, the devil's plant. (the d--- wouses & hypocrites.)*"[48]

I did not understand Charlie's anger then, but now I'm sure he missed us; he just wanted us back in Australia.

Mother had written to Uncle Thomas in England hoping to get back some of the money she had sent him, so we could get a place of our own. In October she got a letter saying that he had been robbed and murdered.

I found out the true story years later from Uncle Thomas's grandson, Brian Powell. "My grandfather, Thomas Buchanan, was an underwriter at Lloyds of London, a very honest and upright man. He had a partner named Mr. Harrison. Thomas discovered that his partner kept two books, one for Thomas and everyone else, and another accurate one, seen only by himself. When Thomas found out, he was very distressed. Then one evening he failed to return home. The family waited up all night. A fortnight later the police recovered his body from the River Thames."[49] The Police and the family believed he took his own life, but that was never reported in the papers; nor did my mother ever hear about it.

Uncle Thomas's family never sent us any money for there was no money left in England. We lived that winter with my Aunt Lil in St. Cloud. Although Mother managed to get back to Minnesota, she had lost everything. Depressed, Mother sat staring into space.

In December, my brother Charlie wrote a letter in answer to Marjorie's letter written November 5, 1923, "*We were glad to have your letter of Nov. 5th, thought your hands were frozen stiff as we have not had letters for a long time.*" He described that first Christmas without his Mother and sisters in Australia. "*Christmas has*

---

48. Letter, August 23, 1924. On file.

49. This information given by Brian Powell, Thomas's grandson, when I went to visit him in England and in subsequent correspondence. Brian's mother's children completed their education with help from the Aid Society and friends. Florence's children in America were not as lucky.

come and gone. It didn't seem very much like it although we had a very pleasant day and some big dinner. We were all just on the bursting point. Peggy can tell you at the end of this letter what Santa Claus brought to her and Boy."[50]

Peggy wrote about Boy, my little nephew, who was born after we left for America., *"Boy hung his stocking up, it did look 'huge.' We took another lot of snaps*[51] *today and will send you all some if they are any good. He is growing into a lovely baby and very good, full of mischief and can laugh aloud a little."*

Although my sister Marjorie had loved her home in Canada, she found that living in St. Cloud was difficult. She wrote in her 1936 essay,

> *At first we lived in St. Cloud, and I went to a junior high school. I did not have much difficulty with the work, but my social life was a problem. The girls were very nice to me, but I was much disappointed in them. Nothing that they did interested me. I could not dance, I could not skate, I did not like boys. Nothing pleased me, even the landscape got on my nerves. The neat checkerboard countryside almost drove me crazy after the wild bush and scrub of Queensland.*[52]

Marjorie knew how to speak American. Marjorie knew about the climate, she understood winter.

I did not know what was coming. The first day of school I went in smiling, thinking of the little school in Crohamhurst. The teacher assigned me a seat behind a nicely dressed little girl. I sat down quietly. Some time during that first day I raised my hand.

"Where is the W.C.?" I asked quietly.

---

50. Boy was Charles MacIntyre Buchanan, born September 9, 1923, after Charlie's mother Florence left for America. Later he was called Mac. Letter, December 30, 1923. On file.

51. Photographs.

52. Marjorie Buchanan, essay written about 1930. On file.

"What is a W.C.?" the teacher replied.

Embarrassed, I quietly whispered, "Water Closet."

"A what?" the teacher asked again.

"A ... a water closet," I replied

"A what? We don't have any water closets here," the teacher answered, and all the children laughed.

I sat down and crossed my legs. I had to go really badly. I was afraid I would have an accident.

A little while later, the teacher said, "Girls line up to go to the bathroom."

I was confused. *Were we going to take a bath at school?* I lined up with the other girls and we went to the W.C. I thought, *How strange to call the W.C a "bathroom."*

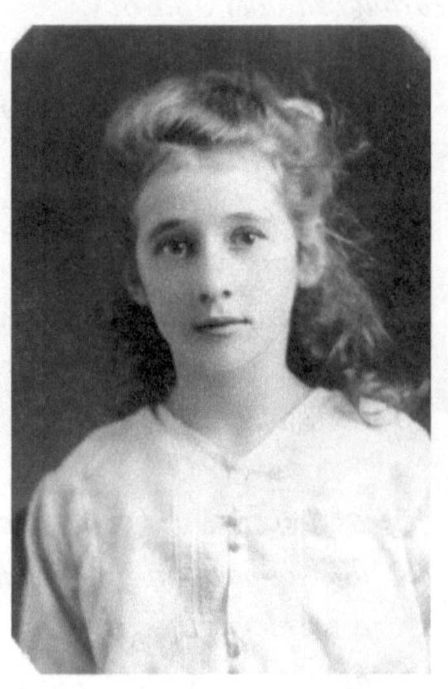

Sheila age 10

The boy behind me teased, "W.C., W.C., what do you mean W.C.?" I turned red in the face. The teacher turned toward us and the boy got quiet.

I'm not sure if it was that day or the next when that boy dipped my pigtails in the ink well. He pretended it was an accident, in case the teacher caught him. I did not say anything; just looked at the end of my braid all tipped in black ink.

That first day of school, the leaves on the trees, though different from the Australian trees, were still green. The days got colder and the trees looked sick. Their leaves turned strange colors of red, yellow and brown and then fell off the trees.

One morning Mother dressed me in long woolen underwear. Under my skirt I wore long stockings that pulled over my legs to the top of my panties. They itched terribly. I was polite, and did not say a word. Under the top of my dress, I wore a long sleeved woolen shirt. I wiggled my arms. They itched from the wool.

Mother said, "Sheila, stay still. You need to wear this to stay warm. It froze last night. You aren't accustomed to the cold, and you might get sick."

My skin prickled, especially under my arms and down the sides, but I was quiet. I did not want to worry Mother. I stepped outside to go to school. A cold wind attacked my face. My eyes grew wide with shock. It looked like everything had died. The plants on the ground were green yesterday, but now they were brown and wilted as if there had been a drought. *"We had plenty of rain, why were all the plants dead?"* I wondered.

I asked my Uncle Cass. He was a farmer and he would know. "Why did the plants die last night?"

"Oh," he said, "there was a frost last night."

I pondered this information. The frost killed them. Mother wanted me to wear this wool, so the frost would not kill me.

I wore the itchy wool and sat at my desk sweating and itching each day. I did not open my mouth to say a word. Even if the teacher called on me, I did not speak. The children laughed when I talked and the teacher did not understand me. I knew I wasn't behaving properly, but I couldn't talk at school.

In December, just after Christmas, I came down with pneumonia, and stayed home in bed. All through January and February I refused to get well. Sometimes I would raise my head and look out the window. I saw white snow, cold and dead trees. I longed for home, for the bush, for something green. Mother, Aunt Lil and my sisters were not sure if I would recover. The doctors thought that perhaps I should go back to Australia, but I would not leave my mother.

Then March came. The ground was still white, but the white was melting, bit by bit. One warm spring day Uncle Cass took me for a walk.

"Sheila, come I wanta show you something," Uncle Cass said. Although his grammar was not perfect, his voice was kind and gentle.

"Should I go out, isn't it cold?" I asked.

"No, it is not cold today," he answered. "But git yer boots."

We walked towards the swamp. The snow crunched under our feet. Uncle Cass held my hand. I slipped on a piece of ice, but Uncle Cass held on tight. My foot crunched down through the snow, oozing in melted water.

"Sheila, look up," Uncle Cass urged.

I looked into what had been bare branches a few weeks before. The branches were covered with little pink-gray buds. Those buds were bursting with life, so soft they felt like a puppy's soft fur.

Uncle Cass bent a branch. "These are pussy willows. They tell us that spring is here. Soon everything will be green." Uncle Cass cut some pussy willows so we could take them home to Mother and Aunt Lil.

After I was grown up, I painted this watercolor on board using the tips of my fingers. Every spring for the rest of my life I went out in the woods to find pussy willows. Pussy willows gave me hope.

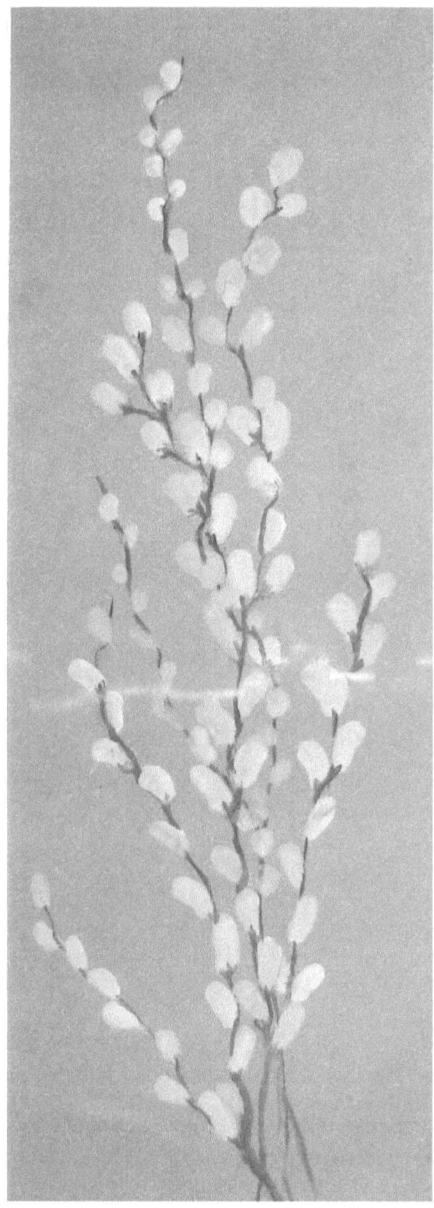

Pussy Willows. To see painting visit blog:
Visionsfromtwocontinents.blog

Spring. Sheila Buchanan Buell, watercolor circa 1960. To see painting visit blog: Visionsfromtwocontinents.blog

CHAPTER 8

ST. PAUL, MINNESOTA

Just as Uncle Cass had predicted, spring came. I could feel the earth push and swell here, sway and give there. The little shoots appeared first light brown, then yellowish, and then they turned that marvelous spring green. There is no awakening on earth quite like a Minnesota spring.

My big sister Lucille left St. Cloud in the fall and found work in St. Paul, Minnesota. St. Paul was the capital of Minnesota. Lucille said it was beautiful, with lots of parks. She told Mother that the schools there would be much better for Marjorie and me. Lucille had found work as a cook and helped Mother find an apartment.

We lived on the third floor of this old mansion in St. Paul, Minnesota.

I lived with my mother and sister Marge in an ugly cold flat lit by gas lights. My poor Mother had always been a protected housewife that had no other job training (outside of housework). There was no help for widows or orphans. We lost all our money in some bad deal in London,

England. It was the beginning of the Great Depression.[53] My poor Mother had to work so hard it was awful. I seldom saw her and she was so tired. She had to work ten hours a day, sometimes even on Sunday, to have food and a few clothes to wear.[54] I was so lonely I would walk to the bottom of the hill she came up walking home (streetcars cost too much) to meet her. Often she was so tired she leaned on me as we walked. I never let her know she was leaning on me, and I felt rather proud, that maybe I was helping her rest. Then she had to have her teeth all pulled out, and she had no money for false teeth, so she could not chew anything. She did not get proper value out of the food. She loved nuts and my uncle used to pick and send us a lot of wild hazel nuts. I used to crack them and put them in a rag and pound them with a hammer til they were powdery for her. She always ate them and gave me such a sad smile.

I had one dress to wear and it was washed on weekends and put back on Monday. Sometimes some of the kids made unkind remarks about my only dress. I cherished Sundays when my mother was home and Lucille would come home from her job sometimes and give my mother some money and maybe take us all to Como and Phalen Park. . . . I tried not to do bad things to worry my mother nor did I ever tell her any of my troubles at school. I was so sad to see her suffer so, but something always sang inside of me. "No matter what happens I still have me." I could see beautiful things and I made some nice friends and took care of little children because I loved them and they loved me.[55]

---

53. In 1981, when remembering their poverty, Sheila states it was during the depression. However, it was actually 1924, the roaring 20's. It was roaring for some, and great poverty for others.

54. She worked as a "Chambermaid" at the St. Francis Hotel, as indicated on her death certificate, February 12, 1928.

55. Sheila, Letter to children, written in 1981.

Florence Buchanan, St. Paul, MN, age 60.

Although my mother Florence was Protestant, she sent me to catechism class because she had promised Father to raise the children in the Catholic faith. She took me to a catechism class as soon as we got to St. Paul. She could not do this in St. Cloud because her sister, Aunt Lil, detested the Catholic religion. A few days after my first catechism class someone knocked on the door of our flat.

Mother tidied her hair and started to get up to answer the door. She was tired from a long day at work.

"Should I answer it, Mother? I asked.

"All right," she sighed. Though it was not proper for a child to answer the door, Mother was just too tired right then.

I opened the door a crack to see who was there. Standing tall in his long black robe was the priest from my catechism class.

"Well hello young lady. Is your mother here?"

"Yes Father," I replied opening the door."

Mother stood up and held out her hand in greeting. "Welcome," she said letting him into our small apartment.

"Would you like a cup of tea?" she inquired politely.

"No, it is rather late for tea. I should not like to inconvenience you. I will only be a minute," the priest replied, sitting down on our worn chair in our small living/dining room.

"We should probably talk privately," he said, signaling that I should leave the room.

I wondered what I had done wrong that would cause him to come to our home. It was evening. We had very few visitors except for my sister.

I went to the small bedroom, but stood with my ear against the door.

"I am very glad you sent your daughter to catechism class. It is very important to save her soul," I heard the priest, speaking in a low voice. "But I have not seen you at Mass."

"My husband was Catholic, but I am not," stated Mother. "I am a widow, but I promised to raise the children in the faith."

"Well, even if you do not attend Mass you need to donate towards her education. Most of our families pledge ten percent, perhaps five percent of your income would cover her expenses," stated the priest, not bothering to inquire about our current situation.

The priest stood up abruptly.

Mother escorted him to the door.

I did not hear any more of their conversation. I knew enough. Although Mother still tried to send me to catechism class the next week I refused to go. We barely had money for food; my soul could wait. I knew my Guardian Angel would watch over me whether I went to catechism or not.

My big sister Lucille had studied at the convent in Canada and Australia. She believed that her prayers would be answered, and that the church would show compassion and care for families like ours. Here in the "roaring twenties" she saw the St. Paul Cathedral looming over the city of St. Paul, a large compassionless pile of stone. Father had always worked with the church, for the workers, writing in Australia for the newspaper *The Catholic Worker*. Lucille walked away from the church that showed no empathy, into the arms of the Communist movement. In 1924, the Communists in the Twin Cities of St. Paul and Minneapolis worked hard to better the conditions of the poor and working class. There, at a party meeting, she met a man about her age, Henry Bartlett. Henry had also been raised Catholic and he shared her faith and compassion for all types of people. His father, Captain George E. Bartlett, had been the U.S. Marshall of the Dakota Territories.[56] Henry's first wife had died and left him with three motherless children. Lucille brought Henry and his daughter, Charlotte, up those flights of stairs to our little flat to meet us.

"Mother, I have brought someone for you to meet, "Lucille said.

Lucille was a small woman, about five feet tall. Next to her stood a thin wiry man, with a smile and a twinkle in his eye.

Mother stood up and put out her hand, looking this strange man directly in the eye.

"This is my fiancé Henry Bartlett, and his daughter Charlotte," said Lucille, a slightly nervous tremor in her voice.

"Pleased to meet you, Madam," said Henry, with a confident smile. Henry turned to me and, still smiling, said, "Pleased to meet you too."

His smile was so inviting that I overcame my shyness. I said, "Pleased to meet you too," shaking his hand.

I could feel a hard working energy in that handshake. I instantly liked this finance of Lucille's. Henry turned to his daughter Charlotte.

---

56. Information provided by Charlotte Bartlett Wasiluk, Henry Bartlett's youngest daughter.

Lucille took over and said, "Charlotte, I would like you to meet your future cousin, Sheila."

Now it was Charlotte's turn to be shy. She smiled, but did not say anything.

I said, "Come, let me show you something." I took Charlotte into the small bedroom I shared with Mother. There on a chair dressed in her lovely dress, her curls just so, was my China doll that Marjorie made sure we brought from Australia.

Charlotte reached out her small hand to touch the doll's hair. She approached the doll with such care I could tell that she did not have a China doll. "It is all right, go ahead, you can touch her," I told her.

Charlotte smiled and said, "She is beautiful."

"Santa brought the doll for me when I lived far away in Australia," I told Charlotte. Charlotte looked young enough to still believe in Santa Claus. Perhaps Henry Bartlett could see that Santa brought her a China doll for Christmas.

We played quietly with the doll, while the grownups talked in the other room.

The best days were the days we received a letter from our brother, Charlie, in Australia. My sisters saved those letters. In April of 1924, Charlie wrote:

Tootles & Jim (the dogs) are still prominent members of the family. Only Jim does not appreciate the baby, he (Boy) can crawl all over the place now and everywhere the 'Jimmy' goes Boy is sure to follow.

In July he added,

Boy is growing into a clean kid, of course he is over nine months old now. He can walk a few steps, and has six teeth or had when I saw him last. He is very forward in many ways and most amusing. Peggy made him a pair of long trousers out of two of her stockings to protect his little legs from splinters when crawling and if you could see him in them it would amuse you. He loves to push his pram along the verandah and sometimes it gets a bit of a go on and Boy strides after it hanging on for dear life and laughs, he laughs at most things even if he bumps his little head. His eyes are still very blue and he has a good crop of wavy hair. Best of all he loves the out of doors and if we put him out in the back yard he crawls way up the hill by himself, doesn't seem afraid of anybody or anything. When we were going up in the train he went to anybody, and used to walk along the aisle of the carriage hanging on to the seats investigating other passengers luggage. Tootles adores Boy. He sits on her, pulls her ears and then her tail, but Tootles takes it all patiently, Jim doesn't though.[57]

Charlie wrote about his love of writing and gave Marjorie some advice on writing in America:

Had another article in last Saturdays paper & will send it along when Peggy sees it, she hasn't read it yet, will send the whole paper and you can cut out the piece and return it to me, they have another article of mine now. Some times I feel sort of bubbling over with a desire to express myself but cannot always find the way, the materials for writing are free, but it takes an author on post to put them down. Suppose I am a sort of journalist, one of those wonderful animals whose take comes out of their mouth. You will probably find Marjorie that your writing is not suitable to U.S.A. Your ideas and ideals are founded on your life in Australia. Perhaps in years to come you will acquire the American style, it might be a doubtful acquisition. The more I see of Yankee papers the less I want to see of them. We may be behind the times, but if being a Yank is the only way to be progressive, God forbid![58]

---

57. Charlie Buchanan. Letter, July 7, 1924.
58. Ibid.

Marjorie must have written about how short money was because Charlie continued:

Yes I know how you feel Marjorie. I often wish I could send you some money and Mother too, but at present I cannot spare it and don't know what would happen if any of us get sick now. Thank goodness we are out of debt to all storekeepers, and if I can get some revenue from Duira this year to pay the interest and taxes, we will begin to look up and have a chance of helping mother a bit, when they get a new road up there the place will be valuable.[59]

Marjorie had just read *Main Street*[60] and it reminded her of St. Cloud. She wrote to Charlie about it. Charlie wrote back: "

I have never read "Main Street" will if the opportunity arises Marjorie & see if I agree with you. No doubt if somebody sat down and wrote about any of us as we are really, we would not be agreeably surprised or pleased.[61]

In her 1936 essay my sister Marjorie wrote:

The next year we came to St. Paul, and I went to one of the large high schools. Here I was much happier. As my mother worked, I had to do most of the housework and had time to brood. I enjoyed going to the museums, the parks were interesting, if tame, the library was a great joy to me, and best of all I found a few real friends. I think my social life began at this time. I was amazed to see Negroes in my classes and to find that they were normal human beings. I was surprised to find that Jews were not all

---

59. Ibid.

60. Mainstreet by Sinclair Lewis originally published in 1920 by Harcourt, Brace and Howe

61. Ibid.

money lenders and peddlers. At the same time I definitely discarded the Catholic religion which had only held me by fear. That set me at a loss for a while because I did not have anything to take its place.[62]

Marjorie & Sheila at Como Park, St. Paul, Minnesota

62. Marjorie Buchanan Benson, essay, written in 1936. On file.

CHAPTER 9

JOY TO GRIEF

On Friday, May 20, 1927, Mother came home from work, very excited. She was carrying a copy of the *St. Paul Daily News*.

"Look what that young man is doing! I just can't believe I've lived to see such a thing. Why, I remember when he was a baby in Little Falls."[63]

"Who? Mother, what are you talking about?" asked Marjorie.

"Look at this. It's Charlie Lindberg, Evangeline's little boy. He's trying to fly across the Atlantic all by himself in one of those crazy flying machines."

Smiling, Mother held out the paper. Marjorie bent over and read it. I peered over her shoulder.

"LINDBERG OFF ON LONG FLIGHT TO PARIS"[64] read the second section headline. Over the picture of Charles Lindberg and his mother was the headline, "STARTS ON PER-ILOUS FLIGHT." Six men had died, in three separate attempts, with larger more expensive planes. Another three were injured in a fourth plane crashed, so no one expected Lindbergh to survive this rash attempt to fly it alone in a single engine aircraft.

---

63. Sheila's father, George Charles Buchanan, was a doctor in Little Falls, Minnesota, from 1892-1907. Her mother told her they were friends with the Lindbergs. Her father and Charles Lindberg, Sr., had similar progressive polit-ical views.

64. *St. Paul Daily News,* May 20, 1927.

"I remember when we used to visit their home in Little Falls. Your father and his father, Charles Lindbergh, Sr., were good friends. He was elected to Congress the year we left Little Falls for Canada. Little Charlie was just five years old," Mother recounted.

"If he makes it, he'll win $25,000.00,"[65] said Marjorie.

"His mother Evangeline, she must be so worried. My Charlie may be in Australia, but at least I know he isn't flying over the Atlantic," Mother mused.

"Oh, I hope he makes it, I hope he does," I said, silently asking my guardian angel to look after him. I could hardly sleep that night. I kept thinking about Charlie Lindbergh flying, flying, flying, all by himself, across the ocean.

We were so excited and proud when on Sunday, May 22, 1927, we saw the front page headline. "CROWD WILD AS DARING MINNESOTAN COMPLETING HISTORY-MAKING ATLANTIC CROSSING."[66] He made it! He left Friday at 7:51 a.m. from Roosevelt Field in New York, and arrived in Paris on Saturday at 5:21 p.m.," read Mother, her voice filled with awe. "When you were little Marjorie, it took us 6 days for our little steamship to cross the Atlantic Ocean on our way to Australia, and I thought that was miraculous. And we were lucky. It was the same year that the Titanic sunk," Mother said, her face darkening.

A few weeks later my sister Marjorie graduated with honors from Mechanic Arts High School. She even won a scholarship to college. But since it was not enough money for her to go, she went to a secretarial school instead. Mother was so proud of her. Soon everything would be better.

Later that summer everyone in Minnesota was excited because Charles Lindberg was coming. On August 23, 1927, I got up early. It was a hot day, but I had a plan. I was going to be in the front row when Charles Lindbergh came in his parade

---

65. The Orteig Prize was first offered in 1925. It is worth an estimated $340,000 in 2015 dollars.

66. *St. Paul Daily News*. May 22, 1927.

through St. Paul. Mother looked up from reading the paper at breakfast and said sadly, "Evangeline is going to be in the parade too. Oh, how I'd love to talk with her about old times."

"Maybe we could find out where she is staying and you could visit her," I suggested innocently.

"Oh no, I couldn't bother her. She will be much too busy," Mother said, excusing herself from the table, with tears in her eyes.

Marjorie looked at me and whispered, "Sheila, I need to get a job so I can help Mother get new clothes and teeth. Without that she will never visit anyone."

Marjorie Buchanan graduation

"Oh," I said, ashamed that in all the excitement I'd forgotten that we were poor.

I went to the parade with Marjorie. I took the little girl from across the street with us. In our neighborhood rich and poor people lived next to each other. This little girl's mother let me babysit her. It was fun because she had such lovely clothes. Her mother had so many she often threw the dirty ones away rather than wash them.[67]

---

67. Sheila often talked about babysitting the children in the neighborhood, and this mother who had so many clothes she could throw them away rather than wash them.

Christmas, 1927, was a happy time. We were all together for Christmas dinner at my sister Lucille's home. It was a crowd – Marjorie, Lucille and her husband Henry Bartlett and their children Charlotte, Myron and Gordon. Mother looked around and smiled, but it was a sad smile. I know she was missing my brother Charlie and his family, still far away in Australia.

In January of 1928, Mother developed a cough. It was winter and bitter cold, but Mother went to work every day. Marjorie and I were both busy with our studies. After school I played with the little kids in the neighborhood. I babysat every chance I could get, usually without pay. I just loved caring for little kids.

Mother wrote to her son, Charlie, on January 25, 1928, and did not even bother to mention her cough.

Suddenly in February the cough turned into pneumonia. My mother, Florence Thompson Buchanan, died February 12, 1928. I was only 14 years old, and I was an orphan. I don't remember anything about the days after she died. I was too sad to remember.

I felt a desperate grief. I had lost my papa, my home, and now my mama. (shown in painting Australia Dreaming)

My brother Charlie was so depressed when he received the news that he was unable to write. His wife Peggy wrote to us:

My Dear Sisters

As you will see the enclosed letter was written before we received your cable with the sad news it contained – We received the word 2 days ago. It has been a terrible shock to us especially to Charlie. He is very much broken up and feeling it terribly. I don't think he can write yet so I am just sending off these few lines so that you will get them at the earliest. We went down on Monday in the hope of sending by cable a few pounds to help along but found when we got there we could not cable it, so we got a money order and sent it there. We are hemmed in by floods and I was afraid the letter would not get away till today and we should not catch

"Australia Dreaming"
Oil on canvas
Sheila Buchanan Buell c. 1946. To see painting visit blog: Visionsfromtwo
continents.blog

the mail as it closed today. It just seems as if everything must go wrong. How you will miss your dear Mother. It seems such a tragic loss. As she has worked so hard to keep the little home together for you all and just when the times was nearly there that might have had it a little easier she is taken. One wonders why? But we are taught that the good God does these things always for the best, so perhaps she is escaping harder day and ended now into her rest and reward. – It is horrid to be so far away at a time like this and able to do so little to help. Please write and let us know what your plans are and how you are faring and what we can do. I know Charlie is worrying terribly over you. I just feel that I wish I wasn't in the way as he'd be able to keep more than he can with the babes and I to think of – It seems strange that we should all be in trouble at the same time. I was lying in the hospital when she passed over. I expect. Then we received the word on the anniversary of my father's death. Mother and I keep talking of her and wondering if she was long ill and what went wrong. It will seem a long time till we hear from you –[68]

Charlie's wife, Peggy, suffered from diabetes. It was so caring of her to feel she got in the way of Charlie helping us. Charlie wrote to me on March 3rd. I wish I had kept the letter. Marjorie kept hers from March 7, 1928:

"Strathroy" Imbi. Q. Aust. 7-3-28

My dear Marjorie,

I wrote to Sheila a few nights ago so tonight will try to write to you. It is hard to know what to say. Over a fortnight ago since we heard the terrible news of mothers death. It came as a shock that I haven't got over yet.. not even knowing of course that she was ill. As soon as Lucille's cable came Peggy and I went to Imbil to

---

68. Peggy Buchanan. Letter, February 22, 1928. On file.

try and cable some money but there is no way of cabling money to U.S.A. so did the next best thing and posted a money order of L10, it will help a bit. We will try to send some more later. It does hurt to think that your little nest is broken up, because it was our one dream to bring the boys along there. We know mother was tired and needed a long rest. God only know how much. You are old enough to know how she had to struggle since she came to Queensland so much against her will. It was all for you children that she battled so hard, children you were then if not now. I was only thinking when reading your last letter I received last night how sudden it must have come to you all, for it was written on Jan. 25, and no word of mother being ill. All your plans will be upset now. It was mother's biggest ambition wasn't it? To educate you and Sheila, and she played her part nobly. Between us we must see that Sheila gets her chance, though I know Aunt Lil will do everything possible for her. It seems to me it would be better for you three girls to stick together if you could, but if you want to come to Queensland there is always a home for you wherever we are. Try to complete your business training.[69]

He goes on to describe how Peggy, his wife, had been ill, and was in the hospital the day his Mother died. She had the youngest son, George Hugh Buchanan, born October 31, 1927, with her in the hospital. Charlie now has three sons, whom he calls, Boy (Charles MacIntyre Buchanan) the oldest, then Jack (John Alexander Buchanan) and George (George Hugh Buchanan) the youngest. Later they will have a daughter, Florence, who will become Florence MacGahan.

The local doctor still has her under observation as she had had two or three bad attacks since, but he hasn't found the cause yet. He has decided it isn't appendicitis or gall stones, the soreness is in that region but deeper down. Just at present she is feeling better, but

---

69. Charles Buchanan. Letter, March 7, 1928. On file.

has lost a fair bit of superfluous flesh. The baby had a rather rough spin during all this as you can imagine, although Peggy had him in the hospital with her. He is a bonny kid very much alive, but fairly cross. Boy is a big help to his mother and the baby simply adores him. Jack is such a funny little soul, and is all eyes.

Write when you feel able and tell us all your plans and if and how we can help you. Next time I write to Margaret Macintyre I am going to ask her if she has any influential friend in the West that could help you. At present she is working on a newspaper.

Will be writing to Lucille in my next spare minute, and then your Aunt Lil. I'm making a try this winter to get appointed to the administrative staff of the Forest Service. I know I will be recommended from here. I can't get any higher here than overseer, my present title. It will be a government appointment, surer, better pay, easier work, shorter hours.

If you know of anything that Sheila wants let us know won't you, poor dear kid she is going to be lonely, cheer her up all you can, I know it's hard but the best way to forget your own

Marjorie Buchanan

sorrows is to help others. Must say good night now dear sister, be as brave as you can because mother will expect it of you. The boys are fast asleep. Peggy is reading and I am just writing and thinking, mostly thinking.

The boys send lots of kisses and love. With much love to you all.

From your loving brother,
Charlie

What a huge burden my brother Charlie laid on Marjorie. Marjorie, too, was totally devastated by Mother's death. Marjorie was only 18 years old. She had worked hard and graduated from Mechanic Arts High School in three years. Mechanic Arts was the high school to attend in those days, and a diploma from there was like a college degree nowadays. Marjorie wrote in her autobiography about that time in her life:

During these years, I became very good friends with my mother, whom I had never understood before. I had hoped to make life easier for her when I was through high school and able to work, but she died six months after I graduated. That is the greatest sorrow in my life.[70]

---

70. Marjorie Buchanan Benson. Essay written in 1936. On file.

CHAPTER 10

WHAT NOW?

I did not remember what happened right after Mother died. I thought I had been depressed. I found a letter I had written, addressed to Lucille Buchanan at 346 Fuller Street in St. Paul, Minnesota, in my sister Lucille's papers after she died. I probably should have addressed the letter to Lucille Bartlett because I'm sure Lucille was married then.

The letter, dated April 12, 1928:

Dear Lucille, & all,

I got here at 12:30 half an hour late. The bus nearly tipped over twice and the last time I nearly went through the top. I surely was scared.

I received a letter from Charlie yesterday. He wrote me a lovely letter. He wants me to come and live with him and I would love to in a way, but I wonder if he thinks I would leave you. I would not on a bet. I'll go and see him when I get older, if I can get some one to go with me. Charlie even said he would send money to me.

Buster, the dog, is just as silly as ever. The cats are not half so nice, they are fighting all the time.

Uncle brought home some crocuses. It takes him to find the flowers doesn't it?

It seems so funny not to have anyone to fight with. Or not to have you kids fight over the dishes. Is that floor dirty yet? I suppose so. Wilbur is to scrub Saturday. Mrs. Broms you be sure he does won't you?

Ruth is playing the piano. She is so lonesome for Grey Eagle, she does not know what to do. I wish I was with you, too. I wish there were about six of me. So I could be everywhere at once. Aunt Lil is busy picking over dried fruit and Uncle is fixing tobacco beds. Some one was here last night and planted the seeds.

The kids over at the little school said I have changed so in looks since I went away. Mildred said I always have had a sad look in my eyes and now they have a sadder look. I did not know that before and I don't believe her. She is the only one I really like over there. Especially since I have been home (In St. Paul) and seen my more refined friends. There is such a difference between them. . . .

Lovingly,

Sheila
P.S
Please read this to the crowd and answer soon.[71]

Oh, the memories that letter brought back. The resiliency of childhood, Mother had died exactly two months before. Although I was an orphan, I was more concerned with helping others than with feeling sorry for myself. My uncle Charlie in Australia wanted me to come and live with him. I wanted to go, but I didn't want to leave my sister Lucille. Lucille and Henry did not have much, but what they had they shared with everyone. Lucille was always going to Communist Party meetings or bringing something to someone in need. Clara Broms, Wilbur's mother, was in

---

71. Letter written by Sheila Buchanan to her sister Lucille, April 12, 1928. On file.

need right now, so they stayed with us for a while. Her husband, Allan Broms, was in prison for having refused to serve in World War One. The stress of it all was too much for their marriage and they were divorced, yet Clara continued to work for the Communist Party.[72]

Clara and my sister Lucille were very close friends. Both had grown up Catholic with a strong faith, and then came to believe that the world needed to change. I remember overhearing them talk.

Clara said, "My dad worked hard yet we did not have enough to eat. We'd go to mass and the priest said how wonderful it would be in heaven. My growling stomach did not want to wait for heaven. I didn't understand why we could not have enough to eat, enough to live on, while we are on earth."[73]

Lucille would nod her head and reply. "Yes, and now the pastoral letter is out telling the priests and everyone that we cannot be both a Socialist and a good Catholic. My father was active in the Catholic Worker movement. He was a good Catholic and believed in Christian Socialist principles. I don't believe any of this church stuff anymore. We have to help each other and create a new Communist society."

Lucille and Henry were passionate that Communism was inevitable and that it would save the world. The workers of the world would unite and rise up. They believed that the rise of Communism in Russia was proof that this was happening

My cousin Ruth was sent to live with Aunt Lil in St. Cloud because her mother, Aunt Lil's daughter, was unable to care for her. Aunt Lil's first husband had been an alcoholic, and Ruth's mother also had a drinking problem. In Grey Eagle, Minnesota, Ruth and

---

72. Information on the Broms family is from the Minnesota Historical Society's 20th Century Radicalism in Minnesota Oral History Project. Transcript of interview with Wilbur Broms on August 7, 1987.

73. Carl Ross, Interview with Wilbur Broms. Quoted from Wilbur Brom's description of his mother talking about becoming a Socialist. Wilbur Broms interview transcript of tape 1. Minnesota Historical Society's 20th Century Radicalism in Minnesota Oral History Project.

I had lots of cousins, who were very open and loving. Aunt Lil was stiff and uptight, as if she was following some unspoken rule.

After a short visit with Aunt Lil, I returned to St. Paul, to help Lucille and to be with my more "refined" friends. I wished there were six of me because I wanted to do everything. I thought I could help Lucille by being a big sister to Charlotte, the youngest child of Lucille's husband Henry Bartlett. Lucille was gone many evenings at meetings for the Communist Party. Charlotte wanted to accept Lucille as her new mother, but Henry's two teenaged sons, Myron and Gordon, wanted nothing to do with Lucille. Gordon, the oldest, was protective of Charlotte and tolerant of me, but Myron constantly teased me. I had never been teased before, and believed he meant everything he said.

"What do you think you're doing Miss Sheila girl?" Myron would say with a sneer whenever he saw me.

"I'm helping Lucille, and you should too," I would answer. Or else I would try to ignore him.

When I came home from school and Lucille was at work or at one of her meetings, Myron would lock Charlotte and me out of the house. We banged on the door, but he would not let us in until just before Lucille or Henry got home. We never told Henry because we were afraid Myron would be even meaner to us if we did. Henry was nice to Lucille and left her lovely encouraging notes each day. Myron made me feel like I was living a nightmare. One day he said, "You and Lucille can both just go away. We were better off before you came." He started to shove me out the door. "You're just another mouth to feed. Dad's got enough problems without you and your sister Lucille too. She's not my MOTHER!"

His words were still echoing in my mind the next morning when I woke up and saw my sheets were covered with blood. I was sure I had hemorrhaged and was going to die. I'd seen blood. I'd seen my father die, and my mother die. Now it was my turn. I stayed in bed, shaking, not wanting to get up. I was not ready to die.

Everyone else was up and about when I sat up and cautiously crawled out of bed. I was amazed that I could still walk. I did not feel like I was dying, but yet I was bleeding. I stuck a handkerchief between my legs and slowly made my way toward Lucille's room.

"Lucille, I'm very ill," I whispered, my lips trembling.

"What's the matter, Sheila?" she asked, her forehead wrinkled in concern.

"I'm bleeding," I mumbled softly.

"Did you cut yourself?"

"No, that's the problem. I just woke up bleeding," I answered, and started to cry.

"Where?" she asked.

I pointed to my private area. We never spoke of those parts of our bodies.

Lucille said, "Oh my, I didn't know you were that old already. Here, I'll get you something for that." She quickly dug in her drawer underneath her underwear and handed me a Kotex napkin and a sanitary napkin belt. She said, "Here, you can use these once a month."

I was confused. The belt was a strange piece of elastic with two metal loops. On the Kotex box was a diagram showing how to use the napkin and the piece of elastic, but it did not explain what it was for. The pictures on the box showed me how to put the belt around my waist and attach the ends of the napkin to the little metal loops in front of my vagina and one in back, in the crack of my butt. I followed the directions. The disposable Kotex napkin had been invented in 1921.[74] My sister thought she was being very progressive providing me with a sanitary napkin, but I vowed that if I ever had a daughter I would tell her about this before it happened.[75]

June turned into July, and my periods were now a monthly occurrence. The heat was unbearable in the crowded upstairs apartment. Myron continued to badger me and tell me what a

---

74. According to the Kotex history on Wikipedia, the first advertisement for Kotex's disposable sanitary napkins appears in 1921.

75. Sheila told me this story shorty before I had my first period, but I had already heard about menstruation from my friends. The times had changed and we talked about these things more openly.

burden I was to his father. I started to believe him. He said, "You know the other day when Dad said he needed to go out. Well, he had to go and borrow money. He had to borrow to get money to feed you. If you weren't here, it would be a lot easier on everyone."

Henry and Lucille did not seem to need me. I quietly cried myself to sleep under the covers, so no one could hear me. I really was a burden. *I'm leaving. I'm going to go away.* I decided to go to Grey Eagle, Minnesota, to my mother's cousin's home. They were warm and friendly people, with lots of little kids. Maybe I could babysit for them.

But how was I going to get there? I had no money. I knew where the railroad tracks were. There were people, bums, who got into boxcars and rode for free. I decided to get in a boxcar and hitch a ride to Grey Eagle. I got up at 5:00 a.m., made myself a cheese sandwich to take with me and tiptoed down the stairs, quietly closing the door behind me. I knew Lucille would not be alarmed because I often went for long walks in the early morning.

I found an open boxcar that looked like it was going the way I wanted to go. Then when I crawled into the back of the boxcar, I heard a voice.

"You're not running away now, are you young lady?" asked the voice.

"Why no, I'm not. I just need to get to Grey Eagle. Is this the right car?" I replied to the voice, afraid this was a bum.

"Well, you picked the right car; this one does go that way. But riding boxcars is not safe for a young lady like you," said the voice.

The voice came out of the shadows and shook my hand, just like a gentleman. But this was not a gentleman. Jake was a bum. But he was a gentleman bum. His clothes were torn but clean, his face was hairy but freshly washed and his manners impeccable. The train did not leave until around noon. In the evening we stopped in Anoka where the bums had a camp. Jake shared what food he had with me. The next day, Jake made sure I hopped off the train near Grey Eagle. I walked until I came to Addie's house.

No one was home so I went in and immediately fell asleep on Addie's bed.

I awoke that evening to a terrible noise.

"There's a body in my bed!" screamed Addie.

I sat up with a start. Just like Goldilocks, I was awake in a strange bed. Addie saw who I was.

"Oh Sheila," she coughed, giving me a big hug. "You gave me such a start. How did you get here?"

"I came by train," I answered, not saying that I did not have a ticket.

"Have you eaten dinner? We don't have much, but I'll give you something."

"Oh, that would be lovely," I answered politely hoping she didn't hear the loud growling going on in my empty stomach. As we walked down to dinner, I noticed that Addie did not seem to be well. Her breathing was labored and her eyes were bloodshot, in addition to her barking cough.

That night Addie developed a very high fever so the town doctor was called. The doctor drove his car up to the house and spent a long time with Addie. When he came out of her room he said that Addie had diphtheria, and that no one could leave the house. Later that day the sheriff came to the house and put a big red "Quarantine" sign on the front door. The sheriff did not even knock on the door. He left as quickly as he possibly could. I was not sick, but I was told I could not leave the yard. Someone, I don't know who, sent Lucille a letter telling her I was there. Aunt Lil knew as well.

Addie's house had a large yard with a vegetable garden and a gaggle of geese. Luckily, when I arrived the day before, the geese were in their pen. If they had been loose in the yard, no stranger could have approached the house. The geese were as effective as a pack of guard dogs. They came after strangers in a moving mass, swaying from side to side and honking loudly. If they caught up with an intruder, they'd bite into his flesh and tear off bits of his trousers. With nowhere to go, nobody to talk to and no books to read, I talked to the geese. The largest one, a male gander, I named Charlie after my brother in Australia. When the gaggle made a move Charlie was always the leader. I put some tasty grain in my hand and offered it to Charlie. Slowly, ever so slowly, I approached him, my hand open with tasty tidbits. Charlie eyed me up and down; he knew I meant no harm. Soon I had Charlie eating out of my hand. The other geese followed him. I looked at that gaggle of geese and realized their true potential. Why if one could harness that power they could pull a cart. That was exactly what I did. To this day I don't know how, but I put a harness around Charlie. I strung the other geese together with him and then they pulled a small cart around the yard. Addie watched out the window and laughed. I think the sight of those geese pulling that cart made her well.

The geese were lovely creatures moving in a group, their necks curved together. Based on my memory of that time I created a watercolour[76] in shades of brown. After an art exhibit someone asked me to create the painting in black and white. I worked on it forever, but it ended up better than the original colour version. The customer I made it for disappeared. I'm glad they did because I really liked that painting.

---

76. Colour is the British spelling of color. I always used that spelling.

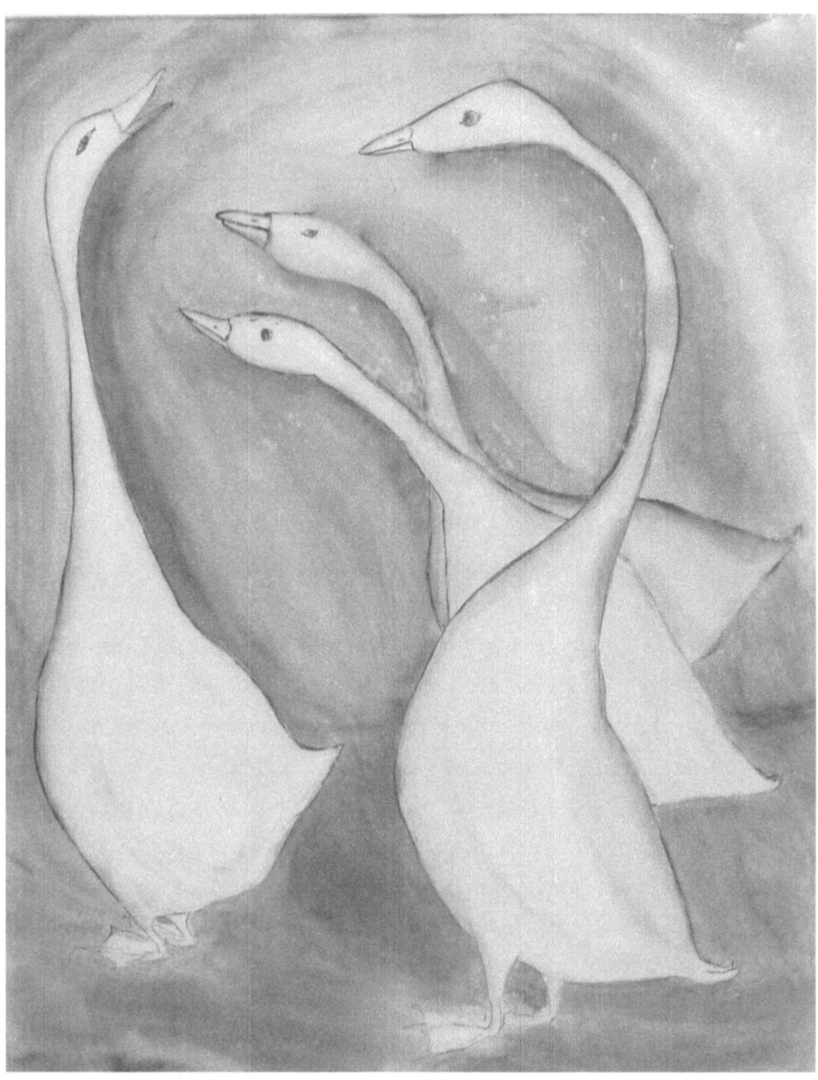

Geese ca 1956 Sheila Buchanan Buell

CHAPTER 11

DRIVING

Aunt Lil came in the Model T to take me to live with them and go to school. I was not excited about living in St. Cloud, but I guessed it would be okay. I wrote this description of my thoughts at fifteen in a letter to my children.

Just before I was 16 I thought I knew a lot. I did not like my sister Marge, I thought my Uncle Cass was a big dumbbell, as he only went to 4th grade and it took him forever to read anything. I corrected his English. I was getting very nasty.

Then one night I did not sleep. I did not like myself and my actions. I turned over many things as I lay there watching the beautiful moon shining in my bedroom window. . . . I guess I grew up in those hours before 4:30 in the morning. Almost like a butterfly coming out of a chrysalis. I knew the things my sister had done when we were children were really creative things that any big sister might do to a little sister when she had nothing to do with her time. My Uncle I felt and knew was a kind and loving self educated man who taught me, next to my father, to be a kind and gentle person, to love and respect all life and to care for animals and plants that needed attention. He taught me respect for all life knowing even then, if we do not and other life dies so do we humans. I thought about all the people who really were in their own ways trying to help me grow up, I really had no one person to help me. At 4:30 am I dressed and went out to the garden and pulled all the weeds. I seemed to be a different me. I had so much more understanding. I heard my Aunt Lil say to a friend. 'I don't know what happened but Sheila is working so hard to help and she is so good to live with again. What happened?' I analyzed myself and grew up.[77]

I loved the gardens. Uncle Cass had a huge vegetable garden and Aunt Lil grew lovely flowers around the house. When I arrived in the late summer, the wild cucumbers covered the front fence with their lacey white flowers. They were native wild flowers, but Aunt Lil picked the seeds each fall and planted them so they would grow where she wanted them.

In late fall I helped Uncle Cass harvest the corn. I was able to work very fast because I could use both hands equally. I picked everything with both hands. The neighbor noticed and wanted to hire me, but Uncle Cass just laughed.

Aunt Lil made sure we went to church each Sunday at the protestant church. I did not mind. I had missed going to church since Lucille did not believe in churches anymore.

Sometimes Aunt Lil would yell at me for no reason, "Don't do that Sheila, you look just like your Father!"

I could not understand. I must be very ugly, I thought, if I looked like my father. Especially the way she said it. Much later when I was grown up Lucille told me why she was angry. Aunt Lil had been engaged to my father, but he broke up with her and went and eloped with my mother. After that Aunt Lil married a man who turned out to be an alcoholic. He was unable to support her and her children. She ended up having to leave her children with her mother and become a nurse to support them. After her children had grown, she married Uncle Cass. Even though my appearance grated on her, she did what she could to

---

77. Sheila wrote this story in a letter to her children in 1982, hoping to help them grow up.

Aunt Lil's Model T

stand in for my mother, her sister, whose death had left me an orphan.

Aunt Lil took me to town one morning in the Model T. That Tin Lizzie hummed along under her strong guidance. The hemline of Aunt Lil's skirt touched her calf, midway down her leg, old-fashioned for 1928. Her sensible shoes allowed her to control the car with apparent ease. At five feet eight inches Aunt Lil appeared to me to be a giant among women. Mother had been only five feet tall, and had always worn her skirts down to her ankles. My sister Lucille was five feet tall and wore modern house dresses that stopped below her knees. But Aunt Lil, at five feet eight inches sat in the drivers seat, straight as an arrow, her long dress accentuated by her long waist. On our way home from town, Aunt Lil suddenly pulled over to the side of the dirt road we were driving on. Dust swirled up as the car rolled to a stop.

She said, "Sheila, you drive home." Not "would you drive home?" or "would you like to drive home?" but "Sheila," my name, "YOU drive home."

"I don't know how!" I responded in total shock. I never thought I would drive a car. I remembered just six years earlier on my first trip to a city, when my nose and ears had been accosted by a horseless carriage. And now I was only 16 and she expected ME to drive one!

"You must learn how to drive. It is a new world and you will need to know how to drive."

No one argued with Aunt Lil, not even Uncle Cass. She left the car running in neutral and we exchanged places. The door only opened on the passenger side. Aunt Lil slid out, carefully dragging her long dress across the seat, and I slid into the driver's seat, my shorter skirt sliding easily across the seat. She then got back in next to me.

"Put the brake lever on the left straight up and down," she said. With my left hand I reached back and moved a lever next to the driver's door to a perpendicular position. "With your left foot push this pedal down, and push the throttle on the steering column up a little bit." I looked down at my feet; there were three pedals there. I stretched and pushed on the left one. The car shuddered. I moved the throttle forward and the car lurched towards the grass on the side of the road.

"Don't let the car go off the road, Sheila, turn the steering wheel!"

With one hand on the brake lever and one on the throttle I didn't have any hands on the steering wheel. The Tin Lizzie had three pedals on the floor, but no gas pedal. To give her gas I had to move the throttle, a little lever on the steering column.

I quickly grabbed the wheel with both hands and tried to turn it back on the road. It did not move.

Aunt Lil quickly reached over and pushed the throttle up, increasing our speed. I was sure we were going to hit a tree, but with the increased speed the steering wheel turned and we were back on the road, heading across the road to the ditch on the other side. Aunt Lil helped me turn the wheel. Suddenly we were back on the road, slowly heading forward.

Aunt Lil left the car in low gear so it did not go over ten miles per hour during that first lesson. Slowly we made our way home. As long as we were moving I could turn the steering wheel. As we approached home Aunt Lil stiffened up. "Listen carefully. In order to stop you have to put the car into neutral and press on the brake, that's the pedal on the far right. If you just push down on the brake you'll ruin the engine."

Now I was scared. How was I going to stop this thing? With my left foot I pushed down on the clutch and it sprang up to neutral. We continued to roll forward until I pushed down hard on the brake with my right foot. "Good job!" said Aunt Lil, obviously relieved, "but we're not home yet."

I put the car back in gear and gave it some gas with the throttle on the steering wheel. We started forward up the hill and down the driveway to the house. I wasn't sure how far ahead I needed to plan the stop. I put the car in neutral, but we were going down hill. I pushed the brake with all my strength. We rolled into the trashcans, finally stopping.

Aunt Lil got out and brushed herself off. She did not say a word. I was relieved, hoping that my driving career had ended.

That evening my cousin Ruth laughed at me. "You sure looked silly driving that Tin Lizzie. Grandma told me to drive once, but I just told her 'No.'" Ruth was the only one I had ever heard say "no" to Aunt Lil.

The very next day Aunt Lil was at it again. "Sheila, start the car. We need to go to Grey Eagle."

"But I don't know how," I answered, as politely as I could.

"Of course you don't. That is why you need to learn," answered Aunt Lil.

I loved going to Grey Eagle and getting to see Addie and the geese. There is no way I would say "No," like my cousin Ruth.

Once again I slid into that tall driver's seat, and Aunt Lil got in right next to me. "Starting is a little tricky, but easy once you get the hang of it. This is a modern car with an electric start. With our first car Uncle Cass had to turn the crank, but this one you just push the little starter button with your foot."

I reached over with my foot to push the button.

"No not yet. Never just push the button. First check and make sure the emergency brake is on. That lever on your left needs to be pushed back. Turn the key, then pull out the choke on the dashboard, and put the spark advance, the lever on the left side, down a couple of notches. Now you are ready to push the electric start button."

I did all that and pushed the button. The car roared.

"Now move that spark advance down so the engine purrs instead of roars."

I did it and the Tin Lizzie started to purr.

"Ok, now release the emergency brake by putting the lever on the left into a vertical position. Push the middle pedal forward so you can move forward."

We slowly started down the driveway. We only went ten miles per hour. I knew we would never get to Grey Eagle going this slowly.

Aunt Lil said, "Now we need to switch to high gear. Push the lever on your left all the way forward, while giving it more fuel with the throttle."

I pushed it forward with my left hand and the car shuddered. I put my left hand on the wheel and used my right hand to move the throttle up a notch. The car surged forward going fast, 15, 20, 30 miles per hour. The trees sped past; dust billowed up from the road. My heart raced, as my hair flew out from my face just like riding a galloping horse only faster.

We made it all the way to Grey Eagle with no problems. But when it was time to go home huge rain clouds appeared in the sky. The Tin Lizzie started up just fine. It was a long ride back to St. Cloud, almost two hours at 30 miles per hour. The rain poured down from the sky turning the road into muddy ruts. The car slid this way and that, splashing through potholes of discolored water. Water sucked at the tires and I wanted to slow down, but Aunt Lil yelled through the roaring rain. "No keep going, go faster! If you stop you will sink into the rut, and we'll have to find a horse to pull us out."

I raced home, splashing and sliding, wishing this ordeal would end. Mile after mile of farm fields flashed by the open windows. At last we turned into the driveway. I put the car into neutral and pressed on the brake at the top of the hill. The car yelped, spun around backwards and slid down the hill. Finally it stopped.[78]

Aunt Lil said, "Great job Sheila. Next week we will go to town and get your driver's license."

I was sixteen, and all I needed to get the license was Aunt Lil saying I could drive. There was no test, nothing, just fill out the form. It didn't ask where I was born, just my name and where I lived. I wasn't sure then, but I found out later, that this was one of the greatest gifts Aunt Lil ever gave me. How my cousin Ruth regretted that she had not learned how to drive.

Ruth and I enrolled at St. Cloud High School in the fall of 1928. I really enjoyed high school. Ruth was not interested in school, except to flirt with the boys. I was not interested in the boys; they just seemed silly to me. I wanted to study. I dreamed of becoming a doctor like my father.

Here is a picture of Ruth and me and two of our friends from St. Cloud High School. I'm on the far right. Ruth is second from the left. Ruth seemed so much more at home with the kids than I did. I always felt I was on the outside looking in. Ruth was in the middle of whatever social activity was happening.

Then she met Ed Parseau. I really didn't care much for Ed, but to Ruth, Ed was everything. All she could talk about was Ed this, and Ed that. It all just bored me to death.

---

78. Sheila told the story of Aunt Lil making her learn how to drive, but of course not with all this detail. The driving instructions came from "Instruction on how to drive a model T Ford detailed – YouTube.

Sheila far right,
Ruth second
from left

In the spring Ruth started to sneak out at night to be with Ed. I didn't think it was a good idea, but I wouldn't tell on her either. One night I woke up and heard Ruth crying. She just wouldn't stop crying.

"Oh Sheila, what am I going to do? What am I going to do?" she sobbed.

"Do about what? What's the matter?" I whispered back, not wanting to wake up Aunt Lil.

"I think I'm pregnant."

"Oh Ruth, don't be silly. How can you be pregnant, you're not married?" I whispered in my innocence.

"That's the problem, I'm not married, and Ed says he can't get married right now," said Ruth.

"What? You did it and you're not married! I thought you knew better than that." I never should have let her sneak out with him,

I thought to myself. I should have told Aunt Lil. It was my fault too. What could we do?

"Don't tell Aunt Lil," begged Ruth.

Maybe she was reading my thoughts, but I did not think of telling Aunt Lil. I thought, *she would be so upset, and angry, yes she would be angry.* I didn't know what Aunt Lil would do if she found out. "We will just have to keep it a secret. You don't look pregnant," I said to reassure her.

"Not yet. But I feel awful, and I haven't had my period for three months."

Three months. I thought about how a mother carries a baby for nine months, so in six more months my cousin Ruth would be a mother!

"What a miracle babies are, Ruth!" I held Ruth in my arms and she sobbed herself to sleep. While Ruth snored in a fretful sleep I laid in bed making plans. I knew the Wilder Clinic in St. Paul had health clinics for pregnant women, and I remembered that there was a home for unwed mothers in St. Paul. I had never gone near there, nor had I known anyone in trouble like that, yet I knew it was there. If Ruth really was pregnant, maybe it would not be so bad. Maybe she should go there.

The next day we started to make clothes for the baby, not telling Aunt Lil anything about the problem. We had no idea how to make baby clothes. We made clothes like we would for a doll, forgetting that real live babies have large necks.

Aunt Lil gave us an allowance to pay for lunch. I started to skip lunch to pay for bus tickets for us. I had some money saved from babysitting and helping on the neighbor's farm. I was not about to try riding the boxcars again. I knew I was really lucky that I had found a nice bum before but now with Ruth, never.

Ruth and I managed to finish that school year in St. Cloud. Ruth ate a lot and pretended that she was getting fat. She was getting fat, but just in her tummy. She wore big blouses and hid her stomach. The 20's style did not include a tight waist so she was able to get by without getting caught.

CHAPTER 12

BACK TO ST. PAUL

I don't remember much about that fateful day. It just fills me with regret and guilt to think about how Ruth and I left St. Cloud, walking out on my Aunt Lil and Uncle Cass, without so much as one word of thanks for all they had done for us. But I just could not let Ruth leave by herself. She was pregnant, and I was the only one who knew.

We got on the bus early on a Friday morning. The bus stopped at every little town along the way, so it took almost the whole day to get to St. Paul. As we approached the huge city of Minneapolis, the bus slowed to a crawl; Ruth glanced nervously back and forth at the traffic surrounding us: cars and trucks of all sizes.

"Where are we?" she asked.

"We are getting close to Minneapolis. We have to stop there before we get to St. Paul," I replied.

"But it's so crowded," she whispered. Ruth, who was always self-assured at school, was suddenly afraid.

"Oh that's right, you've never been to the city," I answered, realizing that I knew much more than she did. I remembered my shock at seeing crowds and cars in Brisbane after having spent my first ten years in the Australian Bush. Ruth was older than I'd been then; I squeezed her hand to reassure her that this was normal. It was okay to be afraid.

The bus sat at the Minneapolis bus station for over an hour. People crowded on and off, dragging their baggage, through the smell of gas fumes. We traveled along University Avenue with the streetcars rattling and sparking next to us. Finally, we reached the St. Paul bus station. Here I knew where I was. I knew how to take a streetcar from the bus station to where I remembered the home for unwed mothers had been the year before. I used to walk by it when I stayed with my sister Lucille. I had wanted to write to them before we arrived, but I had not, because I was sure that Aunt Lil would see the answer when it arrived. So we showed up, unannounced, knocking at their door.

Ruth knocked on the door and a tall lady, with a long black skirt, answered.

"What can we do for you young ladies?" she asked.

Ruth and I looked at each other. We still did not want to talk, did not want to utter that shameful word, "Pregnant." Finally, I spoke. "My cousin Ruth here is pregnant. Can you help her?"

"Come in, please," the lady said, ushering us into the parlor. "Did you write to us?"

"No, we did not. We were afraid to," I said.

"There is nothing to be afraid of here," she answered. "It would have helped if we knew you were coming. Luckily, we have an open bed right now."

The place was clean, but dark. I felt Ruth would be safe here. Hopefully, I could come and visit. The lady left me in the parlor and took Ruth to another room to interview her. I sat and waited, relieved that we had arrived. I thought about my own plans. It was getting dark. How was I going to get to my sister Marge's apartment? I hadn't written to her, either.

I watched the clock tick, tock, tick, tock, in the corner of that quiet room. My stomach was starting to growl, and still Ruth was in the other room. Finally the lady came out with Ruth.

"Ruth tells me you came down from St. Cloud on the bus. Is that correct?" she asked.

"Yes," I answered politely.

"How old are you?" she asked.

"I am 17," I answered.

"It is getting late for you ladies to be out on the streets alone. You had better stay here tonight with Ruth. We have a cot for you."

"Thank you. That would be wonderful." I was relieved. I was not looking forward to going out on the street and trying to find my sister's apartment in the dark.

The next day was Saturday. The lady reluctantly let me leave when I told her my sister was expecting me. Of course she was not, since I had not written. Hardly anyone had telephones, so I could not call her.. I waited at the corner for the streetcar for about an hour. Finally it came, sparks flying on the wire, clattering along the tracks. I asked the conductor the best route to take to my sister's address. It was right on his route, so I was there in no time.

I got off when the streetcar stopped on Fuller Street. I walked slowly up the street, into the dark halls of a brick apartment building and then climbed three flights of steps. I knocked timidly at the door.

"Who is it?" I heard her ask.

"It's me," I said.

"Who?"

"Your sister, Sheila," I answered, louder this time.

The door flew open. "What? How did you get here?" Marjorie asked in surprise.

"I came down on the bus," I answered.

"This morning?"

"No, I came down yesterday."

"Oh, come in, come in," she said. We sat down at a tiny table covered with a linen tablecloth. The apartment was neat and clean, but very small, hardly enough room for one. Marjorie offered me some tea and a bun. I was very hungry since I had not had breakfast, and had not eaten much the day before either.

I told her the whole sad story about Ruth, while I carefully nibbled at the bun so she wouldn't know how hungry I was.

"You haven't been running around with boys, have you?" she asked, looking at me very closely.

"No, Ruth was crazy about boys. I didn't go with them. I just stuck to my school work," I answered.

"I'm glad to hear that," Marjorie said. "Maybe this is all for the good. You should be going to Mechanic Arts High School. It is the best school in the state."

I knew Marjorie had graduated from Mechanic Arts, but I did not know that it was the best school.

"But first, we are going to visit Lucille."

Oh no, I thought. I didn't say anything. I just thought about how I'd left Lucille and Henry not that long ago. I wasn't sure they would want me back. It was only a few blocks walk to the duplex that they rented. I tried to think what I was going to say, and each step I took felt worse than the one before.

Marjorie knocked at their door. Henry came to the door and smiled.

"Well, well, look what the wind has blown in from the country." It was always Henry's way to make a joke about everything.

Lucille came in and looked at me with her piercing brown eyes. She did not smile. "What's the matter?" she asked.

Lucille sat tight-lipped while I once again told my sad story about Ruth.

Lucille said, "I'm not surprised by Ruth. But you, Sheila, I know you know better. Why didn't you tell your Aunt Lil? Aunt Lil is a nurse and she knows a thing or two."

I just sat there with my head down. I felt like a big clumsy idiot, but I did not know anything better to do.

"Well, right now we are going to write to Aunt Lil. She's probably worried sick about you two."

Marjorie then put in a good word for me. "Lucille, Sheila needs to go to Mechanic Arts High School. You remember how

Mother brought us here to get a good education. Besides, I can't see her going back to St. Cloud, after what Ruth has done."

It was decided then and there. I was going to go to Mechanic Arts High School and live with Lucille again, because Marjorie did not have room. The next week Marjorie took me to the school to register. It was a gigantic brick building four stories tall, looming in front of us on the top of the hill in front of Central Park on Robert Street. We walked up the steps and through the large front doors into a long quiet hallway. Marjorie opened the oak door to the office.

The secretary saw Marjorie and smiled. "What brings you back to Mechanic Arts?" she asked, clearly referring to when Marjorie had been a student.

Marjorie said, "This is my sister, Sheila Buchanan. She needs to register for school this fall."

"Come in. Have a seat. I will see if anyone is available to help you."

We sat down in the wooden chairs in the waiting area. I was beginning to think we should leave when the secretary returned and said, "I'm sorry you have had to wait so long. The Assistant Principal is out right now, but the Principal, Dietrich Lange, has offered to see you."

Marjorie whispered to me, "You are lucky. He is usually too busy to see anyone. He is usually off during the summer, writing wonderful books about nature."

We were ushered into a spacious office with lovely paintings of wild flowers on the walls. The Principal himself put together my schedule of classes. I still have my report card from that fall semester, which ended in January, 1930.[79] I took Drawing,

---

79. Information taken from Sheila's report card for the semester ending in January. Grades were reported every month, and the report was signed by Lucille Bartlett for the first two months, and Marjorie Buchanan the third month. The last month is not signed. On file.

French II, History III, English III, Math II and Gym. I had found the classes in St. Cloud to be easy, but here school was a whole different story. I had just one study hall a few days a week, when I did not have Gym, and the homework, especially in History and English, overwhelmed me.

Lucille helped me get a job at the hospital. High school books and supplies were not free, so I needed to work to pay for them. I waited on tables for the nurses, but they did not let me work in the doctors' dining

Aunt Lil, Uncle Cass and the baby Jerry.

room. I did not know why, but years later Lucille told me that it was because I was too pretty and they felt the doctors would try to take advantage of me.

In October, Ruth had her baby; and named him "Jerry." Unlike most unwed mothers at that time, Ruth was able to keep her baby. Aunt Lil went to that home for unwed mothers and demanded that Ruth be allowed to keep the baby. Aunt Lil did not care what the neighbors thought, she was not going to let her great-grandchild go to an orphanage. Although Ed Parseau showed up later and Ruth married him, I never did care much for him. Aunt Lil forgave Ruth and me, but I never forgave myself, for running away like that. Above is a picture of Aunt lil and Uncle Cass with their great-grandchild Jerry as a little boy.

* * *

On October 29, 1929, our local newspaper, *The St. Paul Daily News*, carried the United Press Wire Reports "STOCKS HIT NEW DEPTHS" along with an editorial by Arthur Brisbane warning "Quite an Earthquake. Don't Sacrifice Your Stocks."[80] The editorial told people not to panic or sell their stocks.

My sister Lucille loved reading the newspaper. She and Henry followed every story, and today they were excited. I wasn't sure why, since we didn't own any stock.

Henry said, "This Arthur Brisbane just does not get it does he? He's telling people to hold on to their stocks. Lucille, I think this is it. This is what Karl Marx was telling us about. Capitalism is collapsing, just like he predicted."

Lucille took the paper and studied it. "Don't go counting your chickens before they're hatched," she cautioned.

That was just like Lucille. She loved to quote the old sayings. She sounded just like my father.

I guess we were lucky that we didn't have any money in the bank. People lined up to take their money out of the banks because the banks were not insured as they are today. The banks ran out

---

80. The St. Paul Daily News, October 29, 1927, front page from microfilm at Minnesota History Center.

Bury it and it will grow

of money and closed their doors, so people whose money was in those banks lost their savings. I think I was remembering that time, along with thinking of the Pinocchio story when I made this the cartoon "Bury it and it will grow."

I looked at her in shock. I had never thought of such a thing. *It would be wonderful. I would be able to go to France with her. She went every summer and I was sure she would take me.*

"I don't know," I answered. "My sister Lucille is my guardian. I will have to ask her." In those days one was not an adult until age 21, so even though I was already 17, I would be under Lucille's guidance for four more years.

I told Lucille about it that very evening. "A very surprising thing happened at school today."

"What was that?" Lucille asked.

"Well I was studying with my French teacher, Miss Moosbrugger, after school, and she said she wanted to adopt me."

"She said what?" questioned Lucille.

"She said she wanted to adopt me."

"Well you just tell her that you are a Buchanan, and you will stay a Buchanan. How could you think of changing your name?"

Once again I was surprised. *Yes, I was a Buchanan, and I supposed if I was adopted I would have to change my name. But I wondered why Lucille was so angry about it?*

I told Miss Moosbrugger that my sister would not give permission for me to be adopted, and Miss Moosbrugger did not pursue it any further.[81]

For many, many years I've wondered what my life would have been like if I had been adopted. But at the time I didn't think much about it. I was sure I'd be fine on my own. I studied, and got better at school. I dreamed and I read. I read a book published in 1904 called *Green Mansions* by Henry William Hudson. I felt that the story had been written about me, a stranger in a strange land. The main character was a young girl from a lost tribe, who lived alone in the forest, at home with the wild animals. She wove her clothes from the threads of spider webs. Often, when I sat in class I would dream of being home, back in the Australian bush. I remembered the damp smell of the bush and the clamor of parrots. One spring day I just couldn't stand it anymore. I put my books in my locker and walked out the door.

---

81. Elmire M. Moosbrugger lived from 1898-1974. She never married and never had any children. (http://www.ancientfaces.com/person/elmire-m-moosbrugger/71392276} According to the *University of Minnesota Bulletin* she received her Bachelor of Arts degree in education from there in 1918. She would have been 32 when she inquired about adopting Sheila. She was still teaching French at Mechanic Arts in 1945 when Bernice Fischer attend the school. In 2004, Fischer remembered that in 1945 Miss Moosbrugger wore old-fashioned shoes and print dresses, and how the boys got her angry by taking the door knob off the classroom door. (see above)

The sun was shining and the birds were rejoicing in a chorus of, "It's spring. It's spring." I walked through the city streets, down to the park along the Mississippi River. There I climbed a tree, and sat, feeling calm and totally at peace in my natural habitat. I stayed all afternoon, and then went home. I didn't think about any rules.

When I arrived at school the next day, the homeroom teacher called me up to his desk. "Sheila Buchanan come, here is a note."

The note read, "Sheila Buchanan report to the Assistant Principal."

I wondered, *what is this about?*

I went directly to the office and sat waiting until I was called. I entered the Assistant Principal's office and sat down, looking at him with trepidation.

"Miss Buchanan, I have a report here that indicates you were truant yesterday. Is this true?"

I put my head down, remembering, yes, I had walked out of school yesterday. "Yes sir," I whispered. I was not one to talk back or to lie.

"Did you know that this is not allowed?"

"No sir," I replied. I really had not thought if it was allowed or not.

The Assistant Principal looked at me, tapping his fingers on his desk. "You didn't know?"

"No sir," I murmured, even more quietly.

Again he tapped his fingers on the desk. I wondered if he was going to kick me out of school. Finally he smiled at me and said, "Well, you just tell that young man of yours not to meet you during school hours."

I was shocked, but I did not say anything, I did not correct him and tell him that I had not left to see a young man, rather to respond to the call of spring. Perhaps, if this had been Principal Dietrich Lange who wrote books about nature, I might have said something but I was glad to be sent back to class with just a warning.

Sheila, in her graduation dress, June 1930

Graduation was coming up and I was worried. I did not have a dress for the graduation. It was my French teacher who told me that the school was giving me a dress. I was overjoyed, too overjoyed to feel ashamed that I could not afford a dress. I did not graduate with honors like my sister had, nor did I get a scholarship, but I believed I could get a job and work my way through college. I had confidence in my ability to work hard and make it happen.

But the Depression had other plans for me.

CHAPTER 13

LOSING

As soon as I graduated from Mechanic Arts High School I started looking for a job. Every day I read the want ads in the *St. Paul Pioneer Press* and walked downtown looking for jobs in the stores. It was June, 1930, and everyone was getting laid off from their work. The banks had closed their doors, leaving investors without their savings. There was no unemployment for people who lost their jobs, no insurance on bank-deposits, no minimum wage and Social Security did not exist.[82]

President Herbert Hoover thought the way to get the economy moving again was to cut spending. When campaigning for President in 1928, Hoover said "we are nearer to the final triumph over poverty than ever before in the history of any land. . . . Given a chance to go forward with the policies of the last eight years, we shall soon, with the help of God, be in sight of the day when poverty will be banished from this nation."[83] But in 1930, nothing was working. I just wanted to get a job so I could go to college. There were no government loans for students. Towns and cities provided for the poor but there was no national or state welfare help.[84] Until they ran out, churches and cities handed out a loaf

---

82. Paraphrased from Schlesinger, *The Crisis of the Old Order 1919-1933,* location 77 in the forward to the Mariner Edition.

83. Ibid. loc 66.

84. Greenberg, *Social History of the United States,* p. 23.

of bread and a tin cup of soup if one waited long enough. Usually it was men who stood in these lines, while women stayed home.

Henry and Lucille were constantly in Communist party meetings or off circulating petitions, leaving Charlotte home alone. Henry was on the ballot for the Secretary of State for Minnesota, and Lucille was running for the Mayor of St. Paul.[85] In those days it was unheard of for a woman to run for Mayor. But this was the time for change and they were working to make it happen. The Communist Party platform promoted a national bill to provide social insurance to all workers unemployed or unable to work because of sickness, injury, maternity or old age. The insurance would be paid for by a tax levy on all capital and property over $25,000, and a graduated income tax on all incomes in excess of $5,800 per year.[86]

I walked the streets of St. Paul so much there were holes in the soles of my shoes. I put cardboard inside my shoes and continued to walk, going from business to business asking, "Do you need any help?" I continued to read the *St. Paul Pioneer Press* every morning, looking through the dwindling want ads. They all wanted someone with experience, if they wanted anyone at all. Then on July 6, I saw an ad in the paper that looked hopeful:

LADIES

Time is money. Don't waste yours.
We can place a few neat appearing
ladies in a dignified position where
they can earn $25 weekly and more.
No selling, no collecting. All or part
time employment. Apply in person.
Room 612, 360 Robert St. bldg.[87]

---

85. Minnesota History Center Library Radicals in Minnesota file #119 lists Minnesota Communists Candidates in 1930. This is also mentioned in Lucille's FBI file.

86. Paraphrased from Minnesota History Center Library file #119 flyer listing candidates and platform.

87. *St. Paul Daily News.* July 6, 1930.

The very next day I put on my best dress. I polished my shoes and inserted new cardboards in them. From the top one could not see the holes in the bottom. I found a pair of silk stockings without a run and slipped those over my legs. I was excited, a real ad, and it made no mention of any experience being needed. I was shy, but I could be neat and friendly. The address was about a mile from home, and I practically skipped all the way there. This was it; this was the job.

I arrived at 360 Robert Street, an old building on the outskirts of downtown. It did not look like a business that needed a receptionist. Slowly I walked up the stairs and opened the glass door. A man got up from the desk in the back and shook my hand. "Welcome Miss?" he inquired.

"Miss Buchanan," I answered. "I am here to answer your ad in the *St. Paul Pioneer Press*."

"Oh, yes," he said, with a lecherous smile, looking me up and down. His eyes lingered on my breasts and then lit up as he stared at the curves in my legs.

I squirmed and looked around the room. There were a couple of very sad looking women with painted faces sitting in chairs. They were not working on anything, just sitting there, staring blankly. They did not say anything, but their blank unfocused eyes told me, "Go away!!"

With my heart pounding I stayed calm, smiling, as I listened to this sleazy man.

"We've got just the position for you. There is a company in Chicago that needs a receptionist with your youthful enthusiasm. Why you could even start tomorrow." My palms felt sweaty as I gingerly picked up my purse.

"Oh, that sounds very interesting, but my sisters are expecting me home any minute now. I'll be back tomorrow."

I was afraid he wouldn't let me out the door. I'd heard of operations like this, where they recruited young girls, got them on drugs and turned them into prostitutes. I walked calmly to the door. As soon as I closed the door, I ran down the stairs and all the way back to Lucille's.

I cleaned the house, cooked and kept Charlotte company. I still looked in the want ads but there seemed to be fewer every day. The election came on November 6, 1930. Lots of people rejoiced because Floyd B. Olson, the Farmer-Labor candidate, won. Poor Lucille only got 285 votes for mayor.[88] Henry, along with the other Communist candidates, came in last among those running for Secretary of State. But he did get at least one vote in every county: 1451 votes in Ramsey County (St. Paul), 2101 votes in Hennepin County (Minneapolis) and 1540 votes in St. Louis County (Duluth and the Iron Range). There were lots of unhappy voters interested in changing the way things were going.

It was already the middle of May and the weather was unusually hot and dry. It was almost a year since I had graduated from high school and I still had not found work. One day a letter from my brother Charlie arrived. I was so excited I opened it right away. It was addressed it to Marjorie Buchanan and sisters, so that meant me too. He had started writing the letter in February, but had not mailed it until the end of April. There were really two letters in that envelope.

Charlie wrote:

Imbil Q. Australia
5-2-1931 (February 5, 1931)

My dear Marjorie,

I have been putting off letter writing until a rainy day came along. The rainy day is here now with a vengeance. It's more like a rainy week though....

The boys are quite O.K. Boy & Jack are off to school again and doing well. Jack was put up one class, though he had only

---

88. This is a remembered estimate from the family (Charlotte Wasiluk).

been going six months, the work is a bit hard but he doesn't worry, an earthquake wouldn't worry Jack. Boy is a very different disposition, very merry, easily excited, takes his studies too seriously. George is an absolute wild cat, a talking machine, and very cheeky, but lovable. Last night he went up the road with me while I was doing a bit of weed pulling. He was asking the difference between a footstool and a mushroom. A footstool turned out to be a toadstool, a bit further on he informed me that "that was an onion tree," the "onion" tree was a bunyan tree. You can't open your mouth but he repeats what you say. Boy has a very nice voice for singing and they all love music of any sort. . . .

Unemployment question is as you say very acute here. We have been very fortunate so far. The farmers are receiving very little for their produce now too, but there is a tremendous difference between what he gets, and what we pay. If the difference between the consumer and the producer could be bridged living would be cheaper. Very few people seem to realize that everyone who works is a consumer as well as a producer.

You should not worry about sending us any parcel this year. We are intending to send one along directly for you.

Have leased the paddock along the road that passes our house and intend to buy and rear up some calves to sell, not to go in for dairying, but to sell for a profit. A few cows together with a garden will keep us alive and make a welcome addition to our income if everything goes alright. Just at present there are a large number of men employed here on an unemployment relief scheme, I have twenty under me. Thank God there is no severe winter here or conditions would be desperate. As it is I expect there will be serious trouble in the South.

The next day, still it rains, it makes over a week of it when it does..

Peggy has just driven the boys down to school. They usually ride but it's hard for them to keep dry.

30-4-31 (April 30, 1931)

Dear sisters

Have been a very long time getting this away to you. Your Easter cards for the boys received early this week awakened a dormant conscience, so here goes again. The lads were very pleased with their cards. Your winter will be over now, thank goodness you will say! Have been often worrying about you, since we read so much about the unemployment problem being so acute in USA. The politicians here tell us it is because we borrowed too much money, you have all the gold & your politicians say you don't loan enough money. It looks as if poor old much abused Russia was the only nation that could see daylight ahead the more they produce the worse for the rest of the world. Our dad always used to say that Russia and China would be the two powers that would fight out the final conflict between East & West. . . .

The garden has been a huge success, all the beans & tomatoes we could eat, sweet potatoes, ordinary ones, carrots, beet root, parsnips, peas, lettuce, rhubarb, broad beans, pumpkin, cabbages, the melon were late. Peggy sold quite a lot of tomatoes and I have 600 plants in now for the winter, if they are good we should have a small cheque. Peggy has been caring for artistic side of the garden, has had beautiful roses, dahlias, gainais, chrysanthemums, sweet peas are now in. It's wonderful how a few flowers improve or rather make a house a home.

A friend has been giving us the National Geographic Magazine to read and we think of subscribing to it. It is the best Yankee production I have seen and the boys spend hours pouring over it. Had an Easter card from Sheila yesterday, evidently she has been sick again, goodness how I wish I could get you out of that detestable climate. George is a seeker after knowledge yesterday he asked "how many feet has God got" and when there was no answer his philosophic brother Mac of 4 years quoted "the questions of a

*child confound the wise man," but you want to be an encyclopedic
alright. We all send you all, fondest love*

Your loving brother,
Charlie Buchanan.

How I longed to see him and to meet his children. It was so
hard to be stuck here so far away from my real home.

Things here in America seemed to be getting worse every day.
One quarter of the population had no income and there were no
food stamps. I could not help but see the headlines while I read
the want ads. In February there was a "food riot" in Minneapolis. Several hundred men and women smashed the windows of a
grocery store and made off with fruit, canned goods, bacon and
ham. A store owner pulled out a gun, but the looters leapt on him
and broke his arm. The riot was brought under control by 100
policemen.[89]

My sister Marjorie still had a job, but she took some time off
and went to a Communist convention in Chicago. There she met
a very nice gentleman from Sweden named Alfred Benson. Alfred
was very kind and gentle and spoke with a heavy musical Swedish
accent. He was well-educated. As a younger son there was nothing
for him to inherit in Sweden, so he had immigrated to America.
Alfred came to Minneapolis and proposed to Marjorie. Marjorie
was not one to talk about her feelings but I know she loved this
man. Without hesitation, she said "Yes." They never kissed or even
held hands in front of me, but the look in their eyes said "Love."

Marjorie and Alfred were married by the Justice of the Peace.
Someone snapped this photo of us on the courthouse steps.

Lucille thought this was just wonderful, and she wanted me to
be happy too. I just looked for work and stayed home. I really did
not want anything to do with politics or marriage.

---

89. Timeline of the Great Depression www.pbs.org/wgbh/american
experience/features/timeline.

On the left Marjorie and I on the courthouse steps. On the right I'm feeling shy next to my new brother Alfred Benson

"Sheila, you really need to get out more," Lucille would tell me.

"I don't want to go anywhere."

Sometimes I would dream about what my life would have been like if I'd been adopted by my French teacher Miss Moosbrugger; or if I was still in Australia.

Lucille kept badgering me to get out, so finally I went out to a picnic that the Young Communist League had organized.

I wore an old dress I'd had in high school. It fell straight down in the style of the 1920's, and did not enhance my curvy figure. My shoes were the same ones I wore to the job interview, complete with cardboard.

Elm trees lined the streets of St. Paul, forming a canopy over the road, and the parks were some of the finest in the United States. The hot air hung on into the evening, and the flowers bloomed where they had been watered. When I reached the park I saw picnic tables covered with checkered table cloths. Some people were seated at the tables and others sat on cloths spread on the ground. I approached a table overflowing with food that someone with money must have donated. There were apples, potato salad, hot dogs, tomatoes and even fresh watermelon. I hadn't had watermelon for ages.

A young man walked away from a group of guys and approached me, "Hi, Sheila, I'll get you a plate."

It was Ernest Heikkinen. He was not much taller than me, with dark hair and intelligent eyes that never stopped looking around the room. He'd been to the house a lot to do work for Henry and Lucille. I knew they liked him and said he was a hard worker for the party.[90]

Ernest came back with a plate and I gingerly picked up some watermelon and potato salad to put on it.

I fixed my eyes on that luscious watermelon as I sat down on the edge of a picnic table. I licked my parched lips anticipating the sweet moisture of the watermelon.

"Sheila, I'm so glad you came."

"I didn't know you were going to have watermelon," I answered.

"That's not all we have. We've got home brewed wine and beer too. Let me get you a glass of sweet wine."

I was shocked. It was prohibition. Liquor was illegal. They did allow some home brewing, but Lucille and Henry never drank.

Ernest placed a glass of wine in front of me. I ignored the wine and sank my teeth into my watermelon instead.

Ernest sat down beside me with his drink and said, "You know, don't you Sheila, you're the prettiest girl here." All the guys laughed. "In fact, I was telling everyone how I was hoping that you'd come."

"Don't be silly; there are lots of pretty girls here," I said, turning red.

---

90. The description of Ernest working for the Party was provided by Henry's daughter Charlotte Wasiluk. The exact scene is made up. Sheila told me that Lucille talked her into attending this Communist League party in St. Paul and Ernest raped her in a park on her way home.

"None that compare to you," he whispered in my ear, so the others wouldn't hear. He took my hand in his.

I pulled my hand away. "That's just silly talk."

Everyone was holding a drink and laughing really loudly. The guys and gals were all sitting in couples, really close to each other. Some were kissing in public which shocked me. My sisters did not even kiss their husbands in front of me. It was beginning to get dark. This whole thing had been a bad idea. Looking around I got up quickly and said, "I need to get home."

"I'll walk you home," Ernest said.

I didn't want him to, but I didn't say anything. After all, young ladies were not supposed to walk around town alone in the dark. I just grabbed my handbag and headed towards home.

Ernest thought he was a gift to every pretty girl in town, but I wasn't interested. As I walked quickly down the street towards home, perspiration started to drip into my eyes. The normal coolness of evening had not arrived. Ernest followed me. I started to walk faster, and he walked faster too. He was gaining on me. Finally when the street got dark he caught up and put his arm around my waist. "Go away,." I said.

"Oh, you don't really want me to go away, do you?" he asked.

"Yes, I do. Just go away! It's too hot out for this," I replied, pulling my body away from him.

He grabbed my arm and pressed against me, covering my mouth with his lips.

"See how nice it is, just a kiss. You are so beautiful. I don't want any other girl, just you, Sheila."

"Let go of me! Let me go!" I hissed, pushing him away and thinking I did not want to cause a commotion.

We were still walking in the park, with no houses nearby. It was all so sudden. He pushed me down onto the ground, covering my mouth as he pulled up my skirt and pressed into my body. I struggled against his sweltering body. I tried to scream. I tried to pull away. He was strong. I felt him bang against me, shoving his

Ernest with two girls

penis into my body. It burned like someone had lit a match inside me. He panted against me, his hand still over my mouth. "Oh Sheila, you are so wonderful," he moaned.

As soon as he released me I jumped up and ran home, tears streaming down my face, my hair plastered against my neck, wet from perspiration. No one saw me tear into my bedroom and close the door. I lay on my bed gasping for breath, trying to understand what had happened. I was bleeding. What had I done that caused him to do this to me? Was I asking for it? That's what they said if a girl got on with a boy, she was asking for it. I was ashamed, so ashamed I did not tell anyone.

CHAPTER 14

MARRIED

The next day Ernest came to Lucille's apartment. He knocked on the door and Lucille answered. I just wanted to hide.

"Oh, come on in. Sit down, have a cup of coffee." She greeted him like she would anyone, especially someone she knew from the Communist Party meetings.

"Thank you Ma'am, but I really came to see Sheila."

"Sheila, come out here, you've got a visitor," Lucille's voice sang out joyously.

I stayed in the bedroom trembling, every part of my body tensed. I said, "I'm not feeling well today." I truly was not well. My arm ached painfully where he had grabbed me and my insides burned where he had violated me.

Ernest said loudly so I could hear. "I'm so sorry she is not well. I'll come back tomorrow."

He left and I felt like I could breathe again, as my tense body relaxed.

True to his word, the next day Ernest came back, and Lucille let him in. I was feeling better so I agreed to talk to him. I wanted to tell him myself, "Go Away!!"

As soon as Lucille left the room he got down on his knees and said, "Sheila, I'm so sorry I hurt you. You are just so beautiful, I just got carried away. Please forgive me. I'll make it up to you, I promise."

It was strange to see this usually quirky smirky guy kneeling on the floor.

He looked like a sick puppy dog. He was so funny that I relaxed a little bit. I looked at him with sad eyes, but I failed to say "Go away!" like I'd planned.

He got up and sat in the chair. "I'm so sorry, Sheila, I was drunk. If you let me see you I will never do that again, unless you want me to."

He left, saying, "I'll be back tomorrow."

I was confused. He seemed sincere. What if I was pregnant?[91] I'd better let him see me just in case.

Ernest came almost every day. He did not try anything again and seemed very nice. He took me for walks and talked of grand plans. He was going to make the world a safe and fair place for the working man. He was going to write a book.

Marjorie got a letter from Charlie dated February 7, 1932, in response to the news of her marriage to Alfred Benson:

My dear sisters

First of all Marjorie, let me wish you, belated as it is, a wish full of feeling, much happiness, and contentedness on your new venture, congratulations to both of you, to our new brother. I never had any brothers, but you girls are doing your best to remedy this deficiency. The nationality doesn't matter a tinkers ass. There are always ups and downs in matrimony, as the man said a cat and dog can live quite peacefully together, but if you tie their tails together you start a first class row. You received some very nice wedding presents and still have one to come from us when we can send it. We would very much like to see you all but unless the Golden Casket (winning the lottery) comes our way, it seems a long way off yet.

---

91. All abortion was illegal at this time even in case of rape.

> *Peggy and three boys, plus sister Florence are just home from a fortnight in the briny ocean at Noose Heads. We have been having a very hot summer and since Christmas very dry, and as you wrote in your first letter we are also having an epidemic of infantile paralysis (polio) 150 cases in Queensland so far and no sign of it abating. We wanted to give the boys a change before school, and in the meantime the schools have been closed. We are not panicky, but a bit nervous of course as there have been two deaths in Imbil. The new serum is giving good results as long as it is taken in time...*
>
> *We are anxious to hear from Sheila again. Here's hoping you are all well and happier than in your last letter.*
>
> *Your loving brother*
> *Charlie*

Reading this letter made me wish I could win the Lottery, or at least get a job. There was nothing to do; I went to the library, and Ernest came by to visit. In March the weather was unusually cold, and I longed for the heat Charlie complained about.[92]

I even helped Lucille by taking care of the little kids at Young Pioneers, the Communist Party Youth Group.

People continued to lose their jobs. In March, 1932, I read in the *St. Paul Daily News* that three thousand unemployed workers marched on the Ford Motor Company's plant in River Rouge, Michigan. Dearborn police and the Ford company guards attacked the workers, killing four and injuring many more.[93]

Ernest did manage to land a job as a cook. He proposed to me. I believed that what he had done was a mistake and would never happen again. Besides who would ever marry me now? I said yes and we were married in the court house on June 15, 1932. My

---

92. Description of 1930's weather from St. Martin, *Decade of Disconsolation,* umn pdf.

93. PBS Timeline of the Great Depression.

Sheila, back row, Pioneers, St. Paul, 1930

sister Lucille and her husband Henry were our witnesses. Lucille had not wanted me to be adopted, but yet here I was, married and my name had changed. I became Sheila Heikkinen

Right after we were married Ernest lost his job. The beginning of July, after being married only two weeks, we moved in with Henry and Lucille.[94] It was very crowded, and there was hardly anything to eat. After a week Ernest came back from looking for work and standing in a bread line. He was tired and angry.

"Sheila, let's get out of here. We don't have to stay here. We can go to my family's farm in Phelps, Wisconsin, near Upper Michigan. There are lots of deer in the woods to eat and we always have potatoes."

"But Marjorie is going to have her baby any time now," I said, startled at the idea of leaving.

"Look there's nothing for us here."

"Uncle Cass planted tobacco last spring. He worked hard

---

94. Henry Bartlett's daughter Charlotte remembers the newly married Sheila and Ernest living with them. She said they appeared very much in love, and was surprised to learn Ernest had raped Sheila.

raising it and watering it through the drought. The buyers only gave him half of what he spent on seeds and fertilizer. After all that work he ended up in debt. All they managed to keep was the Model T," I argued, thinking Ernest's family would not be able to feed us.

"My family doesn't owe anything on the farm in Phelps. They always raised what we ate so it will be just fine. It is close to Lake Superior, which is not going to dry up. They'll be happy to have us. You'll see."

"I've got to stay and help Marjorie. She doesn't know anything about babies."

"And you do?" Ernest asked incredulously.

"Yes, I did lots of babysitting. Marjorie has never cared for a baby."

"All right, we'll try to hang on a little longer," he agreed grudgingly.

Marjorie's baby, Cathleen Anne Benson, was born July 11, 1932. I stayed with her, and taught her how to take care of the baby. We were both glad that I'd done that babysitting. Ernest and I left in August. Tiny baby Cathleen was just a month old, and I hated to leave, but we had no way to stay.

Ernest had a very old car. Sometimes we had to stop to make sure it did not overheat. We went up one hill and down the next, then up another hill and down the next, each one a little higher, and the road a little narrower. The air got cooler as we got closer to Lake Superior. The woods on either side got more and more dense. This was not an oak woods. Actually it was not a woods at all, but rather a pine forest. How I longed to stop and walk. It reminded me so much of the Australian bush, but we just drove on and on.

Finally, we turned down a little rocky road, more like a path than a road. At the end of the road was a cabin surrounded by fields of potatoes. The fields were fenced with rocks piled around them. Just beyond the small cabin was a very tiny cabin which seemed too small to possibly be a house and further back a very simple barn. As we approached Ernest yelled out in words that I did not understand. Ernest had told me his parents were Finnish immigrants.

A very small woman, perhaps four feet tall, came to the door. Her long gray hair was pulled back from her face. Ernest said something to her and motioned towards me. The woman smiled a smile that spoke more than any words. She took my right hand in both of her strong wrinkled hands and pulled it up and down. "Tervetullut tytar, tervetuloa kottin!" She looked into my eyes and touched my hair. "Tytar" she said again. Ernest had not told me his mother did not speak English. She did not need to speak English. Her body language welcomed me. She was overjoyed to have a daughter.

I came to know her as "Aiti," Mother. She always called me "Tytar," Daughter. She had only had sons but no daughters; no one to help her in the house. I helped cook, and peel potatoes; we hauled in wood and cooked over a wood stove. Potatoes were the only vegetable that they ate. We had lots of food, mainly venison (deer meat), fish, potatoes, eggs, chicken and a little pork.

At the end of the week, we hauled wood to the tiny cabin that nobody seemed to live in. Walking into the tiny cabin I saw just two rooms. There was an outer room with hooks and a bench, and an inner room with a pot-bellied stove, surrounded by rocks and benches on the walls, one higher than the others. Aiti filled the small stove with wood and lit the fire. She placed pans of water on the stove. Then we went back to the house. After about an hour the boys and her husband went to the tiny cabin and went inside. They made lots of noise and stayed there a long time. Then I saw them come out, naked and laughing, throwing buckets of water on each other. I looked away, embarrassed. Soon they dressed and returned to the house. Ernest said, "Now it's your turn."

Sauna 1932 sketch Sheila Buchanan

"My turn for what?" I asked.

"Your turn for a sauna," he replied, laughing.

I followed Aiti to the small cabin and she undressed. She motioned me to undress too. I had never undressed in front of anyone since I was a child, but I followed her lead. We went into the room with a stove. It was very hot and perspiration flowed from my body and into my eyes. Aiti gently poured warm water over me, and motioned for me to sit. I felt the warmth seep into every pore of my body. All the dirt from traveling and working flowed out of me. After what seemed like an eternity, she motioned me out of the stove room. She took a bucket of cold water and poured it over my steaming body. Pores that had been opened by the heat, closed, and I shivered. She gave me a towel and I got dressed. I had never felt so clean in all my life.

The next day was Saturday and that night the boys got some moonshine and went drinking. Ernest came home late. He threw me down on the bed in our little corner. Behind the curtain he raped me just like he did that first night. He didn't kiss me, he was not tender, he just forced himself on me. Not just once but again and again. I cried out in pain, but I could not run away. This was my husband. I had married him.[95]

95. Sheila told me he apologized to her. But many times she would say, "Why did I marry him. I wasn't pregnant." In 1932 women had the right to vote, but very few other rights; there was no such thing as wife rape.

CHAPTER 15

CHANGING TIMES

The next morning I woke up early. Ernest had left for the day. My body was bruised from Ernest banging on me. I crawled out of bed and dragged myself into the kitchen. Aiti put her arm around me. She kept repeating in my ear, "Olen pahoillani. Olen niin pahoillani että hän kohtelee sinua niin." I felt a warm security from those words that I later learned meant, "I'm sorry, I'm so sorry he treats you that way."

I walked quickly away from that tiny cabin into the forest. Thimbleberries appeared along the path, soft and sweet, begging to be eaten, but in my grief I ignored them. My feet stepped without a sound on the soft moss that blanketed the floor under huge pine trees. I lay down in the soft moss next to a fallen log. A tear fell from my eye and landed on a lovely little flower, reaching through the dark forest, searching for the sunlight. A small black insect crawled across the forest floor minding its own business. I looked up and saw the light slanting through the trees. The peace of the forest held me close. Here there was hope.

A red squirrel played boss of the forest. He traveled down the tree complaining all the way. "Who is this in my woods? Look there is something, someone lying there. I'll jump a little closer, a little closer, chip, chip." The red squirrel squeaked and ran up the huge pine tree. Oh, to live in a tree, to stay in the woods and not return to that crowded cabin, to Ernest, to sleepless nights with demands from him. Ernest had promised me he would not hurt me again, but now. . . .

When Ernest came home in the afternoon he seemed unaware that he had hurt me. He said, "Sheila come, I want to show you someplace magical."

I hesitated, remembering last night. "I'm awfully busy right now," I said, heading towards his mother in the kitchen.

"Oh come on you'll love this," he said, saying something in Finnish to his mother. She smiled and nodded.

I looked at her. She smiled and nodded again, motioning me to go with him.

Reluctantly I got in his old car and we went down a very narrow road, actually just a path through the trees, not a road at all. We stopped and walked into the forest. I saw in front of me a small lake surrounded by thick spongy moss. As we walked closer to the lake Ernest said, "Sheila, watch where you step. If you aren't careful you will fall through."

"What?" I asked, wondering if he was trying to trick me or do something nasty. I felt the ground tremble as I gingerly stepped on it. The moss I was walking on formed a thick mat that floated on the surface of the water. Dragonflies fluttered all around me. I saw flowers so lovely I felt I was back in the Australian bush; ferns so delicate one would think they were fairy wings. A strange plant had red veined cups surrounding a thick stalk with a vibrant red flower drooping down towards the moss. The cups held water that intensified the colors

Ernest explained, "In those cups the pitcher plant catches insects and dissolves them in liquid. "

I bent down and stared inside the veined pitcher. I watched a mosquito floating dead inside the liquid. So beautiful, yet so vicious. "Oh my," I said. Ernest held my hand and gently guided me over the bog, helping me to be careful where I stepped.

Sometimes Ernest was nice but then he would turn nasty and attack me. I never knew when he would change. Often it happened when he was drinking, but sometimes he had not been drinking. Suddenly he would yell, "I saw you looking at that guy. Remember, you're married to me." I hadn't looked at anyone.

* * *

In the fall of 1932, the rest of the country was excited about the elections coming up, but on the farm everyone worked to get ready for winter. Ernest was 21 and it was his first chance to vote. I could not vote. I was not 21 yet, nor was I a citizen since I had not been born in America.

"Who are you going to vote for?" I asked Ernest.

"Sheila, don't you know? I'm certainly not going to vote for that Hoover, and his Hoovervilles.[96] But I'm not going to vote for the rich Roosevelt either. Of course I'm going to vote for William Z. Foster, the Communist Party candidate. He's the only one running for the people. He knows what's going on. This is the end of capitalism and soon we will have a workers' republic."

I didn't really know who was running, as I hadn't paid much attention to all the political talk. But I decided not to say anything, rather than have Ernest yell at me. I did pay attention to the results. William Z. Foster came in fourth after the Socialist candidate Norman Thomas. Franklin D. Roosevelt won 472 electoral votes to Herbert Hoover's 59 electoral votes. It was an overwhelming victory for Roosevelt. People with money were scared. A Los Angeles banker said "The farmers will rise up. So will labor. The Reds will run the country—or maybe the Fascists. Unless, of course, Roosevelt does something."[97]

---

96. The name that was given to the shacks that homeless people built on the edge of the cities. Democratic National Committee publicity director and longtime newspaper reporter Charles Michelson (1868-1948) is credited with coining the term, which first appeared in print in 1930. http://www.history.com/topics/hoovervilles.

97. Schlesinger, *The Crisis of the Old Order.*

The snow piled higher than I had ever seen it in Minnesota. It came up to the roof of the house. The path between the house and the barn was like a tunnel that went by the sauna. After a sauna, instead of having cool water thrown on us, we would jump into a snowdrift. That was the best time of the week, and the only time I really felt warm.

If we were out and saw someone on the road we would stop and pick them up, for if we did not they would likely die from the cold. Even for Minnesota the winter of 1932 was extra cold. On November 26, it was 30 degrees below zero near St. Paul, and when Lake Superior froze it was even colder in Phelps, Wisconsin. The winter air was so cold I had to cover my mouth and nose, or my breath would freeze. Icicles formed on my scarf as the moisture from my breath cooled. The snow was pure white, and sparkled like silver in the sunlight. The colder it got the more it sparkled. The cold yet deadly beauty surpassed anything I had ever seen before.

On January 30, 1933, Adolf Hitler became Chancellor of Germany. I knew he was a Fascist and the Communists hated him, but I didn't know much else. He was far away in Germany. Surely this was not anything for us to worry about.

On March 4, 1933, with snow still on the ground, Ernest, his brothers and I crowded into our car and went to town. There was no radio on the farm because, like most of rural America at that time, they didn't have electricity.[98] Gathering around the only wireless radio in town at the local café, we strained our ears to hear the inaugural address of Franklin D. Roosevelt. "This is a day of national consecration," the radio crackled out in the voice of our new President. "Let me assert my firm belief that the only thing we have to fear is fear itself—nameless, unreasoning, unjustified terror which paralyzes needed efforts to convert retreat into advance." The radio crackled on.

---

98. There were very few farms in rural Wisconsin with electricity until the REA, Rural Electrification Administration, was established by Roosevelt in 1937. wisconsininhistory.org "Turning Points in Wisconsin History"

"Tell that to the hungry people standing in line in St. Paul," scoffed Ernest.

"Shh," his brothers and I looked at him straining to hear.

"There must be an end to a conduct in banking and in business which too often has given rise to instead of a sacred trust the likeness of callous and selfish wrongdoing…. This Nation asks for action and action now…We must act and act quickly. Our primary task is to put people to work… We must move as a trained and loyal army willing to sacrifice for the good of a common discipline, because without such discipline no progress is made… It may be," he added, his rich voice brimming with solemnity, "That an unprecedented demand and need for the undelayed action may call for temporary departure from that normal balance of public procedure"

I wondered, *temporary departure from what?* Then he clarified it. "I shall ask the Congress for the one remaining instrument to meet the crisis—broad Executive Power to wage a war against the emergency, as great as the power that would be given to me if we were in fact invaded by a foreign foe."[99]

"He's going to declare himself dictator. He's nothing but a rotten Fascist!" said Ernest.

I thought, *Give him a chance, he hasn't done anything yet*, but I didn't say anything out loud.

Later that week, the comedian Will Rodgers reflected on the mood of the whole country when he said, "America hasn't been so happy in three years as they are today, no banks, no work, no nothing."[100] Roosevelt did shut down all the banks and they did not open until March 9, when Congress passed the Emergency Banking Act in just eight hours.

When Ernest heard the news he scoffed, "Of course he'd do something to help out his rich cronies."

---

99. Listen to the entire 20 minute speech on line: google YouTube President Roosevelt 1933 inauguration C-CPAN originally published January 14, 2009.

100. Schlesinger, *The Crisis of the Old Order* Vol 2 p.13

Spring came, with pussy willows bursting out of the swamps around Lake Superior. In April, I received a letter that my sister Marjorie had forwarded from my dear brother Charlie:

March 27, 1933

My Dear sisters,

I was very pleased indeed to have your letter of Feb. 3 a couple of weeks ago. Marjorie I have intended to answer it every day since, but between laziness, tiredness and ceaselessness it keeps being put off.

Glad to hear Cathleen Ann is progressing so well, long may it continue, only if she could know her cousins our own Florence Margaret is the lovelist thing on earth, so we think, she is talking quite a bit now, and is a real scamp.

How the devil am I going to write to Sheila, she hasn't condescended to write to me, and you haven't told me her name, but above all I wish her happiness because, well just because I love her so!!

The photo of her was very good, everyone admired it, thanks for sending it Lucille. Sheila hurry up and tell us all about yourself, this Finn of yours. There is a colony of Finns near here growing bananas one I know called Nurrenkin, they are very decent industrious chaps....

I felt tears well into my eyes as I read this. How could I answer him? He would know how unhappy I am. I just kept quiet and did not write. But then I discovered that I was pregnant. It was a miracle; there was a child growing inside me. I thought, *what can I do to help this little one?* Suddenly it came to me.

I got some seeds and started a garden. I needed to eat good food for this little baby, something more than venison and potatoes. In May it rained. I harvested lettuce and spinach in the rain.

Ernest's family said, "Peura ruoka, peura ruoka" deer food, and turned up their noses. They would not even taste it.

After May it stopped raining and I hauled water to the garden from the pump almost every day. When the carrots came they feasted on them. I ate my lettuce and spinach. I ate everything I could for the little one growing inside me.

I told Ernest, "We have to go back to St. Paul. I need to be where there are good doctors to have the baby. Pretty soon we will have a new President and things will get better."

I'd been hearing about all the new laws that Roosevelt had passed and I hoped things would be better soon.[101]

"I don't know that anything will be better until after the Revolution," he declared. It almost sounded like he hoped things wouldn't get better.

I was going to go back to St. Paul, with or without him. I wasn't going to spend a winter in that cold little cabin with a tiny baby. Finally he agreed to come with me.

I gave birth in St. Paul on October 16, 1933, at Bethesda Hospital. On the birth certificate Ernest's occupation was "Unemployed," and mine was "Housewife".

---

101. These are most of the laws passed in Roosevelt's first 100 days:

March 9, The Emergency Banking Act;

March 20, The Economy Act;

March 31, The Civilian Conservation Corps established;

April 19, Abandoned the gold standard;

May 12, Federal Emergency Relief Act so there would not be a national relief system;

May 12; Agricultural Adjustment Act;

May 12, Emergency Farm Mortgage Act;

May 18, The Tennessee Valley Authority Act;

May 27, The Truth in Securities Act;

June 13, Home Owners' Loan Act for refinancing of home mortgages;

June 16, The National Industrial Recovery Act, a system of industrial self-government and a public works program;

June 16, The Glass-Steagall Banking Act, divorcing commercial and investment banking and guaranteeing bank deposits;

June 16, The Farm Credit Act;

June 16, The Railroad Coordination Act.

Information from Schlesinger, Crisis of the Old Order, vol. 2, p. 20.

Now Cathleen Ann Benson, my sister Marjorie's baby, would have a playmate. Being a mother was overwhelming. I loved my little boy with all my heart. My milk flowed and my breasts swelled so that I had to wear a towel all the time. Ernest did not help me, he just laughed at me.

I was filled with the joy and awe of motherhood. I wrote to my brother Charles and told him all about my little boy, Brian.[102]

---

102. His name has been changed because he did not want to be included in this book.

CHAPTER 16

THE DECADE OF DISCONSOLATION

Although Ernest was unemployed, everything was much better than before. The new relief agencies gave out real food and the hospital delivered little Brian without charging us anything.

On November 12, 1933, when Brian was barely a month old, I looked out the window at dark massive clouds, and called to Ernest.

"Look. Look at the sky. What is that?"

Ernest looked toward the window and then opened the door. The wind blew the door wide open, allowing dirt to fly into the apartment.

"Shut it!" I yelled, clutching Brian's face to my breast, while fine dust blew right into my face, eyes, and even into my teeth.

Ernest banged the door shut, but everything was already covered with dust. "I've never seen so much dirt," he said.

I picked up a cloth and tried to clean the dust up, but it just flew into the air, swirling like a flock of blackbirds. I got out the mop and a bucket and mopped the furniture and floors. After they dried, I used the dust cloth again, while Ernest sat idly by, watching me.

The winter continued to be strangely warm.[103] In January it was 50 degrees with very little snow. Uncle Cass and all the farmers

---

103. All weather facts are from: St. Martin, *Decade of Disconsolation* http://climate.umn.edu/pdf/Decade_of_disconsolation.pdf.

had plowed the fields in the fall so they would be ready for spring planting. Normally the earth would be frozen solid, and the fields covered with snow, but in a winter without snow or rain the soil just blew away. April brought the first big dust storm, followed the next week by pitch-black clouds from the Dakotas just west of us. They blew across Minnesota and all the way to North Carolina. In May, the temperatures were in the high 90s, which was simply unheard of for St. Paul. Then a cold front again blew the dust in from the Dakotas, turning day into night. The sprouting wheat was picked up from the fields and blown away.

I remembered that just the year before, under the Agricultural Adjustment Act, there was so much surplus that the government killed baby pigs and plowed under cotton to raise prices. They had planned to plow under the wheat as well, but now with the wind blowing the sprouting wheat away I did not know if there would be enough wheat to make bread. When I visited St. Cloud and went to church with Aunt Lil, the preacher declared that, "the drought and dust are the judgment of God on men who dared to plow under cotton and slaughter baby pigs."[104] Many people appeared to agree. I hoped the preacher was wrong. Washington rushed seed and feed to distressed areas and began to develop a plan to protect land and water.

In order to give the workers a way to get higher wages without government involvement[105] Roosevelt had created section 7a of the National Recovery Act. It stated that workers could bargain collectively, through unions of their own choosing. Under the new law, the unions tried to get organized that summer.

------

104. Schlesinger, vol 2, p. 70. Schlesinger says some people claimed this. Aunt Lil could have been one of those "some people."

105. Garrison and other labor relations experts persuaded Roosevelt and Congress with the argument that labor's right to organize was essential to a democratic society, not only as a matter of simple justice, but as a means of achieving economic and social balance. The bill was a safety measure, because he regarded organized labor as the chief bulwark against Communism and other revolutionary movements. Paraphrased from Ibid p. 403-404

On Monday, May 13, Ernest picked up the *St. Paul Daily News.* "Look," he said, "the truckers that planned a strike on May 12th for a closed shop have agreed to a modified agreement calling for recognition of the union.[106] Those chicken livers! Now is the time for action not compromise." At that time a third of the people in Hennepin County (which included Minneapolis) depended on public support for their bread.[107] Truck drivers' wages had gone down to less than $2.40 a day ($42 in 2015 dollars)[108] and sometimes they were paid in bruised vegetables. Everyone became involved trying to help on one side or the other. Lucille, who was always looking for a way to become involved, went to help in the kitchen serving the strikers. Ernest went over as an observer for the Communist Party.

The Citizen's Alliance, an organization of trucking companies, refused to agree to the compromise negotiated by the truck drivers and the Governor. The strike began tying up truck traffic. The Citizen's Alliance hired some students and football players from the University of Minnesota to either be "scabs" (strike breakers) or to protect the scabs. They were paid $5.00 a day, more than twice what the truckers were paid.[109] Tensions grew, and everyone in the two cities wondered, *how this would end?* Then on May 22, 1934, "over twenty thousand people crowded into Minneapolis's Central Marketplace. Many were police and special deputies, determined to clear the market for trucks. Others were workers, determined to keep the trucks off the streets. There was an ominous interval of waiting. Then a scuffle: a striker tossed a crate of tomatoes through a plate-glass window; and, in a moment, the square dissolved into a melee. Clubs rose and fell; people screamed, cursed and ran. Two special deputies were killed. Governor Floyd Olson ordered the mobilization of the National Guard."[110]

---

106. *St. Paul Daily News* May 14, 1934, Home edition.
107. Kennedy, *Freedom from Fear,* vol 1, loc 5502.
108. http://www.coinnews.net/tools/cpi-inflation-calculator/.
109. Wilbur Broms interview by Carl Ross, Minnesota Historical Society.
110. Schlesinger vol. 2 p. 388.

Lucille said, "You'll see what is going to happen now. That union is just going to give in, because it is run by that scoundrel Trotskyite Vincent Raymond Dunne. We kicked him out of the Communist Party in 1928."[111]

This time the union accepted a compromise on the basis of indirect union recognition, but the employers, hoping to smash the unions, broke off the talks. On July 16, 1934, the truckers voted again to strike. And again the trucks stopped moving. "The police sent out a truck with an armed convoy. A strikers' truck, manned by unarmed pickets, tried to block its way. The police, without warning, let loose a barrage of shotgun fire at the second truck and into a gathering crowd. In ten minutes they had shot 67 people, many in the back; two lay dying."[112]

"It was awful," Ernest said. "I'm glad I stayed on the sidelines observing."

I was glad I was not a widow.

Federal mediators worked out a new plan to settle the strike. Governor Olson declared that if both sides did not accept the plan, he would impose martial law. The union agreed but the employers refused, so the National Guard took over the city.

When Governor Olson ordered a reduction of pickets[113] and allowed some trucks to move, the workers demanded a voice in who decided who moved. Olson arrested the strike leaders. When Lucille heard she said, "You see that Olson, he's just a Fascist,"[114] shaking her head.

But then two days later Governor Olson ordered a similar raid of the businessmen's group, the Citizens' Alliance. This got the

---

111. There was a big split in the Communist Party between followers of Trotsky and Stalin. Charlotte Wasiluk remembered how Henry and Lucille disliked Trotskyites. Stalin later had Trotsky killed.

112. Schlesinger, vol 2, p. 388.

113. Pickets are strikers that line up in a picket line to stop the work from continuing, or in this case the trucks from moving.

114. Governor Olson was a very progressive Governor and had even encouraged the strikers. In this action Lucille and Henry would call him a Fascist.

negotiations going again and the employers began to sign up with the unions. It took four months of constant struggle in the heat and dust of that awful summer, but the workers finally got the right to be represented by their own union (in contrast to one created by the company). Other unions that tried to organize under section 7a were not so lucky. At the end of 1934, the National Labor Relations Board was created to help enforce the new law. Both the Communists[115] and the businessmen were against it. The Communists were against the National Labor Relations Board because it undermined the revolution and the businessmen because it might actually cut their power to fire workers who joined unions.[116]

* * *

Ernest got part-time work as an accountant, and helped with Communist Party activities like spying on the Trotskyite strike. My sister Marjorie had a job at the library, so I took care of Cathleen, her younger sister, little Marge and Brian. Her husband Alfred worked in construction and did some minor work for the Party, but did not take an active role because of his heavy Swedish accent.

At the end of the summer we took little Brian to Phelps, Wisconsin, to meet his grandparents. The family found a big sombrero to put on his head. He is pictured standing in front of their barn. The clothesline stretched from the barn to a single pole holding the clothes Aiti had washed by hand with water

---

115. This was especially for the creation of the National Labor Relations Board, Ibid. p. 405.

116. Ibid. p. 405 The *United States News* described the campaign against the National Labor Relations Board as "the greatest ever conducted by industry regarding any Congressional measure." The Associated Industries of Oklahoma said it "would out-STALIN Stalin, out SOVIET the Russian Soviets, create a despotism from which non could escape or appeal."

Little Brian with his cousin Cathleen

pumped from the well; a sad testimony to the poverty of that beautiful place.

Little Brian grew and never stopped moving. He looked just like a little boy doll. I lost most of his pictures in a fire, but here is one of him and my sister Marge's little girl Cathleen. He had my curly hair and none of Cathleen's shyness about having his picture taken.

Brian was healthy, but I kept getting sick. I had migraine headaches almost constantly. Ernest was sure I was faking. One day he said, "Sheila this is just so much nonsense. We're invited to dinner with the Mackie's and I'm not going alone. Just buck up and come along."

Marjorie had agreed to watch Brian, so I went along. Maybe I could do it. I held my head, desperately trying to feel better. I managed to smile and sit down to dinner. I looked down at my plate. The smell of the food made my stomach turn inside out. I held a napkin to my mouth, but the vomit spewed out onto my fingers. I was so embarrassed, but finally Ernest had to acknowledge that my headaches were real.

Little Brian in Phelps Wisconsin

The next winter, 1934-1935, was the coldest winter on record. It was so cold that my brother-in-law Henry bragged about cranking up his Model T to go to his WPA,[117] job, only to find no one there. Work had been cancelled because of the cold. He was irritated, yet proud of his Model T that ran no matter what the weather. One day it hit 34 degrees below zero. On January 4, 1935, during this cold spell, President Roosevelt, in his annual message to Congress, declared that "social justice, no longer a distant ideal has become a definite goal"[118] and he outlined his proposal for Social Security. Social Security, I thought, *how wonderful it would have been for my poor widowed mother; this law would have helped her.*

But, the weather did not make us feel very secure. On January 22, a blizzard stopped all traffic. Everyone hoped all that snow would bring an end to the drought and Roosevelt would bring us the social justice he had promised.

---

117. Works Progress Administration, one of the jobs created to help the unemployed. The story reported by Charlotte, Henry's daughter.

118. Kennedy, *Freedom from Fear,* vol 1, loc 4653.

During a cold spell I came down with rheumatic fever. I had a high fever and my joints ached. I simply did not get well. Even after the fever went away, I continued to be constantly tired. I caught every cold that came around and struggled to catch my breath. I went to see Dr. Moriarity, the children's pediatrician. She told me I needed rest. The months passed, February, March, April, May and still I was not well.

That sweltering summer Roosevelt kept Congress in session and they passed what is sometimes called the Second New Deal. It included the Emergency Relief Appropriation Act, the Banking Act, the Wagner National Labor Relations Act, the Public Utility Holding Companies Act, the Social Security Act, and the Wealth Tax Act.[119] The most important was the Social Security Act. This was not a program like the Socialists and Communists had imagined but a unique American insurance plan requiring contributions from both employees and employers.[120] Some members of Roosevelt's team thought the taxes were regressive, but Roosevelt "intended to establish his social security system not as a civil right but as a property right. That was the American way."[121] Furthermore, Roosevelt stated, "We put those payroll contributions there so as to give the contributors a legal, moral, and political right to collect their pensions and their unemployment benefits. With those taxes in there no damn politician can ever scrap my social security program."[122]

July that summer was hot, above 100 degrees almost every day. I couldn't sleep at night because it was so hot. There was only .06 inches of rain for the whole month of July. I still could not breathe and coughed constantly, so once again I dragged myself in to Dr. Moriarity's office.

---

119. Ibid. loc 4556.

120. Ibid. loc 4996. "Virtually alone among modern nations, the United States would offer its workers an old-age maintenance system financed by a regressive tax on the workers themselves."

121. Ibid. loc 4988.

122. Ibid. loc 5005, quoted from Perkins, *The Roosevelt I Knew.*

She looked at me and said, "Sheila, you need a change of climate in order to get well. You need to go to Arizona."

"Arizona! How can I do that?" I asked, astounded at the idea.

"I think if you spend another winter here, without getting any better, you may die."

"But I've got little Brian to take care of, and my family."

"I think I can find a job for you in Phoenix, Arizona, and you can bring your son with you," Dr. Moriarity insisted.

I went home and went to bed. I had no idea how to explain this to Ernest or what he would say. Finally I got the courage and the strength to tell him.

"Ernest, Dr. Moriarity says I'm not going to get well, and that I might die this winter, unless I go someplace warm and dry."

Little Brian in Phoenix

"What?" he said, shaking his head, almost like he didn't hear what I'd said.

"I need to go to Arizona!"

"How do you plan to do that?" he asked, with a smirk on his face, like he thought this was just silly.

"I will take the train down there."

"What are you going to do there?"

"I have a job in an orphanage, and Brian can come with me."

"What?" he said again. I didn't ask him, I just told him. I had to go. I had to live for my little boy. I had to get away.

I was scared and happy at the same time. I was going to get well. We got our train tickets. We would transfer trains in Chicago, and then go straight through. I couldn't afford a sleeping berth, so we slept in our seats. We brought our own food. Finally we arrived, and a lady from the orphanage met us at the train depot. Phoenix seemed so different. It was not like up north and not like Australia either. I got a quick tour, and was shown our quarters. The next day I started work. I cooked for all these lost children. It was a very sad place, but I was happy. I was going to get well. The air was dry and warm, and breathing was easier. I felt better. I felt free. I did not have to worry about what sort of mood Ernest would be when he came home. I missed my sisters and my little niece Cathleen, but I did not miss having to worry about Ernest.

One day in October I saw the most beautiful sight I had ever seen. The Monarch butterflies arrived en masse, following their annual migration from the northern states down to Mexico. I was inspired by the beauty of it. I simply had to go out and buy some watercolors and paint them. Every spare minute I had I spent working on this painting. I felt I had just begun to be whole again. If something as delicate and beautiful as a butterfly could travel all the way from up north down to Arizona, what could I do?

"Monarchs Migrating." Watercolor by Sheila Buchanan Buell 1935, Phoenix, AZ.[123] To see painting visit blog: Visionsfromtwocontinents.blog

123. When I found this painting among her papers I asked her for it. She then told me the story of how it came to be, and that she could never part with it. It was her first major painting.

CHAPTER 17

ON MY OWN

Ernest wrote to me, "Sheila, I'm sure you are better now. I expect you will return soon."

He didn't say he missed me, or that he loved me. He even told Lucille, "If she doesn't come back soon I'm going to divorce her."[124]

I felt stronger now, and I didn't want Brian to grow up the son of a "divorcee," as that would be a disgrace. I wanted to go back before it got too hot. I boarded a train in May and headed north. The train passed miles and miles of dry dusty farm fields. The winter had been extremely harsh in Minnesota. Blizzards in February had stopped the railroads, closed the roads and kept the airplanes from flying. People hoped that would end the drought, but it continued. From the train I saw the devastation I had seen in the film *The Plow that Broke the Plain*.[125] As I was traveling toward Minnesota a dust storm approached the capital in Washington DC. Hugh Bennett timed his speech on soil conservation to coincide with the dust storm. His plan worked and Congress passed the Soil Conservation Act.

---

124. This is something her cousin Charlotte Bartlett Wasiluk remembered, Sheila did not save the letter from Ernest, this is from what she remembered.

125. This movie can be downloaded from http://www.savevid.com/video/ the-plow-that-broke-the-plains-ca-1937.html. It is also on youtube.

In June, I was back with Ernest. I had dreamed that my being away would heal more than just my body. I had married him for better or for worse but things just continued like they were before. I never knew what mood Ernest would be in.

On June 27, we listened to President Roosevelt give his acceptance speech at the Democratic National Convention. To this day I remember his words. "There is a mysterious cycle in human events. To some generations much is given. Of other generations much is expected. This generation of Americans has a rendezvous with destiny."[126]

This speech sounded just plain silly; "a rendezvous with destiny," what nonsense, I thought, *poverty maybe, but destiny?*

In July, 1936, the newspaper headlines shocked us when Hitler announced he was sending aircraft to help Franco defeat the Spanish Republic. I asked Ernest, "What's going to become of Marty?" The month before, we had helped our friend, Marty Mackie,[127] raise money for clothes so he could join the Lincoln Brigade and help the Spanish Republic fight against the Facist Franco. Marty was someone who acted on what he believed.

Most of the people I knew were decidedly against any involvement of the United States in any sort of war, especially a war in far-away Europe. That fall, the University of Minnesota students, including Wilbur Broms, organized a Strike for Peace. Governor Olson spoke at the rally. This call for peace ended the compulsory ROTC training at the University of Minnesota. Students could still do ROTC, but it was no longer required of all students as it had been.[128]

The economy at home seemed to be improving, and people turned out to vote for Roosevelt on November 3, 1936. Through

126. Kennedy vol 1 location 5256. Q quoted by Kennedy from *The Public Papers and Addresses of Franklin D. Roosevelt* 1936, pp. 230-36.

127. Mother often spoke of her friend who fought in Spain in the Lincoln Brigade. I got Marty's name from the interview with Wilbur Broms, Minnesota Historical Society.

128. Ibid.

the WPA Roosevelt employed seven percent of the workforce in 1936. He had saved the homes of four million people through the Home Owners Loan Corporation. Now everyone's savings were insured by the Federal Deposit Insurance Corporation. Roosevelt won the electoral votes in every state except two. The House Democrats won 331 seats to the Republican's 89. Of course Lucille and Henry voted for the Communist candidate, but this time he only got 2,000 votes in the whole State of Minnesota compared to 6,000 in 1934.

In 1937, unemployment rose. It was so bad that some people called it the Roosevelt Recession. Marjorie's husband Alfred was unemployed. Marjorie wrote to Charlie about it and Charlie wrote back in August 1937:

You and Alfred had rather a tough trot during the winter. Thank heaven I have not had the worry of unemployment and if ever I prayed for anything it is that I may be spared that. Normally I don't worry but the thought of it makes me shudder. I take my hat off to the brave hearts who fight the depression with a smile and do without for their children. It's worse than the war.[129]

I stayed for the next two years, hoping now that Brian was older, that Ernest would be a good father. Ernest would run into the house, grab some food and rush right out again, hardly ever looking at his son. I did some sketching and I was thinking about making a children's book. Inspired by the Monarch butterflies I had seen in Arizona I started studying insects and telling Cathleen, her little sister Marjorie and Brian a story about Ants. I wanted my story to be a fantasy and yet a true story, that would teach the children about insects and an appreciation for nature.

In the spring I sat with the children and explained the beginning of the story:

---

129. Charles Buchanan letter to Marjorie dated August 30, 1937. On file.

Little Six Legs on Parade

Spring is here. All the plants and animals are waking up after a long winter sleep. Bright yellow green leaves are bursting out everywhere. Flowers, of yellow, blue and purple hue cover the ground even under the trees. Two little girls and a young boy venture out into the cool spring air. They have a package, and are all trying to open it at once.

Opening the package the children found a glass. It had a light blue handle to hold it.

"Oh, I know! That is the glass that makes little things look big," said Cathleen. "It's a magnifying glass. Here is a note tied to the magnifying glass. It says: 'Use me to find out all about little six legs. Who can they be?'"

"Insects!" cried Marjorie, jumping up and down. "Ants! Butterflies! Bees! and all the little animals with six legs. Let's see who can find some insects first," she called as she ran into the yard.

"Look!" cried Brian. "Here are two ladybird beetles. See! They have six legs so they are insects. How big that one looks under the glass. What do you suppose they do?"

Cathleen took the magnifying glass and said, "Let's go find some ants." The kids jumped up after her, leaping with excitement and went out to look for ants. I followed them, observing how they watched the ants after that short introduction. My heart soared at the thought I could share the love I felt for these little creatures through my paintings. Every free moment I spent drawing the small creatures around me. This was much better than reading the newspaper and listening to endless political debates.

But I struggled with a constant fear of when Ernest might go into a rage. I had to keep that fear in check to keep being there for the children. I knew I had to get out on my own, I had to get away from Ernest or I was going to get sick again. One night

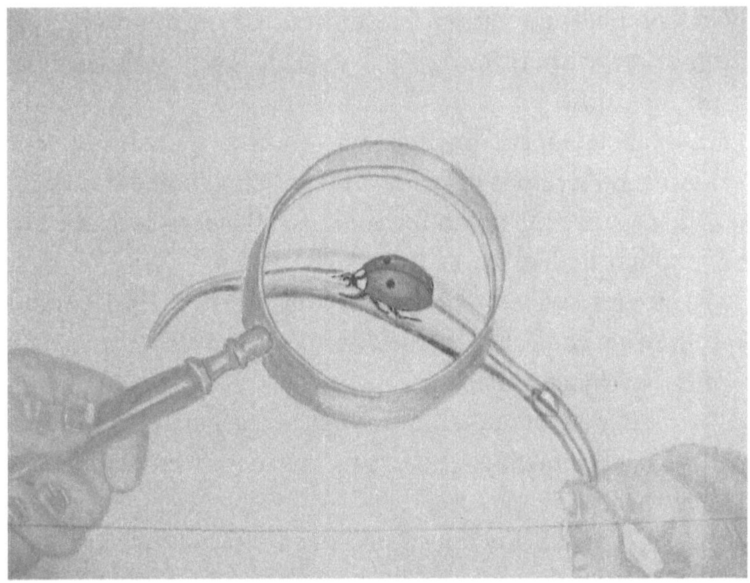

"Looking through the Glass" watercolor Sheila Buchanan Buell c. 1942. To see painting and insect story visit blog: Visionsfromtwocontinents.blog

Ernest came home late. I was feeling happy because I'd done a lot of drawing that day.

"What were you doing sitting outside today? Don't lie to me, I saw you. Who were you going to meet?" demanded Ernest.

"I was outside drawing."

"What were you drawing, sitting right there next to the sidewalk?"

"I was drawing the ants."

"Really, show them to me."

I showed him the paper I had drawn and redrawn on. I was just getting the hang of drawing these tiny things.

"That's just silly. I don't think that was your plan at all."

I did not say anything. It was useless to talk with him when he had his own ideas. But that night, when he came to bed, he ended our relationship forever. He started to make overtures to me indicating that he wanted to make love. I turned away, hurt by what he had said earlier. He turned me on my back, pulling my legs apart, with a weird grin, and said, "You think I'm not big enough for you."

He grabbed a broomstick and shoved it inside of me. I screamed and cried out in pain.[130] He quickly pulled it out.

"Oh, was that too much for you?" he whispered, surprised, but not sorry, that he had hurt me.

My insides burned, and I curled up into a ball. I could not believe anyone could be so cruel. *Using an ordinary household item he had ripped my soul to shreds.*

The next day, barely able to walk, I gathered up Brian, my clothes and my drawings. I went to my sister Marge and said, "I can't live with him anymore."

She did not ask any questions, and I did not give any details. She just opened the door and let us in. She helped me with my bags, and asked if there was anything else we needed to get from the apartment. Not wanting to be a burden, I started to look for work and find an apartment of my own. Thank goodness Alfred was employed now. He had found work in North Dakota. Little Brian started school in the fall. Maybe I could get a job and be on my own.

* * *

I started pouring through the paper looking for work, but it was the headlines that jumped out at me. BRITAIN AND FRANCE DECLARE WAR ON GERMANY. It was September 3, 1939. *Oh no, not again,* I thought, as I imagined my Aunt Bella and cousins I had heard about in England. I finally turned to the want ads. There were more ads than I had seen in years, even in the

---

130. Sheila never wanted Ernest's son, or anyone, to know about this. She told Linda Buell, her second son's wife, this story many years later and Linda Buell told me.

women wanted section. There was an ad for an apartment manager that included free rent. Wearing my best clothes, I went to apply, walking into an old brownstone apartment building near the Capitol. These lovely buildings, built in the late 1800s, were old, but spacious. I tiptoed up to the door, hesitated then pulled the metal knocker that hung on the door. It clanged so loudly I jumped.

"Come in," said a woman's deep voice.

I walked in the room and behind a large desk sat a very large woman. She had short curly dark hair and dark blue eyes that looked intently out from her soft round face.

"How can I help you?" she asked.

"I came to inquire about the apartment manager position," I replied.

"Are you inquiring for your husband?" she asked.

"No, no." I hesitated to answer. "I'm on my own," I added.

"Well, you look pretty strong. Do you know how to clean?"

"Yes I do. I am very good at cleaning," I said, encouraged that she had not sent me away.

We walked across the street, or more correctly, I walked and she waddled. She was in good shape for carrying all the weight she had on her. She didn't even get out of breath. The apartment was small. It had a bedroom, dining area and kitchen. The bathroom, down the hall, and was shared with two other apartments. My job was to keep the bathroom and my apartment clean and to clean all the halls in the building. My pay was simply free rent.

"You can start the beginning of next month."

I went back to Marjorie and told her all about it. "Marjorie, I found an apartment! I can move in the first of October."

"Where is it?"

"It is at 768 Cedar Street."

"Who is the owner?"

"I think her name is Irene Buell."

"Oh I know her. She is very nice, she's helped out a lot folks in the Party," said Alfred. Alfred rarely spoke so when he said something I knew it was important.

I moved in October 1, 1939. Brian was in school all day and I went searching for a job. I had my own apartment, but I still babysat for Marjorie's children, and she made sure I had food and clothes. I didn't have a real job yet. I found out I needed a Social Security Number to get a job, and for that I needed my citizenship papers. I started to take classes to become a citizen. Soon I would be a citizen and be able to vote, so I paid close attention to the news.

On May 10, 1940, I listened to Edward R. Murrow's "This is London," on CBS Radio News. I sat, unable to move, as he described history being made "too fast." The British suddenly had a new Prime Minister, Winston Churchill, and Germany had invaded Luxemburg, Belgium and the Netherlands.[131] It sounded awful, but I didn't worry too much about it. Surely they wouldn't get too far. But then in just four days the Dutch surrendered. On the 19th I heard Churchill's first chilling speech describing Hitler's victories in France and proclaiming we will "wage war until victory is won, never to surrender ourselves to servitude and shame, whatever the cost and agony may be."[132] On June 2, I thought about my Aunt Bella and British cousins as Edward R. Murrow described a young pilot who had been shot down and bombed. He could hardly hear from the bombing, yet he was anxious to fight again.[133] The Allies had to evacuate everyone they could from Europe to England. They ended up leaving their tanks, machine guns and other equipment behind.

Finally on June 16, 1940, I became a citizen of the United States. Marjorie took off from work and went to the ceremony with Cathleen and little Marjorie. Now I was going to be able to vote; maybe I could make a difference in this world.

---

131. You can listen to this 2.43 minute broadcast by going to: https://archive.org/details/1940RadioNews and scrolling down to #42.

132. https://archive.org/details/1940RadioNews #57.

133. Ibid. #75.

Sheila Viola Heikkinen original citizenship certificate[134]

I was lucky I had gotten my citizenship straightened out because on June 28th Roosevelt signed The Smith Act. That would have required me to be fingerprinted as an alien. This law also included federal criminal penalties for anyone who was a member of or affiliated with "subversive" activities. It did not define exactly what those activities might be, or what affiliated with meant.[135] I wondered *might that include Henry and Lucille?*

As I listened to the political campaigns I felt angry when I remembered how my friend Marty had fought so hard against the Fascists in Spain. After Stalin signed the non-aggression pact with Hitler,[136] the Communists had changed their directives and

---

134. On file with author.
135. Katznelson, *Fear Itself,* pp 332-333.
136. August 23, 1939 also called the Molotov-Ribbentrop Pact

were encouraging people to let the Fascists win, and that included my sister Lucille.

Lucille said, "Just let those Capitalists fight it out. They'll destroy each other, and then we can create the new order." She simply believed whatever came out of the Kremlin.

I didn't say anything out loud but I thought, *I'm not going to support the Communist candidate*. I listened to the Republican candidate, Wendell Willkie, and his warning that a third term for Roosevelt might bring "the destruction of our democracy."[137] I heard the Republican radio commercial that said, "When your boy is dying on some battlefield crying out, 'Mother! Mother!'... blame YOURSELF, because you sent Franklin D. Roosevelt back to the White House."[138]

Roosevelt assured us that it was not our boys that were needed but our manufacturing might. We needed to replace the war material that the British lost during their hasty retreat from Dunkirk across the English Channel.

In June, July and August the radio reports worsened daily with news on the bombing of London. We heard how Germany bombed London for 57 consecutive nights, but still they did not surrender. I tried to keep the radio turned off until after little Brian went to bed. My mind kept seeing my Aunt Bella in London helping the injured, while bombs dropped and windows shattered.[139] These reports made me realize how much the British needed our help.[140]

I felt relieved and guilty when I got a letter from Aunt Bella in December. She was alive, but upset that we had not written for over a year. I'd been writing to her since I was four years old.[141]

---

137. Marrin, *FDR and the American Crisis,* p. 157.

138. Ibid.

139. https://archive.org/details/1940RadioNews #146. You can listen to this very vivid account of what an air raid was like.

140. Before the bombing only 16% of Americans favored aiding the British. Within weeks the number rose to 52%. From Marrin, *FDR and the American Crisis.*

141. Letters and cards from Aunt Bella Buchanan. On file.

I stayed away from Ernest. I didn't want anything to do with him or any man. He tried to reach out to me, with what sounded like an apology, but this had been too much. I couldn't believe him anymore. I had tried to be a good wife, but in return I had gotten hurt. My body seemed to be alright. I did not go to the doctor but I was afraid of being touched by anyone.

I went to work on my book. It gave me hope. I felt maybe teaching children about nature would let them learn something other than the war news that filled the radio waves.

I wrote to Edith Patch, an entomologist and well-known children's author. I was excited when she agreed to look at my manuscript. I sent her my drawings and the text that I had carefully typed on onionskin paper so that it would not weigh so much when I mailed it to her in September.[142] I mailed it third class because I did not have money for first class postage or insurance. I had no idea if, or when, she would respond.

When the election came on November 5, 1940, I, along with the majority of people in 38 other states, voted for Franklin D. Roosevelt to be President for a third term. This was despite, or perhaps because, one week before the election Congress passed the first peacetime draft in the history of the United States.

I still had not heard back from Edith Patch. Then finally in December, she returned my manuscript, mailed first class and insured. She really liked my pictures, and had some suggestions for the text. She wanted me to change honey to nectar. She recommended that I find a publisher, but did not suggest one. I was glad to get my pictures back, but sad that she could not help any more than that. She encouraged me to try to send it to a lot of publishers, but I could not afford to send it out to just any publisher and probably have it be rejected.

---

142. Edith Patch, letter to S.V. Heikkinen, dated December 12, 1940. On file.

CHAPTER 18

UNITY

We were one year into a new decade. On January 6, I listened intently to Roosevelt give his State of the Union Address. I hoped everyone was listening when he said, "No realistic American can expect from a dictator's peace international generosity, or return of true independence, or world disarmament, or freedom of expression, or freedom of religion–or even good business. Such a peace would bring no security for us or for our neighbors. Those, who would give up essential liberty to purchase a little temporary safety, deserve neither liberty nor safety."[143] Towards the end of the speech I sat next to the radio, inspired, my heart uplifted, when he described a future world which would defend four essential human freedoms: "The first is freedom of speech and expression–everywhere in the world." *Then people would not need to worry about promoting unions or different economic ideas like Henry and Lucille did.* "The second is freedom of every person to worship God in his own way–everywhere in the world." *Then people could stop picking on each other for being this or that or maybe nothing at all.* "The third is freedom from want– which, translated into world terms, means economic understandings which will secure to every nation a healthy peacetime life for its inhabitants—everywhere in the world." *No one would have to suffer like Mother did.* "The fourth is freedom from fear–which,

---

143. http://voicesofdemocracy.umd.edu/fdr-the-four-freedoms-speech-text/

translated into world terms, means a world-wide reduction of armaments to such a point and in such a thorough fashion that no nation will be in a position to commit an act of physical aggression against any neighbor–anywhere in the world."[144] *Fear, that is where we are right now. Just think, if the world had these freedoms there wouldn't be any need for war, Communism, Nazis, or even politics.*

Just a few weeks later he gave the inaugural speech for his third term as President. He tried to get Congress to pass the Lend-Lease Bill called H. R. 1776. This bill would authorize the President to transfer ammunition and supplies "to the government of any country whose defense the President deems vital to the defense of the U.S."[145]

I heard as the President claimed we were preserving democracy by passing such a law, yet I thought *weren't powers like these the powers of a dictator? Wouldn't this just get us into the war?* The President and even his Ambassador to Britain, Joe Kennedy,[146] said aiding Britain was the best means of avoiding war. Charles Lindberg gave a powerful speech against the bill, warning it was "another step away from democracy and another step closer to war."[147] All this back and forth arguing had me confused.

Just three days after the President's inauguration Lindberg testified before a Congressional Committee. He said that the United States should seek a negotiated peace in Europe because we were not capable of creating an Air Force that could beat the Luftwaffe (the German air force). "Our own air forces are in deplorable condition. Regardless of how much assistance we send it will not be possible for American and British aviation to equal the strength of German aviation." He warned that if America joined the war it "would be the greatest disaster the country has ever had."[148]

---

144. Ibid.

145. Goodwin, *No Ordinary Time*, p. 210.

146. This was President John F. Kennedy's father, who had previously opposed giving aide to Britain.

147. Ibid. p.213.

148. Baime, *The Arsenal of Democracy*, p, 103.

I couldn't believe it. America is a huge country; if we would just unite, surely we could beat the Nazis!

In February Churchill gave a speech where he said, "Mr. Roosevelt, put your confidence in us. We shall not fail nor falter. Give us the tools and we will finish the job."[149]

My heart reached out to Britain and I hoped we would help them. I was amazed to hear the Republican candidate who had lost, Wendell Willkie, testify for the bill by saying if we sat back and did nothing, there was no telling where "the madmen who are loose in the world might strike next."[150] When the debate started the country was split fifty-fifty, but after the hearings 62% of the people supported the bill,[151] including me. Finally in March, after six weeks of testimony and debate, the American democracy decided to support the democracy across the sea.

As I listened to these political debates I thought of my Aunt Bella in England, and how much this bill would help her.

Every day the headlines told about a new factory making something for the war effort. The Depression was finally over and people were working. Most of the workers who wanted to join unions had done so. All of the car companies, except for Ford, had unions. Henry Ford hired a special private police force headed by former boxer, Harry Bennett, to beat up anyone who wanted to join or organize a union. The Ford Motor Company had negotiated big contracts to make planes for the war effort, and the unions were angry that Ford was not following the law. The workers planned a strike for April 3. Bennett had a plan to break the strike. He had 2,500 black strikebreakers trained and hired to keep the plant working, and to create a race riot. As soon as the strike began he "cabled the White House that the Rouge plant had been seized by 'communist terrorists.'"[152] He asked the President to send troops.

---

149. Ibid.
150. Ibid.
151. Ibid. p. 215.
152. Baime, *The Arsenal of Democracy*, p. 116.

When Lucille read this story in the paper she said, "Well I'll be! Look! I sure wish we had the power to take over the Ford plant. It's too bad the Communists didn't do that."

The President had his own informants. He sent Walter Francis White, head of the NAACP, and Thomas Dewey to negotiate a settlement. There were 2,500 strikebreakers locked inside the plant, surrounded by pickets blocking all roads and entrances to the plant. Ford plants in all 48 states, including Minnesota, were in lockdown to prevent further violence. The strike went on for ten days, until finally Ford agreed to sit down to talks. Ford's son and his wife persuaded him to let the workers vote for or against a union. He was very disappointed when they voted 70% for CIO union, 27% for AFL, and 2.6% to stay a non-union shop. The contract the CIO negotiated brought an end to the terror of the private police force, as well as the reinstatement and increased pay of union workers who had been fired.[153] I read all of this with amazement, realizing the workers were making progress without the revolution that Henry and Lucille advocated.

Workers were in demand because Congress had passed the draft. All young men between the ages of 21 and 36 had registered for the draft, including my brother-in-law Henry's sons Myron and Gordon. Fifty percent were rejected for health reasons or illiteracy. Many had started to serve their one year of training. Myron ended up in the Air Force and Gordon served in CB unit of the Navy. CBs went in ahead of the troops to create landing strips and infrastructure. Since the Lend-Lease Bill passed companies needed workers, even women workers, and I needed a job. There was an ad for a job working on the assembly line at Honeywell in Minneapolis and, anxious to get one of these new good- paying jobs, I applied.

I didn't put on my best dress; this wasn't an office job, a pretty job, this was a factory job. It paid real wages. I'd be able to save money so I could take art classes and work on my book later.

---

153. Goodwin, *No Ordinary Time*, pp 229-230.

Five blocks from my apartment I got on the streetcar. It rattled along tracks in the pavement, powered by electric lines that sparked over the top of the car as the wheel moved on the power lines. It was noisy, but it did not give off any fumes. The University Avenue streetcar passed into Minneapolis and I transferred to the Third Avenue line, which stopped just two blocks from the factory. Walking into the waiting room my hair curled up out of control, as nervous perspiration dampened my forehead and neckline. There were lots of other gals, and some guys, sitting and waiting nervously. They all looked larger and stronger than me. I was only five feet two inches tall with small hands.

A voice called, "Sheila Heikkinen."

I wasn't divorced from Ernest so I still had his name. I got up and walked into a small room. A thin blond guy with a ready smile asked me to sit down.

He said, "Oh Heikkinen, that's a good Finnish name. I know you're agile and smart. You're hired."

"Oh, thank you so much." I didn't tell him that Heikkinen was my married name. My face beamed with joy as I left that room.[154]

The next Monday was my first day on the job. I worked from 8:30 a.m. until 5:00 p.m. Every weekday I got up at 6:30 a.m., got dressed and made lunches for Brian and myself. Then at 7:00 a.m. I made sure Brian was up and dressed. I had to be on the streetcar at 7:30 to be at work by 8:30. Brian played with the neighbors until school and after school came home by himself. He was just eight years old. I hated leaving him like that but I had no choice. I worked on an assembly line, making small things with wires attached. They never told us exactly what they were for, just what to do. It was exhausting to stay constantly alert, making sure my

154. Sheila often told this story about her interview. I verified the possible dates and the hiring of women at Honeywell at http://www.hon-area.org/history.html. "M-H had hired women for the production lines as early as the 1920's, because it seemed that their smaller hands and fingers provided them with a distinct advantage in delicate assembly line work." It was probably her small hands that were more helpful than her name. The sketch was done in the 1970s when she worked at Honeywell for a second time.

Myself as a kangaroo working on a line

piece was perfect before I passed it on. I went home with just enough energy to make us a quick supper. Often we ate something easy like Chef Boyardee spaghetti or Campbell's soup. I read him a story and we went to bed. On weekends Marjorie's eldest daughter, Cathleen, came over and helped me clean the halls in the apartment building. And I did manage a little time to paint, but I didn't have time to make the changes Edith Patch had suggested for my manuscript.

June 22, 1941, was a lovely summer Sunday evening. Lucille and Henry had invited Brian and me over for dinner. We were just sitting down to eat some of Lucille's wonderful apple pie, when Henry turned on the radio. "Special alert. Hitler has invaded Russia. Churchill will speak to Parliament shortly." Lucille stopped in her tracks.

"What?" Henry said, shaking his head in disbelief.

I couldn't take one more bite of my pie, as we all gathered around the radio, straining our ears to catch every word.[155]

---

155. Listen an excerpt from the speech at http://ia700402.us.archive .org/3/items/Winston_Churchill/1941-06-22_BBC_Winston_Churchill _Germany_Invades_Russia.mp3

"Guttersnipe, he called Hitler a guttersnipe," exclaimed Henry. "He's far worse than a guttersnipe, he's a damn double crosser!"

Lucille looked so sad, and murmured, "Oh those poor, poor Russian people. They were just getting on their feet, creating a new society."

I didn't say anything. I thought *I'm so glad I voted for President Roosevelt and Congress passed the Lend-Lease Law. I'm doing what I can to stop this Nazi menace.*

So it continued. I went to work every weekday and came home exhausted. Then came another blow, again on a Sunday. It was Sunday, December 7, when I heard on the Radio, that Japan had attacked Pearl Harbor. We did not get any details until I came out of work on Monday. The newsboys yelled, "Extra, extra, read all about it." I anxiously reached in my purse and gave the boy a nickel. On the streetcar ride home my heart sank as I read, "U.S. DECLARES WAR ON JAPAN, 3,000 Killed or Injured in Attack on Hawaii; 2 American Warships Sunk."[156]

This could not be true, yet it was. I went home and hugged my little boy. How I wanted to protect him from the horror this world had become. That evening Brian and I gathered around the radio to hear President Roosevelt address the nation. I didn't try to put Brian to bed. He had just turned nine and he needed to know we were at war.[157]

The next day at work they put black air raid curtains up covering all the windows. Honeywell had a night shift and the company did not want us to be sitting ducks in case of a Japanese bombing raid. They also put up air raid curtains at the telephone company in St. Paul.[158] It seemed insane to think the Nazis or the Japs could drop bombs on Minnesota. A Berlin bomber could fly

---

156. *Minneapolis Star Journal,* December 8, 1941, front page.

157. You can hear this speech on youtube https://www.youtube.com/watch?v =5eml6lxlmjY

158. My cousin Charlotte Wasiluk was 20 years old at the time and working for the phone company. She remembers the air raid curtains they put up in the panic after the attack on Pearl Harbor.

from Greenland to Minnesota as easily as New York, and flying across the wilderness of Canada there would be no one watching. On July 16, 1942, at 10:00 p.m.[159] a siren screamed steadily for five seconds, then stopped for three seconds.[160]

Brian woke up screaming, "Mommy, Mommy!!"

The siren blasted again. I wrapped my arms around Brian and yelled into his ear so he'd hear above the siren. "It's O.K. Remember at supper I told you we were going to have an air raid practice."

"But you didn't say it would be so loud."

"That's so everyone knows, and everyone covers up their lights."

"Can I light a candle?"

"Only as long as the curtains are tightly closed."

I lit the candle and it flickered against the curtain. It looked strangely dark outside. We had been told to "see that our blackout is as black as soot." They said not to stand outside staring at the sky, but since this was a practice I blew out the candle and we stepped outside into pitch blackness. The stars, billions of stars, twinkled peacefully down at us. If we could just turn off the lights and open our eyes to this peace instead of the constant fear of war.

"Wow, it looks just like the sky at Grandma's farm," Brian whispered in my ear.

"They are always here, just hidden by the city lights."

After twenty minutes a whistle blew, and the stars disappeared behind the veil of city lights again.

After the Russian invasion and Pearl Harbor the war was in our backyard, and the country started to unite. Everyone wanted to help, even those who had campaigned so hard against American involvement before the attack. Charles Lindberg had done everything he could to keep Americans out of the war. He had resigned from the Air Corps Reserves. Now he wanted back in and asked the Air Corps to reinstate him.

---

159. Malen.

160. Kenney, *Minnesota Goes to War.*

The Secretary of the Interior told President Roosevelt, "Lindberg is a ruthless and conscious Fascist, motivated by hatred for you personally and a contempt for democracy." He concluded that it would be "a tragic disservice to American democracy to allow this loyal friend of Hitler's . . . a chance to gain a military record."[161] The President agreed. Lindberg was blackballed and no one would hire him. Depressed, Lindberg wrote, "I have seen the science I worshiped, and the aircraft I loved, destroying the civilization I expected them to serve."[162] He was hired in March by Henry Ford, who was also under suspicion because of his involvement in the anti-war movement. Although Lindberg was offered more, he agreed to a salary of $666.66 per month, the equivalent of what he would have earned in the Air Corps. He went to work testing the bombers that Ford was yet to get off the assembly line.

We were constantly bombarded by newspaper articles, radio news and newsreels at the movie theater about the war. I was excited when Lucille told me that Wilbur Broms, a childhood friend, was home on leave. I remembered how Wilbur and his mother lived with us when my mother had first died. He was a very talented musician and a wonderful singer. Both he and his parents were very active in the Communist Party. I went to a party at Lucille's house for Wilbur. It felt like a family reunion. Lucille used her precious sugar rations to put together a few of her wonderful pumpkin pies. We gathered around Wilbur listening as his penetrating baritone voice told us the story of his induction and service in the Army. Wilbur said:

> I was inducted on April 3, 1941. Right away the commanding officer sat next to me on the train and said, "Broms, I'm assigned to watch you." I didn't say anything, and he didn't say why.

161. Baime, *The Arsenal of Democracy*, p. 151.
162. Lindbergh, *Of Flight and Life*, p. 5.

At first I was sent to Oakland, California. I was with the other guys and I was on guard duty the night of Pearl Harbor. I heard a shot. Everyone was kind of edgy. That night all the guys were talking about getting on with the war, getting the dirty Japs. We thought we might be shipped out tomorrow. When I was relieved of my guard duty shift I found that shot I'd heard was one of the sergeants who'd shot himself in the foot to get out of combat duty. In spite of all the rah, rah, rah stuff in my outfit no one was really anxious to get fighting.

Right after Pearl Harbor I was transferred to Presidio, San Francisco, to what they called a casual unit. I was shocked to find myself there. The Articles of War stated that all deserters from WWI were to report to the nearest Army station. I was certainly not a WWI deserter, or any deserter, but because they had special records about me because of my Communist Party activities I was assigned to this Detached Enlisted Men's List (DEML). This included people who had deserted in WWI as well as some guys roughly my age who were drafted recently but had gone AWOL or Absent With Out Leave. I was in a barracks with all these people, a special category of misfits. I was not sent out to drill, and they didn't even issue me a rifle. I had been issued a rifle before, but not now. I gave myself a title: Sergeant of the Latrine. Every day I went down and scrubbed the latrine, then polished floors in the barracks, and for quite a while I was in the kitchen, on permanent kitchen duty.

I was called in by the commanding officer because I'd been complaining about just getting KP duty. I know you Henry, and my Dad too, told me not to get into any discussions, to be careful not to open myself up to criticism, just do what I'm told, and that's it. But I just couldn't keep my mouth shut.

The officer said, "Well Broms, I hear you've been complaining about your assignments. Could you tell me why you are being treated this way?"

"Well sir, from the very beginning I was told I was under surveillance. I've made several attempts to get sent to a combat unit so I could be sent overseas."

"Well why weren't you sent overseas?" he asked, confused.

"Because I'm an anti-Nazi, this is what I was before and I went in the Army and what I still am. But the outfits I've been sent to give me special treatment."

"We're all against the Nazis, Broms."

"Well that's true. We all are, on the surface, but the commanding officers I've had, they're always, they're not that way, they're racist, they're pro-Nazi, they're anti-Semitic, they're anti-black. They don't believe anything. They regard everything that comes out from Germany and Hitler as just propaganda. They're not the same Army and I want to go overseas. I would like to be a part of the second front but I'm assigned to KP duty, I'm assigned to menial janitorial duty in the barracks."

"What did you do in civilian life?" he asked.

"I've been a singer, and a radio singer, on KSTP in St. Paul which is a National Broadcasting Company. I've been in opera and concerts and I've also sung in church on Sunday mornings. I made a few bucks here and there in nightclubs."

"Well Broms, I'll see what I can do," he said.

The next thing I know I'm assigned to the chaplain, an Episcopalian chaplain in the church at the Presidio.

It was OK, kind of a dog-on-dog assignment, I mean the chaplain was a decent sort of chap and I was his musical assistant, but it didn't get me out fighting the Nazis.

Presidio, San Francisco is a streetcar ride away from the San Francisco Loop so while on leave I went to parties for the GIs in San Francisco. At one of these parties an officer from an IBM unit, a Machine Records Unit, talked to me. I told him how I was being treated and the next thing I knew

I was transferred to a Machine Records Unit. That was awful; it was clerical work since I didn't know anything about the machines they were using. It still did not get me to the front.

I interrupted his long-winded story. "Wilbur do you think now that you are going to officer's training? How did that happen? He continued his story:

Well, from the Machine Records Unit at Presidio I was transferred to another Machine Records Unit in Fort Lewis, Washington. This was a mobile unit where you were trained to operate machine records under conditions of combat. This seemed promising; at least now I'd get to go overseas. But it was not to be. I was assigned to motor pool and supply. I learned to operate a jeep and weapons carriers. Even though I did know how to drive a car I really didn't care much about motor vehicles.

While I was at Fort Lewis my mail and records were still being constantly examined.

Henry asked "Well then how on earth did you end up being recommended for officers training school?" After this interruption Wilbur smiled broadly and continued:

One day I was called into Military Intelligence. I figured this is it. They've found some reason to lock me up. I was interrogated by M-I (Military Intelligence,) a sort of FBI, a sergeant, a fellow from Chicago.

The guy says, "Do you know so and so? Where did you meet him? Why did he transfer you?"

I answered, "I met him at this party in San Francisco and he said he could get me a transfer."

"Do you know anything about his politics?"

"No I didn't know him from Adam," I answered honestly.

"How about the other people at the party?"

"I didn't know anybody there or about their political beliefs. I was invited to the party and I went."

"Did you ask to get transferred to get out of being sent overseas?'

I laughed. "No, the problem is I've been trying for years to get overseas duty." I told them about all my attempts, and my work organizing choirs and building up moral. And you know what?

"Yes, tell us what happened."

'They sent me to take a test for office training. My sergeant just called me in before I left on leave and told me I scored in the top one-third. I got interviewed too, so now it looks like I'll be going to officer training![163]

Wilbur was really excited, but I'd rather he'd stay in the States where it was safe. He was still not sure he'd actually get to go to officer's training.

163. Adapted from an interview with Wilbur Broms, part of the 20th Century Radicalism in Minnesota Oral History Project at the Minnesota Historical Society. Tapes 5 and 6.

CHAPTER 19

DEXTER

It was hard to believe it had only been a year since I'd gotten out on my own and President Roosevelt gave that Lend-Lease speech. Now we were at war, huddled around the radio listening to another State of the Union message. "Exactly one year ago today I said to this Congress: 'When the dictators . . . are ready to make war upon us, they will not wait for an act of war on our part. . . . They—not we—will choose the time and the place and the method of their attack."[164] He said we needed to produce sixty thousand planes, forty-five thousand tanks, twenty thousand anti-aircraft guns, and six million tons of merchant shipping. *When will this ever end? How can we do this?* In 1939 the USA produced less than 6,000 planes, but in 1940 we had managed to double that.[165] But 60,000 that was just a crazy number.

The War started badly. The news from the weekly radio broadcasts sounded like we were losing. In January, while trying to move materials across the Atlantic Ocean to our Allies, forty-five merchant ships were sunk and 1,000 lives were lost to German submarines. We had been building only four ships a month in 1940. In a few weeks Japan had taken over a million square miles

---

164. The American Presidency Project. http://www.presidency.ucsb.edu/ws/?pid=16253.

165. The American Aerospace Industry During World War II http://www.centennialofflight.net/essay/Aerospace/WWII_Industry/Aero7.htm.

of land, including Hong Kong, Thailand, Malaysia, Burma and the Dutch East Indies. That land was home to nearly 100 million people who were now controlled by Imperial Japan.[166] *Maybe Lindberg had been right? What if we continued to lose?*

Everyone was riveted by war news. The President asked everyone to get a map so we could follow the war. In late February Brian and I hurried out to buy ours. Roosevelt gave a Fireside Chat at 10:00 p.m. Eastern time (only 9:00 p.m. in Minnesota) so I let Brian stay up and listen. Eighty percent of the nation listened to Roosevelt describe how we might have to suffer more losses before we could turn the tide of the war. He had confidence in us, the American people, to stick it out. The oceans, which have protected us before, are now endless battlefields.[167]

More losses, I thought. My heart sank. I felt sick and wished I hadn't kept Brian up.

Aunt Bella was back in London, after having spent 1940-41 in Oxford, avoiding the worst of the bombing. My sisters and I were amazed when we got a letter from Aunt Bella in March. It had managed to survive the passage across the battlefield of the Atlantic Ocean.

She wrote:

February, 1942

"I think we all stand together against the common enemy, and now America has come to help, it will make a difference, the Japs coming in has made me worry, and I hope it won't get to Australia. I hope Marjorie's two girls are keeping well, they will be getting big now, how I wish I could see you all. I don't see many people these days, some have left London I know, and many of my old friends have passed on, that is the way it is when one gets

---

166. Goodwin, *No Ordinary Time,* p. 316.
167. Ibid. p. 320.

Aunt Bella, London 1930s

older. Give my love to all, wishing you all a happy New Year, and we will hope for peace before very long.

With love from your

Affectionate Aunt
Bella Buchanan[168]"

She put our worries into words. How was Charlie doing in Australia? Were the Japanese, with all their victories in the Far East, going to invade Australia next?

On April 7, Roosevelt gave another Fireside Chat where he explained a seven-point economic plan to get us through the war.

168. Bella Buchanan, Letter dated February 4, 1942. On file with author.

It included heavier taxes, war bonds, wage and price controls and comprehensive rationing. The plan, he said, was designed to ensure an equality of sacrifice by everyone.[169]

Finally with the Battle of Midway in June, we heard some good news from the Far East. Rationing started in earnest that summer. Men were wearing "Victory Suits," made without cuffs, and women wore shorter skirts without pleats, so the cloth could be used to make uniforms. When they tried to eliminate girdles, to save rubber, which was in short supply, a ladies health magazine said that women over 30 needed girdles to stay upright without tiring. They decided to continue making girdles. I would have been happy to do without a girdle, but, like everyone else, I wore one. I was too busy working to worry about style, but a girdle, that was what every woman wore

In August, I nearly jumped for joy when a letter arrived from Australia. Charlie wrote:

Box 17 Imbil. A.
24-8-42

My Dear Sisters,

I don't suppose you think I will have time or the inclination to write to you all. It is some time since I have written and just as long since we have heard from any of you.

We are still alive and well and not yet feeling any war strain. Though as a family we are scattered a bit. The censors surely won't object to my writing about your countrymen who are with us for the Japs definitely know they are here. Haven't met any of them personally and if you happen to know of any here extend them a cordial invitation to write or visit us. They are very popular here (especially with the girls) and very well behaved.

Mac has been in the army ever since he was 18. His weak eye kept him out at first but he got around that and is in a specialist

---

169. Goodwin, *No Ordinary Time*, p 340.

unit near the front line. Likes the life, is just over 6 feet high and weighs 133kg [290lbs]. We miss him very much, but wouldn't have him do anything else. . . .[170]

So far I am not in the army, much as I want to be. They say I am too old. I am in the Volunteer Defense Corps as Home Guard, and should have a commission soon, we will of course be called up in a time of emergency, we never know when that will be. We drill every Sunday and one night a week. . . . The spirit of the people is marvelous and the Japs are going to have some task to establish their New Order here, we are going to be first to take the bump of course. (Queensland is the closest to Japan). Of course we are rationed in many things, but there is no real shortage of anything and we are going to see this through, we aren't going to be Jap slaves. . . . Be sure we know some tough times are ahead but we will win through, but will be glad of all the help the U.S.A. will send. Hope all the children are well. We all send fondest love to you all. Send this letter on to the others Marjorie, please.

Bye, bye and good luck,
Charlie[171]

I read and reread that letter, praying that my guardian angel would watch over my brother Charlie and my nephew Mac. They were so close to that awful fighting over there. If the Japanese

---

170. Removed this part about the other children shown here: *"Jack is at college near Sydney doing his service a second time as a preliminary to becoming a priest if the war doesn't overtake him, he is just 17 of course. George is at school in Dalby his school, Downland Toowoomba, was taken over for national use, and they shifted to Dalby. He is doing his junior year, promises to be the most brilliant pupil of all the boys, even though Jack had a brilliant career. Let us hope they will be able to use their education. Florence is going very strongly at school always head of her class and has had honours in her music exams."*

171. Buchanan Charles. On file with author.

Mac December 28, 1942

decided to attack Australia they'd land where they lived in Queensland first.

Marjorie got a letter back from his son Mac too! He had written it at the end of July, but it did not get to us until after his father's letter arrived. The envelope was marked "PASSED CENSOR." That's probably why it took so long because it had to be read by the censors to make sure he didn't share any military secrets.

July, 25, 1942

Dear Aunt Marjorie

I am very pleased to receive your letter that Dad forwarded on to me . . .

You say you are getting much news from Aussie now. We are not going short of news from the States here either. The newspapers have special columns devoted to news from USA and the radio stations feature a news session of home news for your lads twice a day. I have often heard President Roosevelt speaking over the radio.

I hope you all will be able to visit down under some day and myself I am hoping to visit you over there.

As you can see by my address I am in the army now. I volunteered for service exactly five months ago and following my old occupation I went into the Survey Company. I cannot tell you anything about my work but I am having a very good time.

All your lads who are over here are enjoying themselves but I think the majority of them are like me in as much that they would like to get home and see their people again. I have picked up quite a number of your colloquialisms as have most of my pals and as a result I find myself speaking more like an American than an Aussie half the time. I think most of your fellows have picked up quite a lot of our not as good expressions also.

The American cigarettes are "tops" in comparison to ours. I have had a few from some of your soldiers and I enjoyed them immensely.

You may be a little surprised at the last sentence, but I have been smoking for some time now. I am not a chip off the old block with regards to the tobacco habit.

I do not think there is much else I can say now so with fond love to you and yours. I will say good-bye.

Love from your nephew
Mac[172]

I sat down as I read the letter, absorbing each word. Knowing they were safe,
I could feel my body relax.

* * *

One Saturday in September, Brian had gone to Phelps, Wisconsin, with his father and I was alone. It was lonely without Brian there and I felt very sad that things had been so terrible with his dad. Resolving to make the most of this quiet time I got out my paints. I was concentrating on painting aphids, when a man's voice said, "Why that's simply beautiful!"

I nearly jumped out of my skin. I was in a second floor apartment and there were no men here. There was a knock on the window. Bright blue eyes danced from the face of a handsome man, with a mischievous grin and a high forehead, standing on a ladder.

"Oh, allow me to introduce myself. I'm Dexter Buell, Irene's son. I'm here fixing your windows."

"Goodness sakes! Don't scare me like that," I said, still short of breath from the shock. Then I remembered *the neighbor pointed him out saying he was Irene's son.*

---

172. Buchanan, Charles MacIntyre. On file with author.

"Would you mind if I come in and take a closer look at your lovely painting?" he asked, very politely.

"Yes, you may," I said, expecting him to climb down the ladder and come in through the door. But he just climbed in through the window, which was no small feat for him. He pretzeled his long thin body through the open window. When he unfolded himself, he stood at least a foot taller than me.

"That was a smaller opening than I thought," he said, laughing.

"I don't think we've ever been introduced. I'm Sheila Heikkinen," I said.

"It's nice to meet you. Don't you belong to that great little boy Brian?" he asked.

"Yes, that's my boy, "I said, smiling. I was glad he knew about Brian so I didn't have to explain anything.

"Where is Brian today?"

"Visiting his grandparents," I answered, not wanting to mention Ernest.

"Now tell me about this painting," he said, gesturing towards the picture I was working on.

"The little green creatures are aphids that the ants raise like cows."

"I've seen them on plants before but I never realized that they were farming the aphids," said Dexter, expressing true interest in my painting.

"If you look closely you will see the ant in front is stroking the aphid to get nectar out of it," I said, looking at the painting and back at his dancing blue eyes.

"Really, that's just amazing. Your drawing shows it so clearly, yet I've never seen such a thing," said Dexter

"I've been studying entomology. I had a scientist check my drawings and he said it was accurate."

"I'd love to see more, but I've got to go back to work. Can I come over tomorrow, or maybe this evening?"

I was fascinated by Dexter, but I didn't want him to think I was an "easy" woman just because I had a child and lived on my

"Ants caring for Aphids" watercolor Sheila Buchanan Buell c. 1942. To see painting and insect story visit blog: Visionsfromtwocontinents.blog

own. I answered, "I'm free tomorrow morning. I'll show you more of my paintings then."

"I'll see you at 9:00 then," he said.

I woke up the next morning before the sun was up. Every pore of my being was streaming with energy. I didn't hear a sound, *Where is Brian?* I wondered. *Oh, that's right, Ernest took him to Phelps for the week.* Then I remembered the appointment I'd made. *Oh I shouldn't have invited him to come here, to my apartment no less! Remember you're not going to see any men!* I told myself. Then I reasoned, *It's all right, he is just coming to look at my paintings.*

Quickly I took a bath, before the people who shared the bathroom were up. I hoped my hair would be dry before he arrived. As I brushed my hair it sprung back into my face, the natural curls never wanting to behave.

I studied my paintings and found the perfect one to share with him first.

The Monarch telling the ant not to bother her egg seemed like a perfect fit. The leaves weren't quite finished, but I think I caught the interaction of the ant talking to the lovely butterfly.

Promptly at 9:00 a.m. there was a knock on the door. As I opened it, the sight of him nearly took my breath away. I had to tilt my head backwards to see his mouth, perfectly formed into a welcoming smile. I could tell he'd just had a bath too, by the smell of fresh aftershave. In his right hand he held a thistle flower with a towel wrapped around the stem.

"I tried to find one with aphids on it, but I failed," he said, with a twinkle in his eye.

"It's lovely. It's better that you didn't disturb any aphids," I said. "Let me find a vase for it."

I went into the kitchen and he followed me. In the excitement of seeing him again I forgot that he was coming to see my paintings and not me. I forgot to tell him to sit down on the couch and wait while I went into the kitchen. In the kitchen I turned and asked, "Would you like a cup of coffee?"

"Oh yes," he said, smiling with an innocent, slightly askew, grin that put me at ease.

Seeing the coffee pot was full, he said, "Let me pour."

This took me totally by surprise. All the men I'd ever known, except Lucille's husband Henry, expected to be waited on.

He poured our coffee and we sat across from each other at my little kitchen table, like we'd known each other for ages. He shared how he loved being in the country and asked me where I'd learned about insects. But mainly he looked into my eyes and I looked into his. I felt like I was melting.

He reached across the table and very gently touched my hand. I felt an energy spark between us. I quickly stood up. "Oh you came to see my paintings. Let me show you what I'm working on now."

"Ant talking to Monarch Butterfly" watercolor Sheila Buchanan Buell c. 1942. To see painting and insect story visit blog: Visionsfromtwocontinents.blog

We walked back into the sitting room where I'd placed the butterfly picture up on a chair. Dexter stood next to me, looking at the picture.

"Oh, look at that ant. That's me trying to talk to you," Dexter said.

"Don't be silly. You're much taller than me. You're obviously the butterfly," I responded, blushing at the idea that I might be as attractive as a Monarch.

We both laughed. He gently put his arm around me and I snuggled closer. He kissed me and I kissed him back, with a passion I did not know I possessed. It was like the worst silly romance novel I had ever heard of. I knew I did not behave like this; yet my body had a mind of its own.

We locked in a passionate embrace. My heart raced; my body wanted him. I was unaware of moving towards the bed. Never in my life had I been touched the way that he touched me. I was helpless. My brain simply refused to control my passion, as I kissed him back.

He whispered, "Don't worry Sheila, I have a rubber." He pulled out one of those new-fangled things that keep people from getting pregnant and put it over his penis. I almost came out of my trance, but then he touched me again. I did not wake up enough to resist him. We flowed in and through each other, our bodies moving in perfect rhythm.

As we lay there in each other's arms, totally relaxed, Dexter suddenly said, "Oh shit!!!"

"What is it? " I asked, concerned by this strange outburst.

"My rubber broke," he explained. "Don't worry dear, it's happened before, but I've never gotten anyone pregnant."[173]

---

173. This story is based on what Sheila told us about meeting our father. She said, "I met him when he was working on a window of the apartment and I was working on my paintings. We only made love once." Also she warned my brother, Gene Buell, about the unreliability of condoms. Also see the history of condoms.http://www.yourtango.com/2013189729/condom-timeline-detailed -history-wrapping-it, they had become much more popular in the 1920s when they started to be advertised.

Suddenly coming to my senses I thought, *I'm just one of many women. I bet he thinks I'm just a cheap whore.* But I didn't say anything.

The next day I got up and went to work. I was more determined than ever to keep men out of my life, and especially out of my apartment. But in my heart I did hope against hope he would come by again.

CHAPTER 20

PREGNANT?

I got up each day, fixed Brian's lunch and went to work. I felt sad, lonely and betrayed. What a stupid person I was to let that guy into my apartment. I wasn't going to have anything to do with men. He didn't rape me; I just fell for him. How could I be so stupid! A month went by, and I did not hear a word, after we'd been so passionate.

I woke up one morning and vomited, sure that I had the flu. I just couldn't keep anything down. Since I didn't have a telephone in my apartment, I went to Mrs. Buell's office to use hers. She'd been so kind, almost like a mother to me, and a grandmother to Brian.

I knocked on the office door, holding on to my churning stomach, "May I use your phone, please?"

"Yes, of course," her voice rang out into the hall. "What's the matter dear?" she asked as soon as she saw me.

"I seem to have the flu."

Mrs. Buell stepped back so as not to catch anything from me.

I picked up the phone and dialed O, my finger hurrying around the dial. "Hello operator, please connect me to Honeywell in Minneapolis." Click, click. The switch board operator made the connection.

"This is Honeywell, with whom would you like to speak?"

"This is Sheila Heikkenin. I need to report that I can't come in to work today. I'm ill," I said.

"I will relay that information to your department. We hope you feel better soon."

The receptionist hung up, and I felt relief. My stomach seemed to calm down right away. This was the first time I'd had to call in sick.

"Thanks for letting me use the telephone, Mrs. Buell."

"You're welcome. I hope you feel better soon. Please ask if you need any help with Brian," she said, looking at me with concern.

I went to my apartment and lay down, staring at the ceiling. *I'm sure lucky to have this great job, and an apartment of my own. I hope Mrs. Buell doesn't think I'm too ill to clean the halls.* Suddenly I remembered feeling like this before. My stomach sank and tightened into a knot of fear. *It could not be. It must not be. Was I pregnant?*

The next day I went to work, even though I vomited in the morning. I found if I ate a saltine cracker I could control the nausea. But it didn't stop. Every day I woke up this way, vomit, rinse, cracker, keep going. Finally I forced myself to make an appointment to see Dr. Moriarity.

Dr. Moriarity would know what was wrong. When I was so sick in 1935, unable to recover completely from rheumatic fever, she had found me a job in Arizona. Surely she could fix this problem, whatever it was.

"Sheila, what is the matter?" she asked, with a caring smile.

"I've been very nauseous," I said, not wanting to say *maybe I'm pregnant.*

"Have you missed your period?" she asked gently.

"I'm not sure. I haven't been keeping track," I answered, looking down at my shoes.

"Well, let me take a look at you."

I lay down on the examining table, and she examined me. She listened to my stomach, and felt my breasts. My breasts were swollen; they were always rather large, but now they were beginning to seem enormous.

"Why, Sheila, I think you're pregnant," she said, smiling. Then she looked at me.

"You're not happy about it?"

"I can't be pregnant, not now!" I said, trying desperately to control the tears seeping out of my eyes.

"You and Ernest aren't getting along?"

"No we are not." I did not say that this was not Ernest's child. I couldn't say such a thing.

"With war raging everywhere it is difficult to think of having a child, but a child is a blessing, especially in a time like this."

"I can't be pregnant. I can't have this child." The tears started to fall. "I have a job, a good job, at Honeywell. They will make me quit if I'm pregnant. I need to work. I need to help the war effort and support my child."

"There, there, it will be all right. Honeywell can find someone else. Don't worry about that. Did you know that I was engaged in World War One. I wish that I had gotten pregnant. My fiancé died, and I never married. I never had children. Every child is a blessing." Her eyes got a faraway misty look as she told this story.

I was shocked to hear her tell such a personal story; she was usually all caring, all loving, yet all business.

"Come back next month. You should be able to work for another month. Then I'll write a note for you to give to Honeywell."

I walked out of the office, dreading every step. I thought this could not be, but Dr. Moriarity had confirmed my worst fears. *I had sinned and now I'm suffering the consequence. What am I going to do?* I did not want to be with people, so I didn't get on the streetcar. I walked slowly, forcing one foot in front of the other. As I crossed the bridge over the Mississippi River I wanted to jump, to have those cool waters take me out of my misery. I moved toward the railing, then quickly hurried on across the bridge. *I can't leave Brian alone with just his father to raise him.*

* * *

What would I say to Marjorie? She was always perfect; the perfect student; the perfect happily married wife. Even when I told her good news the corners of her mouth just turned up slightly. She was reserved and did not show her emotions. The very next weekend Brian went to see his Dad and I went to see Marjorie. She was the only person in the whole world I could trust. The girls jumped up and down, eager to see me.

"Aunty Sheila, Aunty Sheila, we've missed you so. Where have you been?"

"I've been working." I picked up Cathleen, then little Marge, giving each one a big hug. "My, how you've grown," I said, realizing I probably should not have picked them up in my condition.

I liked my job at Honeywell, but I missed caring for Marjorie's children and my son Brian and sharing my stories with them. But now I felt my stomach churning, and knew I needed to speak to Marjorie alone. I gave her a stare, my eyes saying, *something is wrong.*

"Girls, girls, go outside and play please. I don't think your Aunt feels well."

I sat down on a kitchen chair and put my head in my hands.

"Sheila, what's wrong?" she asked.

"I'm . . . I'm pregnant."

"Are you sure?"

"Yes, I went to see Dr. Moriarity."

"Did you tell Ernest?"

"No not yet, but it's not his child," I said, twisting my scarf in my hands.

"What?" her eyes widened.

"I haven't been with him since I left over a year ago."

"Where is the father?"

"I . . . I don't know, he disappeared."

"You don't know?" she looked at me incredulously, her head shaking. "I just can't believe this Sheila. You know better.""Of course I know better. I can't believe I did this," I said, looking at my feet.

Alfred came in from the next room. "Well she'll hae to hae an abortion, that's what. She should hae an abortion. That's what we'll do," he said, speaking logically with his lovely soft Swedish accent that dropped the v sound at the end of have.

Marge said, "No she can't have an abortion. Abortions are illegal in America."

"Dare must be a way," Alfred said in his accent.

"No, we are not even going to look for one of those quacks. She'll just have to come back here, and the girls can share a room. Maybe Brian can stay with his Dad until after the baby comes," Marjorie said, her voice flat with resignation, but not anger.

"It's my fault. Oh Marjorie, you don't deserve this. I'm so sorry." I wished I could sink down into a hole and disappear.

* * *

I caught a streetcar and hurried back to my apartment in St. Paul. Ernest would be bringing Brian home soon. When I left Ernest over a year ago I had hoped that he would file for a divorce, even though I just couldn't bear the thought of divorce. Ernest never did, but surely he would divorce me now.

"I hope you had a good time," I said, when Ernest and Brian returned.

Brian looked at his Dad and smiled a big, secret smile. For once Ernest had actually followed up on what he had promised Brian. I was glad that I had never told Brian how his father had treated me. Ernest was his father and I wanted my son to love him. Usually Ernest promised to do things with Brian and then never showed up.

"It's a secret, Mom," Brian said, as he ran into our apartment. I looked at Ernest and quietly whispered to him, my heart pounding, "Could you come back after Brian is asleep? I have something I need talk to you about."

"Oh sure, I guess so," he responded, looking at me strangely. We had been married long enough for him to know this was a strange request.

I read a story to Brian, trying to keep my mind on what I was doing, but constantly rehearsing what I was going to say to Ernest.

At 10:00 Brian was sound asleep and Ernest returned. I wore some loose trousers with a large paint shirt covering my bulging stomach. I wore a scarf on my head, trying to look as unattractive as possible.

"Well, what is it you have to say?" Ernest demanded, standing there with his fists clenched.

"You have to divorce me," I blurted out, trembling, unable to control my fear and shame.

"Why should I give you a divorce?" he asked, looking surprised at my sudden demand.

"Because I'm pregnant."

"Oh you stupid, Bitch. If you'd stayed with me this never would have happened. Let me get my hands on that bastard."

"He's not a bastard," I lied.

"Then where is he? Why isn't he telling me? What a lily-livered cad. You don't know where he is, do you?"

I just stood there trembling, unable to say another word.

"Well, I'm not going to give you a divorce. I'm not going to have you go through the shame of having a child out of wedlock. Why you should get an abortion." He stormed out the door, banging it behind him.

* * *

We stayed in the apartment and I continued to work. I didn't know what to tell Brian, how to tell him he would be staying with his dad, or how to tell his dad that myself. Then it was time to go back to Dr. Moriarity. She heard the heartbeat as she put the stethoscope on my swollen stomach. She had me listen. I pretended to be interested. She gave me the note:

Sheila Heikkenin is pregnant
Please excuse her from work.

I took the note and handed it to my supervisor. He looked at it and smiled, "Congratulations, Sheila, and the best of luck to you and the lucky guy."

I smiled politely. "Thanks, I'm going to miss all of you," I said, looking around the room.

Everyone suddenly looked my way. I think they heard despite the clatter of noise from the machines. I turned and walked quickly from the room. I didn't want to hear any more congratulations.

I stayed in the apartment until after Christmas, trying to keep things the same for Brian. I wore baggy dresses to hide the bulging fact of my pregnancy. Since I was only five feet two inches tall, it was difficult. The song "I'm Dreaming of a White Christmas" sang out from the radio, making me want to sit down and cry. But the Christmas I dreamed of was hot and green, in the Australian bush. The song was wrong and I was wrong. I should have gone home to Australia when Charlie asked.

Marjorie had made Thanksgiving dinner so it was Lucille's turn to make Christmas dinner, but she was in the hospital. Lucille just sat and stared, unable to use her hands. She could not lift, write or pick anything up. Henry said she had a "nervous disorder." Lucille was convinced that her hands had given the fatal dose of medicine that killed our Father. She was getting treated with insulin shock therapy, and the doctors said this would help her forget.

Marjorie and I worked hard to create a Christmas for the children. The city was quiet and there were no special displays in the shop windows or a lighted tree at the Capitol. We combined our sugar rations and got enough sugar to make Swedish Christmas cookies and the children all helped. I babysat the children while Marjorie and Alfred worked Christmas week. On Friday, Christmas Day, we woke up early to cook dinner. Henry and his grown daughter Charlotte joined us. His two sons had been drafted and did not get home for Christmas. Henry was excited to tell us his good news. "I'm working at the Twin City Ordinance Plant, making ammunition for the war. We're going to win this thing and beat those Nazis." We all nodded our heads and smiled, knowing that for the first time ever my brother-in-law had a well-paying job. He was always losing jobs because of his dedication to the Communist Party.

Right after Christmas, Henry and Alfred moved me to Marjorie and Alfred's place. I carried my paintings and watercolors in my arms, desperate to keep them safe. Brian went to live with his Dad. I had given Mrs. Buell notice at the beginning of December. Now I left a note on her desk with a forwarding address, in case anyone, perhaps her son Dexter, asked where I was. She was not around, so I left it, sneaking out so she would not see my swollen belly. I had shared a lot with her, and she had helped me out so much with the free rent, but I just could not tell her about this problem.

Lucille moved into Marjorie's too,[174] and I took care of her. She was still unable to do anything, and with Henry working she needed constant care. The treatments she got at the hospital made her very confused. Then Henry switched to a new job at the Gopher Ordinance Plant they were building south of town. Suddenly in March he wasn't working there anymore.[175] Henry took it all in stride, but one day he came over to see Lucille, laughing his head off.

---

174. Lucille Bartlett's FBI file, on file at the Minnesota Historical Society, states Lucille was ill and living with her sister at this time.

175. This was reported in Lucille's FBI file, dated May 4, 1955. It refers to a report of special agent Willard I. Stapes, dated January 20, 1943, that Henry Bartlett was working at the Gopher Ordinance Plant, that he was a member of the Communist Party and that *The Daily Worker* was sent to his address.

"Well you see, they came to the house, two of them, one banged on the front door and one ran around to the back door. I guess they thought I was going to run out or something," Henry said.

"Who came? Two of who?" I asked. Lucille just sat looking into space.

"Well, two FBI guys of course," he said, still laughing and shaking his head. "I just invited them in the house. I didn't have anything to hide. They searched the house, didn't find anything and then went on their way."[176]

"What were they looking for?" I asked, confused.

"I really don't know. I guess they decided I was un-American."

Since Henry was unemployed, Lucille went back home and slowly recovered the use of her hands. But without Lucille to look after I started to fall apart, just sitting and staring into space myself.

For three months I stayed, waiting, listening, ashamed, not wanting to go out, not wanting to eat, not wanting to live.

Finally Marjorie said, "You've got to get out. You've got to eat. You've got to live for your children if not for yourself. I'm going to take you to talk with Dr. Foote, the minister at Unity Unitarian Church. I think he can help you.

It was March and the pussy willows would be blooming on the farm in St. Cloud. But Aunt Lil didn't have the farm anymore. They lost it in the Depression. Even the thought of pussy willows did not bring a smile to my blistered lips. I was thin, except for where my stomached bulged from the baby. Marjorie and I took the streetcar to Unity Church. The snow was melting in the streets as we rode past the lovely houses on Summit Avenue. The church was only two blocks off that street of fancy houses, where my

---

176. Henry's daughter Charlotte Wasiluk interview, and also from Lucille Bartlett's FBI file. Henry and Lucille were given Custodial Detention Cards at the request of John Edgar Hoover, Director of the FBI, after informants at the plant told the FBI that Henry Bartlett was a Communist.

father had visited the famous railroad baron, James J. Hill. How ashamed my father would be if he could see me now.

I shouldn't go to a church. I have no right to go in there. I should be wearing a red letter "A" like the woman in The Scarlet Letter,[177] I thought to myself as Marjorie pulled me through the stately wooden doors and into the church. It was quiet. Calmness descended on me as I passed through the door into the entryway.

We went down the hall to the minister's office. He came out from behind his desk to greet us. "Hello Marjorie, I'm so glad you could come."

"This is my sister Sheila," she said. I was glad she did not say my last name. I really wish he had given me a divorce; it was such a lie to wear his name.

"I'll wait in the next room," Marjorie said, taking a book out of her purse.

I was shocked. I didn't think she would leave me alone with this strange man.

"Please Sheila, have a seat."

I looked at the soft chair behind me and sat down, looking at the floor. He sat down across from me, not behind his desk.

"I understand that you have been feeling very sad lately, and not taking good care of yourself. Your sister is very worried about you."

I just sat there. What he said was true. I was unbearably sad. I really did not want to eat; I just wanted to sleep, to forget what I had done.

I heard his voice say gently, "Do you know, Sheila, that God is Love? He loves all his children, especially you now, in your time of need."

I shook my head. I really did not know. I felt I had become pregnant as a punishment. "Are you sure?" I asked.

---

177. *The Scarlet Letter*, a novel by Nathanial Hawthorne about an adulterous woman, was first published in 1850.

"Yes, I am sure. You are one of God's children. He loves all of his children. Think of his love for you and the child you are carrying. Let your mind be filled with Love and come back next week and tell me about Love."

I was only there about 20 minutes, but it felt as if it had been hours. It was like a huge stone had been rolled off my shoulders. I came out smiling, and told Marjorie we could go home, I'd return on my own next week. I went every week, then every two weeks.[178]

* * *

The government asked for 18 million home or community gardens, called Victory Gardens. Marjorie and I were going to have one. We started tomatoes and green peppers in egg cartons. I brought in frozen dirt from outside and heated it in the oven, thawing and sterilizing it at the same time. I would be doing something. I would be helping Marjorie, Alfred, myself and the war effort.

I was planting peas in the plot when the pains started. I made it to the hospital all by myself on the streetcar. The hospital called Marjorie. They asked about calling Ernest, but I said no. I had read a new book on natural childbirth and practiced the breathing exercises. I knew what to expect—breathe, pause, puff and push. The pains came and went and suddenly I was holding a precious baby boy. He did not look at all like Brian. He was beautiful, with Dexter's high forehead. Marjorie brought Cathleen to see the new baby, and Lucille came with Charlotte. I named him Dennis Lee.[179]

---

178. This story is made up from what Sheila told me, which was that she was very depressed and that Marjorie took her to Unity Church and the minister helped her.

179. His birth certificate states that he was born on May 20, 1943, at the Swedish Hospital, and Sheila lived at 1801 10th Ave South, in Minneapolis. Sheila listed his father as Dexter Lucier Buell, 29 years old, and herself as Sheila Viola Buchanan, 27 years old. In reality her name at the time was still Heikkenin, and Dexter and Sheila were the same age.

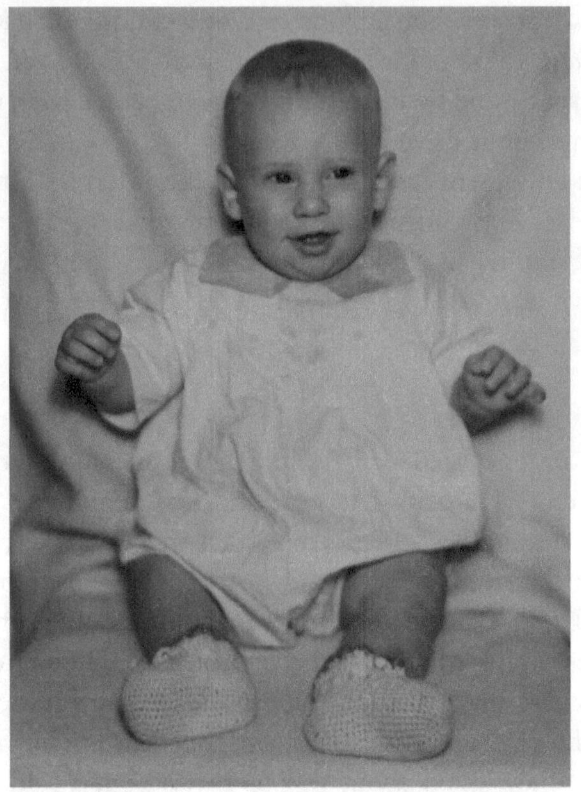

As soon as I could I took Dennis with me every day to the garden. I put him in an old buggy covered with blankets at first, and mosquito netting later. We walked six blocks to our plot. Most of the day was spent pulling weeds and cultivating the soil. I brought a lunch with me. I'd eat my lunch and nurse Dennis on a blanket in the shade of a tree, just out of sight. I was happy outside, surrounded by green growing things, and could forget there was a war going on.

CHAPTER 21

THE WAR ENDS AND . . .

In the fall of 1943, Marjorie, Lucille and I got a letter from Charlie and his wife Peggy.[180] Marjorie asked, "When are you going to write to them? They keep asking about your last name. They want to write to you directly."

"I can't tell them. Just tell them to write to me, Sheila, at your address." I turned away so Marjorie wouldn't see the tears brimming up in my eyes.

"Tell them yourself, I'm not going to write it," Marjorie said, giving me a tired look as she turned away.

I read and reread the paragraph he wrote addressed to Dear Sisters:

First of all to Sheila our sincerest congratulations on that new son, & wouldn't we like to see one Dennis as well as Brian,[181] give them a big kiss for us. Hope by now you have quite recovered from your illness dear, better pack up & come over here on the Clipper, just the same cannot guarantee you won't have rheumatism.[182] You nearly collected Dennis on your own birthday didn't you?

---

180. Charles and Peggy Buchanan,. Letter dated September 10, 1943. On file with author. Both Charlie and Peggy ask for Sheila's last name and address. Long descriptions of gardens and what the children are doing.

181. Ibid. Name changed from the original letter.

182. Charlie is referring to possible complications from the rheumatic fever Sheila had in 1935.

I hadn't even thought about my birthday. *Yes Dennis was a lovely birthday present. But if Charlie knew how he came about, would he still want to see me?* I didn't write.

The war had gotten worse. At first it was like an endless tunnel, but now we could see a light at the end. Hitler was finally losing some battles, and even the relentless push of the Japanese had slowed. Everything was in short supply. Marjorie was very lucky that she had me to watch after the girls and stand in line with our ration cards to get supplies. We never went hungry. We had lots of food from our garden, much of which I canned. Nearly everyone had a Victory Garden. Together American families produced 40% of the fresh produce that was grown during the war.[183] But many children were home alone, their fathers off fighting and their mothers working. In the summer of 1942, at the urging of Eleanor Roosevelt, the President approved the first government sponsored child care center. However, the total number of children covered during the whole war was only 105,000, when perhaps two million children needed care.[184] I knew this well since I was working then and there was no one to care for Brian. He'd come home from school every day to an empty apartment, while I was at Honeywell.

* * *

January 11, 1944, was a Tuesday. Marjorie and Alfred were at work and the older children were at school. I sat down in the old rocking chair with nine-month-old Dennis on my lap. I turned the dial on the Zenith table-top radio, clearing the crackle, to hear the booming voice of President Roosevelt giving his State of the Union Address.[185] At first it seemed like the same old story

---

183. Kenny, *Minnesota Goes to War,* p. 54.

184. Goodwin, *No Ordinary Time,* p. 416.

185. For the full speech go to: http://docs.fdrlibrary.marist.edu/011144 .html State of the Union address January 11, 1944.

of sacrifice, but then the message changed. The President did not want us to return to the 1920's, the so called roaring 20's, the time that left my family destitute, or worst yet the Great Depression of the 1930's, that left everyone broke. His description of a Second Bill of Rights filled me with hope for the future:

"We have come to a clear realization of the fact, however, that true individual freedom cannot exist without economic security and independence. 'Necessitous men are not free men.' People who are hungry, people who are out of a job, are the stuff of which dictatorships are made.

In our day these economic truths have become accepted as self-evident. We have accepted, so to speak, a Second Bill of Rights under which a new basis of security and prosperity can be established for all -- regardless of station, or race or creed."[186]

What he was saying rang out in my mind. *It was the economic insecurity in Germany after WWI that caused people to vote for Hitler.*

---

186. The rights were listed as:

The right to a useful and remunerative job in the industries, or shops or farms or mines of the nation;

The right to earn enough to provide adequate food and clothing and recreation;

The right of every farmer to raise and sell their products at a return which will give them and their families a decent living;

The right of every business man, large and small, to trade in an atmosphere of freedom from unfair competition and domination by monopolies at home or abroad;

The right of every family to a decent home;

The right to adequate medical care and the opportunity to achieve and enjoy good health;

The right to adequate protection from the economic fears of old age, and sickness, and accident and unemployment;

And finally, the right to a good education.

All of these rights spell security. And after this war is won we must be prepared to move forward, in the implementation of these rights, to new goals of human happiness and well-being.

This Second Bill of Economic Rights would secure a future for my children and me. Maybe even an end to all these wars.

Because of this message of hope I voted for him again. He won a fourth term in office and was beginning to work towards a future, a real time of peace and prosperity for all.

I was still able to help Marjorie with money saved from my job. But now, as the war was winding down, women were being laid off from their jobs. Even some of my friends at Honeywell had been told to go home. I wasn't sure what was going to happen to me, a single mother with two children. I probably would not be able to find a job like I did at the beginning of the war. Without a war to create jobs, would the nation once again fall into a Depression? What would I do? I couldn't live with Marjorie forever.

* * *

It was a quiet Thursday evening, I was still staying with Marjorie and she was due home from work any minute. I had my special hamburgers, stretched with eggs and oatmeal, frying on the stove. I turned on the radio to the CBS News. "The President is dead," blared out from the radio. Oil splattered on the wall as I dropped my spatula in the frying pan.

I froze, thinking *I heard it wrong, maybe this is a dramatic show like H. G. Wells'* The War of the Worlds. But then they said it again, "The President is dead." *How could we finish this war without President Roosevelt? What will happen to the Economic Bill of Rights?* I turned off the stove, unable to think about food. My mind raced as I sat down on the couch and buried my head in my hands, overwhelmed by grief. He had been President since I was 20-years-old, guiding us through The Depression and this war. It was like my father had died again. I tucked the kids into bed and then turned the radio back on. Marjorie, Alfred and I listened in silence as the reporters described Vice President Harry Truman being sworn in as President.

* * *

Life went on, with a big hole in the fabric of society. It was a loss felt around the world. My brother Charlie wrote on April 30, 1945:

> *What a terrific loss the world has sustained in the death of President Roosevelt. He was deeply mourned here probably even more than King George would be. Coming so close to the cessation of hostilities and the difficult days ahead it has made his death even a greater loss.*[187]

I saw that Charlie wrote that letter on the same day Hitler committed suicide in his bunker.

Germany surrendered unconditionally, and we celebrated V-E Day (Victory in Europe) on May 8, 1945. Later that summer we all gathered at Lucille's to welcome Wilbur Broms home on leave. I was cautiously optimistic. The war wasn't over yet, and when it was over would we have another Depression?

The first question out of my mouth for Wilbur was, "How was officer training school?" I'd been so excited when he told us he'd done well on the tests.

Wilbur answered, "Oh didn't you know, I didn't get to go. They said I lacked qualities of leadership." His voice took on a sarcastic note since we all knew he was a talented leader.

I was embarrassed that I hadn't heard. I really thought he'd gotten in. "But . . . but you did get to go overseas?"

> Yes, I was transferred to 133rd Engineer Combat Battalion, and had to go through basic training again. I boarded a ship to Europe from the 43rd Street docks on the Hudson River

---

187. Charlie Buchanan. Letter dated April 30, 1945. On file with author.

in April.[188] We landed in Belfast, Ireland, and then went to a camp outside of Oxford.

"Oh, that was after the invasion had already started," I said, relieved that he had not landed on one of those awful beaches on D-Day.

We landed on Omaha Beach 14 days after D-Day. In fact it was Bastille Day, the Day of Independence for France. As we marched we saw a lot of flags flying, American flags, the tri-color of France and the red flag of the Soviet Union. I was proud to see all of these nations working towards a common goal. My squadron was 12-13 people. I had been made Corporal and was the Assistant to the Sergeant. But he had been assigned somewhere else, so I was in charge.

He sat back in his chair, then continued,

I think we put up a bridge a night for all of November. We called them Bailey Bridges and we built them mostly at night.[189] We'd learned how to erect them on the Thames River in England. They had us practice so we could do it blindfolded if necessary. Sometimes when we were there shells came from the Germans across the river, but they usually fell short of our bridge.

Wilbur paused and took a drink, his eyes staring into space like he was seeing the scene. I wondered if sometimes those shells didn't fall short, and they hit his comrades, but I didn't say anything.

---

188. Wilbur Broms said it was on April 3, 1944, in his interview with the Minnesota Radicalism project see note #11.

189. For a one minute twelve second video of the bridge being built during WWII, see

https://search.yahoo.com/yhs/search?p=bailey+bridge+youtube+critical+past+video&fr2=sa-gp-search&hspart=mozilla&hsimp=yhs-003

You know the guys didn't believe, they didn't know what we were really fighting against until . . . until. Well I got sick, they sent me to the hospital, and when I returned the guys said, "Broms, you were right." And they started to describe in detail the bodies of gassed inmates, Jews, Communists, men, women and children that were piled up on the outside of the gas chambers.

"Oh." I gasped, and covered my mouth with my hand to keep it quiet. I remembered those awful pictures I'd seen in the paper of the concentration camps.

Wilbur continued,

This was in April, 1944, at the Mauthausen Concentration Camp. We were part of Patton's Army and we had the Germans on the run. But, you know the war has been romanticized by both the left and the right. It is an awful thing.[190]

Wilbur stopped talking. He got up and went to the rest room. When he got back he laughed and joked with us one-by-one. He did not want to talk about the war anymore.

We just ate and enjoyed being together, for there was still a war going on, and Wilbur didn't know when he'd be sent to the Pacific.

* * *

I pushed the buggy along the sidewalk on my way to my garden plot. It was my third summer working this garden, and the weather had been perfect for growing vegetables. It was July and the corn was knee high. I was looking forward to a morning on

---

190. Dialogue based on the transcript of an interview of Wibur Broms 1/23/88 by Carl Ross as part of the 20th Century Radicalism in Minnesota Oral History Project at the Minnesota Historical Society.

my hands and knees pulling weeds. Dennis sat up in the buggy, no longer a little baby, but an active participant in everything. My trowel, a garden fork and my gloves, were nestled around him. He giggled as he bounced along.

"Sheila, Sheila," I heard a voice yell out.

It sounded familiar, but I couldn't place it. I started to walk faster, my heart racing.

Dennis giggled in the buggy. He liked the bouncing of the buggy as I walked faster.

"Sheila, stop please. I know it's you!"

My heart beat against my ribs. It couldn't be! It had been over two years since he'd disappeared. I wanted to run away, but instead I froze like a rabbit in the garden.

"Where have you been? I've been looking everywhere for you?"

"What do you mean where have I been? Dexter, where have *you* been?" I asked, anger bubbling up inside me, my stomach churning.

"I've been looking for you for more than two years," Dexter said slowly, in a soft calming voice.

"I left an address in the office with your mother, you could have looked! You could have asked her!" The despair I had suffered during his absence blasted out with those few words.

"I did ask, but she said she didn't know."

I stood there staring at him, wondering if he was lying or if Irene purposely did not tell him.

Suddenly, he noticed Dennis in the buggy. Dennis smiled up at him, reaching out to touch this strange man.

"Don't you recognize him? He appears to know you," I said, sarcastically.

Dexter stared at his son, his eyes widened. "Is he, is he really? Oh, my God, he looks just like me. I . . . I'm so sorry I didn't search harder. I really wanted to see you again. I was so upset when I came back from Alabama and I couldn't find you anywhere. Can I . . . do you think he would let me pick him up?" Dexter reached his arms out towards his son.

As I stood there glaring at him, my anger began to subside. I figured that if I ever did see him again, he would argue and deny that Dennis was his son. That's what most of these Don Juan types did. It was always the girl's fault and there was no way to prove he was the father. Instead they seemed to recognize each other. I didn't say anything aloud. I just nodded my head, and smiled at Dennis so he would know it was okay. My hands gripped the buggy, hoping for the best.

Dexter picked him up gently at first. Dennis's smile got broader. Then Dexter threw him gently into the air and caught him. Dennis giggled with delight. My heart melted at the sight. How I'd wished that Ernest would have played with Brian like that.

"Sheila, I want to see you again."

"I think Dennis wants to see you again for sure." I still didn't trust this overly handsome guy, or myself in his presence. He had not changed at all. I felt an electric pull towards him.

"Dennis, that's his name, Dennis," he said.

"Yes, Dennis Lee," I said.

"That's a very nice name. Dennis Lee," Dexter repeated, letting Dennis put his little fingers around his large finger, the lines stained with motor oil.

"I have a lot of explaining to do, don't I? I've missed so much. I'm sorry I wasn't there when he was born. If I'd known, I would have been there for sure."

Again, I nodded my head. I just could not take my eyes off of him or open my mouth. After all this time, it was hard to believe that he was real, and that he was here. If I said anything, or looked away, maybe he would disappear, like an elf in an old Irish tale.

I took a pencil and paper out of my purse. I wrote down Marjorie's address. He gave me his telephone number.

"I'm still living there, that's Mother's telephone, just ask for me. Or here is my number at work. I work at the Ford Plant and actually I'm there most of the time. I'm always on call. If anything breaks down they call me."

"Where were you all this time?" I asked. I'd thought perhaps he had been drafted, but he'd never said anything about that. Why hadn't he said good-bye.

"Right after our incredible day together, I got a call from my grandmother in Alabama. She was ill. I'd lived with her and my Uncle Rubin when I was in high school. Anyway, I hurried down there, planning to come back soon, but then Rubin needed help on the farm with the ripe pecans. Most of the Negroes that had helped before had left to work up north, so I ended up staying until after Christmas. I never dreamed that you were pregnant. I'm so sorry. If you let me I'll make it up to you." He reached out and gave my hand a squeeze. "But, now I've got to get back to work."

Again I just nodded my head. I wanted to say "Yes," but nothing came out of my mouth.

He left and I walked on, thinking it was a dream. When we reached the garden Dennis giggled and ran through the rows. My arms were covered by long sleeves to keep my freckles from totally consuming them and my head boasted a broad-brimmed straw hat. As I worked perspiration dripped down my forehead and into my eyes, but I didn't stop until each row was perfect. I loosened the soil around the carrots, carefully pulling out the largest ones. These would be a feast at dinner. I left a good inch between the remaining carrots, enough space for each one to mature. My mouth watered as I worked. I wiped the dirt off of a carrot and took a bite. It crunched in my mouth. This was reality. About the rest I wasn't at all sure.

* * *

Dexter came back the very next day, and the next day. If he did not come by, I'd hear from him. He was constantly on call at the Ford Plant. They were making tanks and jet engines. When he wasn't there, he was working for his mother in the apartment buildings, repairing windows or furnaces. He could fix anything.

It was 6:30 p.m. on August 14, 1945, and we had finished eating supper. The music on the radio was interrupted with "The war is over. The Japanese have surrendered." I almost dropped the plate I was holding.

Within 15 minutes Dexter was at my door. "Come on Sheila, Let's celebrate!" He took me in his arms and spun me around.

It was not until later that I learned the horror of the atomic bombs that were dropped on Hiroshima and Nagasaki. Burned bodies of women and children, the scarred land and the sickness that stayed with the survivors.

But then, we were in a state of pure joy. The war was finally over! Dexter and I stayed in the neighborhood, hugging each other, but in towns and cities throughout the country people fired guns in the air, honked horns and kissed anyone within sight, especially any soldiers.

"Why don't you see if Marjorie could watch the kids tomorrow night and we could go out, just the two of us?" Dexter asked. "But be sure to wear slacks."

"All right." I bent my head back to look up at him. We had not spent any time together, without the children, since he had reappeared.

* * *

The next night he came thundering up on his large black beast of a Harley-Davidson motorcycle. He picked me up and sat me on the back of it, then climbed on himself, careful to not knock me off. As we flew into the evening air, my arms around his back, I felt as safe as a caterpillar wrapped up in a cocoon, so overwhelming was his presence.

We drove along Riverside Avenue, winding our way to St. Paul and then to the fountain at Como Park. Colored lights lit up sprays of water that flew into the air. Dexter parked the motorcycle and helped me hop off. As we walked, his hand on my shoulder, he said, "Sheila, I want to marry you, not just because of Dennis, but because I love you."

I stammered, "But everything is such a mess. I'm still married. Ernest won't give me a divorce. I have asked him lots of times."

"He'll just have to give you a divorce now. I'm sure he will."

Tears started to well up in my eyes.

"What's the matter? Don't you want a divorce?"

"No, it's not that at all. It's . . . it's just I'm so happy."

CHAPTER 22

A NEW LIFE

Ernest had moved to Chicago. I felt relieved that he was far away, but sorry that Brian did not see him much at all. I wrote to him asking for a divorce, but I received no answer. Finally Dexter said, "Just call him on the phone. Sure it's long distance, but I'll pay for it. If you don't call him I will."

That got me going. I got out the number Ernest had given me in case of an emergency. I had never called another city. Nervously I spun the dial on my phone, placing my finger in the O and spinning it around.

"Hello this is the operator."

"H . . . Hello, I need to make a long distance call," I said, my voice fading to a whisper.

"What city?"

"Chicago."

"Do you have the phone number?" the operator asked.

"Yes, it is CALumet 2837,"[191] I said, reading from the note Ernest had given me.

I listened to the phone clicking, while rehearsing what I was going to say. *Did you get my letter? No, first I needed to say hello, how are you?* I heard the phone ringing.

191.　http://www.wbez.org/series/curious-city/311-chicagos-early-phone -numbers-109135 from 1921-1948 dialers used three letters and four numbers.

The operator's voice interrupted my thoughts. "This is a long distance call for Ernest Heikkinen," I heard her say.

"Oh, just a minute. I'll go get him," a voice said, and I heard clattering in the background.

My heart sank, was this his work?

"What's the matter? Is something wrong with Brian?" asked Ernest in a worried voice.

"I didn't know this was your work number. I . . . I just wanted to know if you'd gotten my letter, and if you'd filed the divorce papers."

"I gave you this number for an EMERGENCY. You're sure in a damn hurry, after all this time. I filed them yesterday. If I could I'd unfile them today, you Bitch." He hung up.

I collapsed on the floor, shaking with relief. I hung onto the thought: *he'd filed the papers.*

Sure enough, on December 11, 1945, the DECREE FOR DIVORCE came in the mail from the Superior Court of Cook County. It stated we "were lawfully joined in marriage in St. Paul, Minnesota, on June 15, 1932, that subsequent to their marriage the Defendant willfully deserted, and absented herself from the Plaintiff without any reasonable cause for the space of over one year immediately prior to the filing of the Plaintiff's Complaint."[192] I left, but it was not without reason. I continued to read this legal gibberish. At the end it said that "the bonds of matrimony heretofore existing between the Plaintiff ERNEST HEIKKINEN and the Defendant SHEILA HEIKKINEN are hereby dissolved."[193]

It was over. The marriage that never should have happened was finally over. I wanted to dance for joy. I called Dexter to tell him the good news.

Despite my desire to be in Dexter's arms again, I refused to make love until after we were married. The sparks that flew between us never stopped.

---

192. From Divorce Decree on file with author.
193. Ibid.

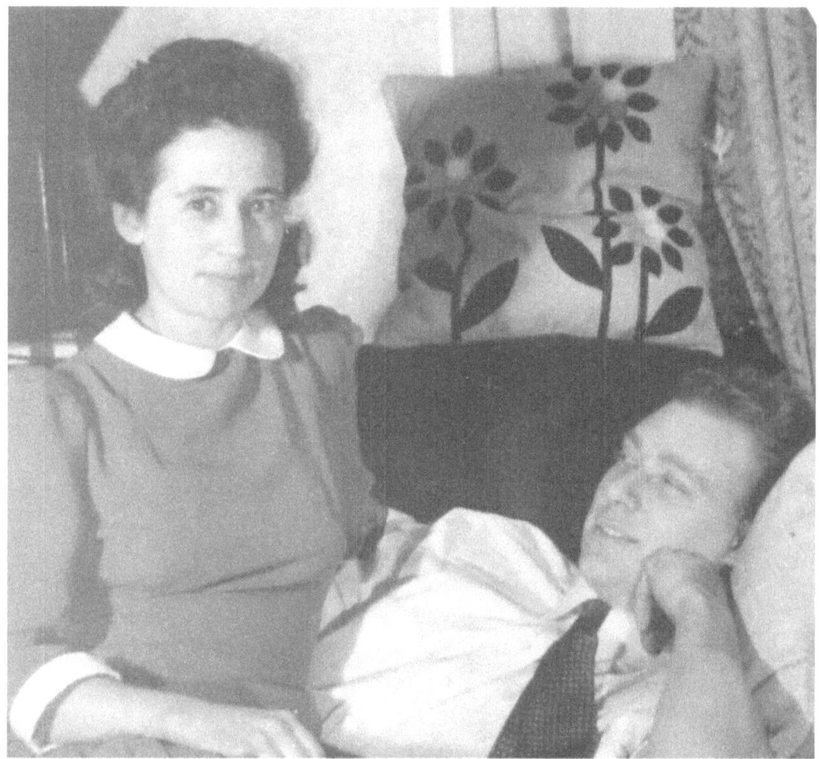

Dexter looking at me, the sparks flying

Dexter loved me, but he loved flying almost as much. He and his friend Kenneth Muxlow had built a plane together and taught themselves how to fly.

One day when we were able to leave the children with Marjorie and her daughter, Cathleen, he took me out to Wold-Chamberlain Field.

"I want to show you something," he said.

"Okay." I wondered what it was, but as we approached the airfield, I knew it was a plane. I had never even dreamt of flying. It was simply too magical to believe I would ever get to be in a plane like Charles Lindberg. Yet here we were, approaching the airport where I knew Dexter flew.

Dexter with the small plane

"I'm taking you up today," he said.

"Okay." I smiled, my heart thumping with excitement, not fear.

It was a small two seater plane with the pilot in front and the passenger seated behind. Dexter put on a cotton flying hat with ear flaps and gave me one to wear as well. He lifted me up into my seat, then climbed into his. We bumped across the airfield, going faster and faster. The propeller spun with a loud whirring sound. He turned the wing flaps and suddenly we were in the air. The wind whistled past my ears. I was glad I was wearing a cap.

Dexter flew with confidence. I looked out, feeling as free as a bird on wing. I was up in a cloud and everything turned white. Then, as we came out of the cloud, I looked down and I saw the beauty of the tiny earth below us. I knew the true meaning of being so happy I could fly. If it was a test to see if I loved what he loved, there was no chance of failure. Dexter and I were meant to fly together.

We got a marriage license. Dexter then called the Anoka County Court House and they said they had an opening for us to get married the following Friday. I needed to find a witness but Marjorie had to work that day. I didn't want to ask anything more of her. Finally I thought of cousin Ruth. We'd run away together from Aunt Lil's house when she was pregnant in high school. Surely she would help me. I'd rarely seen or talked to Ruth since I'd married Ernest years ago. I got her phone number from Aunt Lil and called her on the phone, just saying I needed to visit. She asked me to come over the next morning. She was living out near Anoka, Minnesota, almost an hours' drive from St. Paul. It was a new post-war suburb just being built. Dexter let me use his car and I drove out there with Dennis.

It seemed I'd been driving forever, and I still had no idea where I'd find her. The roads weren't even on the map yet. I turned down an unpaved road, where they were building house after house and they all looked just the same. Finally I rolled down my window and asked a group of kids playing in the street, "Do you know where Ruth and Ed Pareasu live?"

"Sure, they live just over there." They all pointed to a little square house that had not yet been painted. The yard had no grass, just mud with some boards leading up to the door.

Dennis and I walked up the boards and I knocked on the door. "Ruth, its me Sheila." There was no answer, so I knocked louder. "Ruth, Ruth, its your cousin Sheila."

"Heavens, I overslept," said Ruth, still in her dressing gown, her hair rolled into tight rollers on her head, so tight you could see her bare scalp. She hadn't brushed her hair out yet.

"I could come back later," I said, embarassed for her.

"Oh no, come on in," Ruth said, motioning for us to enter. The couch was covered with laundry and the table with unfolded diapers. She shoved the diapers over and pulled out a chair for me to sit on. Her youngest child was crawling around under the table. I put Dennis down to play with her. "So this is Dennis. He doesn't look at all like Brian," she commented.

"Oh Ruth, I just don't know where to begin, so much has happened."

"You're happily married right?" she asked, quickly getting to the point.

"Well, no, you see I'm divorced."

"Really? Divorced? That's exciting," she replied, as if that was the juiciest thing she'd heard in a while.

"No wait, I don't want these things talked about," I said, trying not to to tell her too much.

"I won't breathe a word to anyone."

I paused, unsure what to say next. "You see, I got divorced and Dennis is my fiance's child. We are getting married March 15th. I was wondering if you could be my witness?" I blurted out.

"Sheila, how wonderful! I'd love to!" Ruth practically jumped out of her chair she was so excited. I grinned, relief spreading through my body like a soft wave washing against the shore.

The morning of the wedding we drove out to Ruth's house to pick her up. She was up and ready to go. She had arranged for a neighbor to watch all the children, including Dennis. Brian was in school. I sat next to Dexter in the front seat, wearing a new pink silk suit. Dexter had on a sports jacket, white shirt, tie and a hat. He looked so handsome! I had hardly ever seen him in anything but overalls. I felt like bursting out in song, my heart pounding as the car rolled along. Finally we arrived at the small town of Anoka. The court house was a small classic style building with columns in front. We walked through the door together. I wondered who Dexter had brought for a witness, and then realized he wasn't meeting anyone.

"Dexter, who are you having be your witness?" I asked.

"Do I need a witness?" he asked, raising his eyebrows in surprise.

"I think so," I said, worried that we were not getting married today afterall.

"I'm sure we can just ask the secretary to be my witness," he said, his dimple indenting as his mouth turned up in a grin. I couldn't help grinning too. He seemed to have an answer for everything. .

The secetary, Josephine Pomerleau, did indeed agree to be our second witness. Dexter had a plain wedding band in the pocket of his dress pants. We each said "I do," and at the right moment he slipped the ring over my finger. I didn't have a ring for Dexter. I knew it was not safe for a man who worked with machines to wear a wedding ring.

It said on the Certificate of Marriage that I lived in Anoka County, but actually I gave Ruth's address so we could get married there. I lived in an apartment in Minneapolis that Dexter had found for the kids and me. On our wedding night Dexter came and stayed overnight there. Brian knew he was coming, and he was excited.

Early the next morning Brian came and jumped in bed with us. Dennis was already in the bed. Dexter laughed and tickled Brian. I was so glad. I'd worried that Dexter would be mad at Brian for butting in on us. After a quick breakfast, Dexter hurried off to work on his mother's apartments. He had quit his job at the Ford Plant right after the war.

As he walked out the front door of the building I saw the neighbor stare at him. Her eyes glinted, and the corners of her mouth turned down as she shook her head. After he walked out the door I said, "I'm so sorry I didn't get a chance to introduce you to my husband, Dexter Buell."

She turned her head, her eyes widening in shock, and maybe disappointment. "I didn't know you were married."

"We just got married yesterday," I said, showing her my ring.

"Congratulations," she said, although it sounded more like an apology than a congratulations. I smiled, trying hard to hide my irritation at her snooping on me.

I wrote to my brother and told him I'd married a wonderful man. Very soon after that I got a letter from Charlie's wife Peggy:

You've sinned.

By getting a divorce and remarrying you've sinned against God and all the laws of man. How could you do such a thing?. I never want to see you or have you set foot in my house!

I tore that letter up immediately, but the words burned my heart. I sat down and buried my head in my hands. I told Marjorie about it. Shortly after that, I got a letter from Charlie saying "I'm sure whatever you did, you had good reasons for it." It was a relief to hear he had faith in me, but I did not know how I would ever go home now.

We'd been married for over a month when Dexter finally introduced us to his mother, Irene. We'd been married secretly. I think the real reason we got married in Anoka was so his mother would not see the notice in the newspaper. I have a vivid memory of that day. Dexter brought us into her office. Her huge body was hanging over the edges of a large swivel office chair.

"I'd like you to meet my wife, Sheila Buell," Dexter announced with his dimpled smile.

Irene's eyes widened, then narrowed into small slits glaring out from her round face. The corners of her mouth turned up in a grimace. She recovered her composure and said, "Oh, I remember Sheila," with a menacing whisper.

I smiled at her and said, "It's nice to see you again," remembering how helpful she'd been when she hired me and gave me the apartment with Brian.

She did not look at me. She turned her attention to the children. She told Brian how she remembered him and offered the children treats.

After that Dexter and I got our own apartment. It was a lovely apartment, almost the entire downstairs of one of the brownstone buildings that Irene and Dexter owned. It was around the corner from the building Dexter had lived in with Irene. The brownstone building had a huge front porch spanning the entire width of the building. From our front porch you could see Dexter's mother's building, and her apartment.

One day I took Dennis over to visit his grandmother.

"Oh don't you look more like your Daddy every day," she cooed to Dennis, totally ignoring me. All my senses said, *I'm not wanted here.*

"Has he been getting enough to eat?" she asked, implying that I didn't feed him. She offered him some candy.

He reached eagerly for the candy.

"See there, the poor boy is hungry," she said, her voice brimming with sweet syrup.

As I nervously looked around the room I noticed a pair of binoculars on the sill of the window that faced our apartment.

"Oh what lovely binoculars. I didn't know you were into bird-watching," I said, thinking how my sister Marjorie would love a pair of binoculars like that for watching birds.

"They're not for birds," she admitted. "I like to know when Dennis is coming to visit."

That might have been true, because we did not call before visiting. But there was a smirk in her eyes that said something more. Suddenly I thought, *they were for watching me!*

When Dexter got home I said, "We visited your mother today."

"Oh, that's nice. She always likes to see you."

"Dennis maybe, but not me."

"Oh, she never cared for any of my girlfriends. Don't worry about it, I'm sure she'll get over it."

"But . . . but she's got a pair of binoculars on the window sill. She's spying on me all the time."

"So what. I wouldn't worry about it, honey," he said, smiling at me, "Look, you need to get back to working on your paintings.

You can take classes, and I'll get another apartment that you can use for a studio."

So that's what I did. I started to take classes at the St. Paul School of Art. I studied oil painting for the first time in my life. Dexter often came home with beautiful art books, a large book of Rembrandt paintings that I poured over, and all the drawings of Leonardo da Vinci. Dexter gave me a studio on the third floor of the apartment building. I painted either after the children went to bed or early in the morning before the sun rose. I remember the night I painted the Bamboo. As I painted lighting flashed and thunder roared. The third floor seemed to sway yet the lights stayed on, and my hand never strayed from the brush. The oil paint swayed like the bamboo. In my mind I heard it squeak as it had when I walked through it on my way to school, so many years ago in Australia.

"Bamboo Path" oil Sheila Buchanan Buell c. 1951. To see painting visit blog: Visionsfromtwocontinents.blog

CHAPTER 23

A NEW ADDITION

In June, I woke up nauseated every morning. This time I was pretty sure what it was, but I didn't tell Dexter. I just got up, vomited and ate my saltines without saying a word. In August, I went to see Dr. Moriarity, and she confirmed that I was pregnant. When I told Dexter he grabbed me around the waist and spun me around. "Oh Sheila, that's wonderful. I love being a father. This time I'll be with you every minute."

I carried the baby for ten months, and finally on March 17, 1947, a baby girl was born. The St. Joseph's Hospital nursery was so crowded there was hardly room to put one more little bassinette anywhere. Dexter, true to his word, stayed right by me, as close as he was allowed.

He blurted out, "I even got a girl," as he held her in his arms. "Her nose is flat, all squished over to one side. That wouldn't be so bad if she wasn't a girl."

My cousin Ruth wrote this letter on March 17, 1947:

Dearest Sheila,

My gosh! I'm so excited one would think I was the father. Brian and Dexter called a few minutes ago and told us, and that little girl of yours can be held responsible if all the kids missed the school bus this morning! Such excitement! Brian the little tease, made me wait an eternity before he'd tell me it was a girl. And 8½ lbs!

Holy smoke! That is quite a bundle for such a little girl as you! No wonder you were so blame filled up. I hope you didn't suffer too much Sheila dear, but I know from experience that your tiny girl is ample compensation for whatever you had to go through for her.

My conversation with Dexter was really quite funny. I asked him what time you went so I could have some idea how long you had to wait after getting there, and he told me. Then I said "Well at least she didn't have to lay & suffer too long, & how do you feel Dexter?"

He answered, "Oh I feel just fine, Who, me? Oh yes I feel just fine!" Wish you could have heard it. The expression in his voice was too funny for words. And I know your feelings won't be hurt when I tell you he also said, "It's a homely little thing, but I suppose you'll want to see her anyway!"

Gee, but I laughed, & I reminded him that he couldn't exactly expect her to be a beauty at her very first appearance. He said he supposed not.

Guess he forgot what Denny looked like and what a doll he is now.[194] *I'll bet he will be a proud one.*

Jerry was saying to me yestereday, "Mom you're so anxious about Sheila's baby and when she gets it & you get a chance to hold it you'll melt and say 'I want one, too.' I know your weakness when you see those squeezy little things!"[195] *He is growing up so fast that it scares me a little…*

Sheila, I'm telling you I am still so excited I could cry! I dreamed so many times that you had a boy that I was almost afraid to ask when they called. Of course I never mentioned it to you. I'm so very happy for you both, & so glad it is all over. I hope you don't suffer too much with after pains. Tell those nurses to take extra good care of our little darling. You won't mind sharing her

---

194. Sheila never shared with her cousin Ruth when she was alone and pregnant with Dennis.

195. Jerry was the little baby Ruth was pregnant with when Sheila and Ruth ran away from Aunt Lil's house to St. Paul in 1929.

with me will you? We've always been so very close, & we've been just like sisters so I'm appointing myself official Auntie.

Loads of love and congratulations from all of us,
Ruth, Ed, & Kids.[196]

When Cathleen, Marge's daughter, came to visit she said, "Aunty Sheila, you've got to name her Patricia. She was born on St. Patrick's Day."

Dexter and I looked at each other. We didn't have a name yet. Dexter said, "Why yes, let's name her Patricia, and call her Patsy."

"Lovely," I said, resting my head on the pillow. It had been a hard labor, but I had followed the lastest natural childbirth techniques and had not used any drugs. They kept me in the hospital for a week and when I came home I was weak from being in bed so long.

It took a long time for me to recover my strength, and I was very thin. Dexter tried to get home and spend as much time as possible with Dennis. Dexter's father had died when he was very young. Dexter wanted Dennis to know him, and he wanted to teach Dennis what he knew. Dennis watched and followed his father's every move.

Just before Dennis's fifth birthday Patsy got sick and ran a fever, which went away. Then Dennis got sick; his fever went up and stayed up. He wimpered in pain. We rushed him to Dr. Moriatity and she sent him over to the hospital. They did a spinal tap to check to see if it was polio. In 1946, there had been a polio epidemic, with 1600 cases and 100 deaths in Minnesota between January and August. Minnesota State Fair officials were so concerned that they cancelled the Fair that year.[197] But in 1947, there

---

196. Ruth Parseau, Letter, March 17, 1947. On file with author.

197. For information on the Minnesota State Fair being cancelled see http://www.streetsofsaintpaul.com/2013/05/1946-state-fair-cancelled -due-to-polio.html.

Sheila, Dexter, baby Patsy and Dennis. Christmas 1947

had been very few cases. Surely it could not be polio. Dennis had not been around anyone with polio. However, the spinal tap was positive. I squeezed Dexter's hand and leaned against him. I was afraid I would faint with fear for my precious little boy.

They took Dennis away and put him in isolation. I did not even get to say goodbye or see him at all. I went to the hospital every day, but I could not go anywhere near him. They said he would be highly contagious for two weeks. Two weeks passed and still I could not see him.

Sheila Buchanan Buell first attempt at figures in oil c. 1948. To see painting visit blog: Visionsfromtwocontinents.blog

We were devastated. The separation was bad, as was the fear that he would be permanently paralyzed, or put into an iron lung, unable to breathe by himself.

Finally, I was able to bring him home. He was not the same smiling boy he had been before. He was sad. He thought that we had abandoned him, leaving him in the hospital. Then when I took him for his check up, Dr. Moriarity watched him walk.

"Sheila, do you hear that?"

Australia Dreaming oil Sheila Buchanan Buell. To see painting visit blog:
Visionsfromtwocontinents.blog

"What?"

"That clunk, clunk, when he walks. He is not well, he needs physical therapy."

She arranged for him to go to the Sister Kenny Institute every week. We were lucky that Sister Kenny had developed ways to prevent permanent damage from polio and had built the Institute in Minneapolis.

Finally, after months of therapy, he was able to walk correctly and did not need braces. Many other children were not as lucky.

In the fall, Dennis started school, and I resumed my painting. I put a sandbox in my studio, so Patsy could play while I painted. I continued to work in oil, trying to incorporate what I had learned in the life-drawing class into my oil paintings. My first attempt never got finished. I tried to paint myself and the children in the bush. I was reaching up to pick some fruit. It was a large painting that I worked and reworked, but it never seemed quite right. The figures refused to come alive. (see plate 15)

My instructor Bill Norman told me to loosen up. Just let the figures move with the background and become part of the painting. My mind became one with the tree as it grew and circled around the canvas. The girl bent over crying, remembering her lost home. I let myself and the people become one with the bush. I was in a state of deep meditation, undisturbed by anything, part of the flow, the color, the light. (see color plate #10)

Painting brought me joy, but it did not erase the constant harassment I received from Dexter's mother. She was always breaking into our family time.

"Dexter get over here, there's a faucet leaking."

In the middle of dinner the phone would ring, "Dexter get over here right now."

"Dexter bring me a new coffee pot, the old one's not working."

Dexter would say to me, "Sheila go get a new dress."

If his mother saw me with a new dress, she'd frown and say, "I see you've been shopping again."

I started going out the back door and climbing over the concrete wall in the back yard so she could not see me leave the building. I never wore any new clothes around her.

Dexter said, "Let take a trip to Alabama, to visit my Aunt Helenbelle and Uncle Rubin. I'm sure you'll like them. It's too bad you can't meet my Grandma. She died in 1945. Grandma and Grandpa, Celinda and Jeremiah Lucier, helped start the Fairhope Single Tax Colony.[198] They were trying to create a fairer society, like your Dad was when he went to Australia."

I nodded my head, not understanding what he was talking about but thinking, *not if they're anything like your mother.*

When I agreed to go I didn't realize his mother, Irene, was coming along. It was a long hot drive in the fall, and the further south we went the hotter it got. Irene sat on the front bench seat next to Dexter. Three normal-sized people could sit on the bench seat, but there was no way I could fit next to Dexter with her there. Nor would I have wanted to be squeezed next to her overweight body reeking of B.O. I was in the back with the kids climbing all over me. There were no seatbelts or carseats in those days. Occasionally Irene would take Patsy or Dennis up front on her lap. Dexter liked to drive fast, without stopping. We drove on and on with the open window blowing in bits of cooler air. Dennis constantly asked, "Are we there yet?"

I was almost asleep when Patsy suddenly yelled out in her just-beginning-to-talk voice, "All gone out there."

"What?" I asked.

Patsy jumped up and pointed out the open window.

"Dennis what is she talking about?'

"I don't know."

---

198. On their gravestone in Fairhope, Alabama, is engraved "A Single Tax is a fair tax." The Fairhope Single Tax Community was founded on the ideals of economist Henry George. See http://beautifulfairhope.com/about/history/ for a full description.

But when we got to Alabama Patsy was missing a shoe. Apparently she'd thrown it out the car window.

Dexter's face beamed as we approached a rambling clap-board house with a tin roof. We walked up, entered a large screen porch stretching across the entire front of the house, and were ushered into a small parlor with a brick fireplace on the west end.

"Welcome." Everyone hugged me until I thought I would be squished flat. Irene hugged everyone, with tears flowing down her face. I was surprised by such overt signs of affection, because my family never hugged like that.

"Sit down for a glass of ice tea and cake." Helenbelle had made a pinapple upside down cake, Dexer's favorite, so we all sat down. I was anxious to get out and walk, and to see the pecan orchard.

Finally, we went outside. Dexter narrated the tour, "Here's the washhouse. And a storage building, this is Helenbelle's garden, and our fig trees."

"Oh my, you can grow figs?" My mouth watered at the memory of fresh figs in Australia.

Beyond the garden was the milking barn. The cows were out in the pasture.

Then I saw the pecan trees, six acres of delicious pecans, ready to be harvested. The pecans were dropping to the ground like manna from heaven. I bent down to pick some up.

"Now you just got here. You're our guests, so don't go working already," said Helenbelle.

After sitting on my butt for two days I was more than ready to work.

I was overjoyed when I found out that Irene would not be riding back in the car with us. She had come down to stay with her daughter, Laura, and try to get her granddaughter, Joan, to go to school. Joan had been sent to live with Helenbelle, but Helenbbelle could not handle her, so Irene and Laura were going to stay while Joan went to school. They were sure the Organic School was just what Joan needed. The Organic School had taught Dexter

Irene Buell In Alabama

how to read, when no one else thought he could learn. It was a new progressive program.

Dexter took a picture of his mother standing out in the pasture.

While we were in Alabama we did manage to drive down the coast to the beach just Dexter, the children and me. I loved the smell of the sand and salt and the sound of the waves breaking onto the shore. Patsy played in the sand, and Dexter caught this snap shot of me in my bathing suit:

The children were both healthy the winter of 1949, the country was not at war, yet everyone was in a constant state of tension. The Berlin Air Lift had started on June 24, 1948, and continued all that winter. The news reels constantly reminded us we were not really at peace. The country was festering in what came to be called the Cold War. Congress was chasing Communists, including my sister. She found her birth certificate in a church in Little Falls, so she no longer feared being deported. Many people who had expressed any interest in the ideals of the Communist or Socialist Parties in the 1930s, were ostracized or, if foreign-born, deported.

Lucille's step-sons were back from the war. The eldest son, Gordon, bought an old farm house with his wife and two-year-old child on Idaho Street in St. Paul. That winter they had a new furnace put in. The installer promised he would get it started and the house would be warm when they returned. Instead, the house burned in a tragic fire, destroying everything they owned. The St. Paul newspaper wrote a story about the plight of this young soldier. Donations poured in. In fact they received so much help they were able to buy a place and give land to their father. He knew his Dad had devoted his life to the "cause" and had nothing. At first Lucille and Henry lived in a tent on the land. Then they built a temporary house, and finally a real house.[199]

____

199. This story was told to me by Charlotte, Henry's daughter. I do not have the exact dates and so was unable to find the newspaper story.

Sheila and Patsy on the Beach in Alabama

Lucille and Henry on their Land

An official letter from England arrived, dated January 22, 1949. It was my Aunt Bella's will.[200] I had been very sad to hear that she died. I had never made it to England to meet her, and now I was astounded to find she left her estate to her eight nephews and nieces, including me. It wasn't a lot, but enough that I was able to buy land adjoining the land Lucille had received from her son. Lucille and Henry were able to put a lovely picture-window in their house.

Irene didn't stay long in Alabama. By March she was back, harassing me. She even complained that I had invested my inheritance in the land next to Lucille's. She mistakenly accused me of leaving Dexter off the title. I had had enough. I wrote to a cousin about going to California to get away from her. But finally, Dexter said, "Sheila what would you think about moving out of the city?"

"Maybe if we were out of the city, on an organic farm Dennis would not have gotten polio. It would be a better place to raise the kids."

"That would be wonderful," I said, dreaming of a large vegetable garden.

____

200. Copy of the will on file with the author. It was executed by Lt. Col. P.D.G. Buchanan. Aunt Bella had savings in the bank, and L300 of 3 ½ % War Stock, and a little bit of her Old Age Pension undrawn at the date of death. Each nephew or niece received L95.5.

CHAPTER 24

THE ORGANIC FARM

Moving to the farm was like going home. No, it wasn't Australia, but it was wild, with woods on either side of the farmhouse, and a creek flowing through the pasture. Life slowed down when we bumped off the blacktop unto the gravel road, but Dexter's driving didn't. I held my breath as dust swirled up from the spinning tires and blew in the open car windows. It seeped up my nostrils. Dennis held his arm out the window and waved it up and down like an airplane wing. Then Dexter finally turned down a golden sand driveway. The barn swallows were squeezed along the telephone wire; wing touching wing. They flew off as we approached, then cautiously returned to their perches.

The little old farmhouse had been abused. Despite a fresh coat of paint, it still smelled of sheep dip, some concoction used to clean sheep that the previous owners had thrown on the walls. The house was just a square with a large eat-in kitchen, a small sitting/living room, and three small bedrooms.

Patsy wiggled up and down, crossing and uncrossing her legs. "Where is the bathroom?"

"There isn't one in the house yet. You will need to use the outhouse," I said as I kicked off my shoes. We walked barefoot across the soft sand of the driveway. Patsy smiled gleefully as the sand squished between her bare toes. The golden sand made it seem like we were on the beach. We pushed open the outhouse door and I sat next to her on the two-seater bench. She couldn't see out the little moon shaped window cut in the door so I left it open. A soft breeze floated across the long driveway towards the woods. Patsy seemed confident with using the outhouse. I showed her how to put a small trowel full of lime into the hole so it would not stink.

For our first meal I boiled potatoes, then peeled them, saving the nutrient-rich potato water, and called Dexter in to mash them. I added back some of the potato water and he mashed them in the pan with his right hand and put his left arm around my waist, pulling me close. My heart raced with joy, but I whispered "Not now." I was frying pork chops and making gravy, using more of the potato water, while fresh broccoli from my sister Lucille's garden steamed on the back burner.[201] Dexter laughed and kissed me on the cheek.

I set the plates on the new post-war stainless steel table. The table had an easy-to-clean Formica top and six stainless steel chairs with plastic padded seats, perfect for a growing family. But when Dexter bought it new, his mother insisted that she needed one too. The kids stayed outside exploring until the last minute, but came quickly when I called their names, "Patsy, Dennis." I didn't have to say what for. They were hungry, so they raced in the door and plunked down on the metal chairs, with Dennis coming in first.

Everyone devoured that first meal with gusto. Halfway through dinner Patsy looked at Dexter and said, "Daddy, I'm full. Do you want it?"

"Sure Pumpkin," he answered as he scraped her plate clean. Patsy beamed, her dimples showing on her cheeks; she loved feeding her Daddy.

---

201. Sheila was very careful to follow the suggestions of Adele Davis in her book *Let's Cook It Right*, which recommended steaming vegetables to retain the vitamins. Always cook potatoes with the skins on and reuse the vegetable water.

After dinner we walked down the narrow hallway, past the three small bedrooms and out onto a long porch that spanned the entire west side of the house. There Dexter, Patsy, Dennis and I sat on the front steps and watched the sun set into the clouds in beautiful orange pinks. We were home. The only thing missing was my son Brian. At 19 he seemed unhappy, living in Chicago with his Dad.

The next morning Patsy went to the outhouse by herself, but came running back. "Mommy, Mommy, there's a snapping turtle in the outhouse. I can't go in, he'll bite me."

"Ok, I'm coming." I walked quickly, being careful not to run. My mind raced, thinking of the poisonous snakes in Australia. There weren't any poisonous animals in Minnesota, but a scared snapping turtle could bite, and would not let go.

Patsy did not seem to be very frightened and raced ahead of me, through the outhouse door, by herself. I hurried after her. "Where is it?" I asked.

Patsy pointed down the hole. "See, look, right there."

I looked carefully with the eyes of a child. Yes, I did see the pointed head of a snapping turtle. But it wasn't moving at all. "Look closer, see it doesn't move. Don't worry, it isn't going to bite you." I laughed with relief.

Patsy looked and laughed too, "Well it sure looked like one."

"Yes, whoever dropped that one was very creative."

Directly across from the outhouse was a small shack that Dexter made into my studio. At the far back of the circular driveway was a huge barn. It had a hayloft, and then a long cow barn with stanchions and two almost new silos. Dexter made the large open area under the hayloft into a shop, and installed two furnaces to keep it warm in the winter. He used the pasture closest to the barn for his landing field. He worked hard, but he did not get the bathroom done. When I complained he made a temporary toilet, with a bucket that had to be carried out to the outhouse. He promised to empty it every day. This worked fine until one day Patsy pooped

"Come Play with Me" oil, Sheila Buchanan Buell, 1950s. To see painting visit blog: Visionsfromtwocontinents.blog

in it while he had the bucket out. "How could you do that, can't you look?" He was so loud I was afraid he'd smack her. But he never spanked her, just the boys. She never did that again.

The woods on either side of that little farmhouse beckoned me.[202] When Dexter worked at home I'd wake up early and whisper to him, "I'm going for a walk." He seemed to understand. I followed my heart into the woods. I told Sandy, our shorthaired fox terrier, "Stay home, you just scare the birds." But as soon as I turned the corner there was Sandy following me, with a cat slinking close behind him. *Oh well,* I thought *I'll still get to see some wildflowers.* My feet squished in the damp earth and my pants

---

202. This painting was one of the first ones she did on the farm. If one looks closely you will see that although the foreground is a Minnesota woods, the trees across the water are the trees of the Australian bush.

were wet from the morning dew as I cleared a path across the field, with the dog and cat both following. I increased my speed as the forest drew nearer, hoping maybe I could lose the dog. I slowed at the edge of the woodlot to watch the monarch butterflies feasting on milkweed. I wondered *if there was a baby monarch caterpillar I could take home for the kids to rais*e? *I'll bring Patsy back later to look for one.* I entered the shadow of the forest and the ground under the trees changed to a soft moss carpet. It was fall and there were only a few flowers. I could hardly wait to see what spring would bring. Dolls eyes, white seeds with dark eye spots, hovered above their leaves, reaching for a shaft of sunlight coming through the trees. I did not see Sandy; maybe he had returned home. I sat down on a log hoping to catch sight of a bird, or perhaps a deer hiding in the woods.

I looked up and saw a bright shaft of light coming through the canopy of leaves. *Oh my, Dexter and the kids must be up.* I hurried back to the little farmhouse. As I approached I saw Sandy and the cat sitting on the back steps listening to what was going on in the kitchen. The neighbor's car was parked near the back door. I put my hand on the door latch but stopped. I heard Horace Field, the farmer next door, talking to Dexter. "Don't you wonder what your wife is up to out there, walking in the woods all the time, all alone?"

"Oh, no. Not at all. You see she's an artist, and she's not like the rest of us."

My heart beat faster, and swelled with joy. I didn't know he would defend me like that. It was a big change from how Ernest had behaved.

For Halloween we invited the neighbors over for a bonfire. Janet and Horace Field had not been able to have children so they took in foster kids. They had three foster boys that helped on the farm. There wasn't anywhere to trick or treat, so we made a huge bonfire and roasted marshmallows. Dennis wore the cowboy outfit I'd made for him from deer hide and Patsy dressed as a little princess. The foster kids were older and didn't have costumes, but they loved screaming at ghosts in the dark. Without the glow of city lights, stars filled the sky.

About a week after Halloween the phone rang. I listened carefully to see if it was for me. If I heard six rings it was for our house. There were six families on our party line. As it kept ringing my mind started worrying. *Does Dexter have a problem? Is his mother coming to visit?* It rang six times and I picked it up, hearing the line click as other families set the phone down, but someone just might hang on. One never knew who was listening on a party line.

"Hello, this is Mrs. Sheila Buell."

"Hello Sheila, this is your neighbor Janet. Would you like to come over for a cup of coffee?"

"I'd love to," I said, happy that we'd broken the ice with the Halloween party. We'd already been living here three months but she had not invited me over until today.

It had snowed so I drove slowly along the icy road, about a half mile to their place. They heated with a wood stove, and the place smelled cozy and warm. A springer spaniel was sleeping under the wood stove, and the coffee was hot. Janet said, "Thanks so much for inviting us over for Halloween. The kids had a marvelous time."

"Not at all. I think it was more fun than Dennis had going trick or treating last year in town. But he misses his friends in town."

"Sometimes when the boys are through with their chores they can come over and play," she said, her eyes averting my gaze as if she had something else on her mind. "I'm sorry I didn't invite you over earlier," she blurted out.

"Oh that's OK. You've probably been very busy with the boys and the farm work and all," I answered, wondering what she was getting at.

"No, you're a new neighbor, and I should have invited you over earlier. It's just, well, your mother-in-law, Irene Buell, came over before you guys moved in."

She paused, and I nodded my head.

"Well, she said these awful things about you. Why, she said I'd better keep an eye on my husband. Now I know you're nothing like that."

"Oh my, I'm sorry she said that," I said, my face turning red as I tried to control the rage building up in me. Yes, I knew she did not like me, but to spread rumors like that before I had even moved in.

I stayed calm during the visit. But as soon as I got in the car my hands clutched the steering wheel and my teeth crunched together as I drove home, trying to contain my anger. I couldn't believe she'd say a thing like that.

I went into the house, my jaw still tight. I needed to scream, to hit something or someone, but I just didn't want to do that. It wasn't proper. Dexter was in the city right now, working for that woman. She possessed him. It was like the umbilical cord had never been cut.

Yes that's it, that's the problem. Maybe if I paint a picture, Dexter will understand, and I will be able to let go of all this anger. I poured all of my anger into the painting. It was a large oil painting, in earth browns with a fat lady coming out of the earth, and an umbilical cord coming out of her. Attached to the umbilical cord was a little man dressed in a suit. The colors flowed one into the other, and the anger dissipated into them. By the time the kids got home I was well on my way to completing the painting. By the time Dexter got home I was my calm, happy self again. I hid the painting in the back of the studio.

I brought the painting to class, and Bill Norman, my painting instructor, said it was one of the best paintings I'd ever done. Dexter still hadn't seen it. Finally he saw it. "Is that really what you think?" he asked, amazed, staring at the little man dressed in a suit. He knew right away what the painting was about. I told him about the incident with Janet.

"Oh, honey, I'm so sorry" he said, giving me a big hug. "That explains those weird questions Horace asked me."

That one hug was more than a thousand words. My face softened and my rage melted in his embrace. The next morning, after the kids went to school and Dexter drove into town, I took the painting out to the trash burner and burned it up. As flames licked at the oil paints, I hoped each puff of noxious smoke was taking my anger away.

When Patsy got home from school she skipped into the living room and asked, "Mommy, where is the painting, the one of the fat lady and the little man?"

I hadn't realized that she would remember the painting. "Oh it wasn't any good, so I burned it up," I said, making an excuse for its absence.

"Oh no, I liked it. I liked the brown moving colors and the little man." She said almost what Bill Norman had said. But I was glad it was gone, and hopefully the anger with it.

CHAPTER 25

PAINTING AND FARMING

I needed to get my mind off of Irene and back with my children. Nine-year-old Dennis was home from school, whining about the friends he'd left behind in the city

"Can James come to visit? I haven't seen him forever."

"No, I don't think so. Dad and I don't have the time to drive there this weekend," I said, thinking of an hour's drive each way, since James's parents didn't drive. "Let's go for a walk." It sounded like he needed some of my time. "Just the two of us."

I set five-year-old Patsy up drawing at the kitchen table, and then got my coat, hat and boots.

"Put on your boots Dennis, I want to show you something."

As we walked towards the swamp behind the barn, my mind flashed back to my first winter in America. The snow and wind had been endless, almost like this, our first winter on the farm. I was just recovering from pneumonia, and the snow was melting, when Uncle Cass took me for a walk to the swamp on his farm near St. Cloud. Now it was March, and our swamp was teeming with pussy willow bushes, their thin branches sticking straight up from pools of melted snow. Soft little gray catkins covered the tops of the branches, the first sign of spring. I wanted to show them to Dennis, the way Uncle Cass had shown me.

As Dennis and I walked I said, "Can you hear that crying?"

"What, what? I don't hear anything," Dennis said, turning his head from side to side.

The water from the swamp oozed up around our boots as we slowly tromped towards the pussy willows. Dennis followed, matching me step for step.

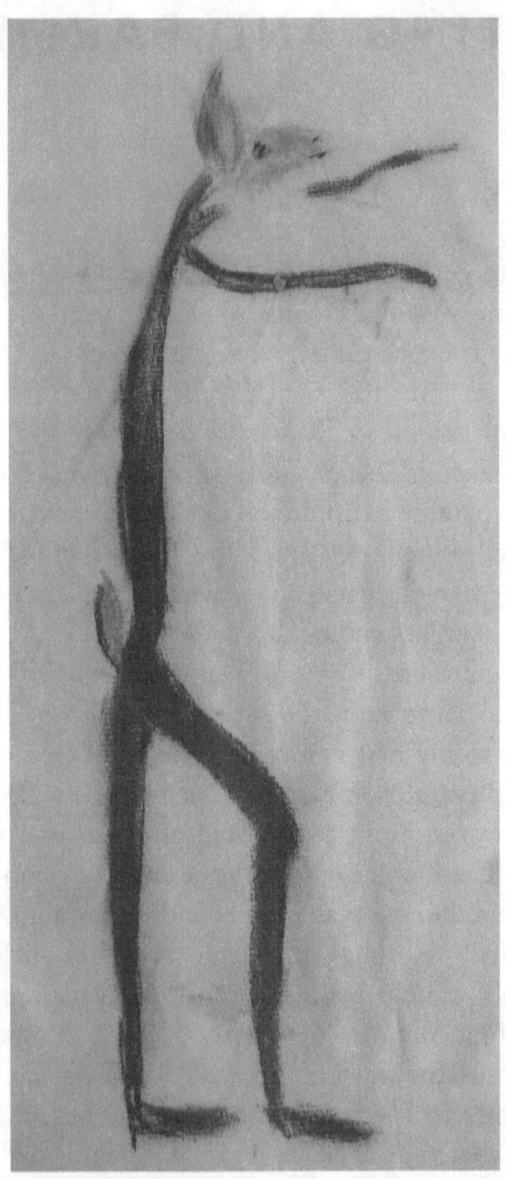

Mr. Pussy Willow sketch 1953

The red-winged blackbirds trilled. "This is my reed. No one else can have it." As the willows swayed in the wind, one mature catkin bud danced in the sun, with a yellow beard around his face. I showed him to Dennis. "See, this is Mr. Pussy Willow. He is lonely and wants you to play with him." I picked it and handed it to him. Dennis gingerly accepted the stick, a confused look in his eyes that said, "It's what?"

When we got back from our walk, Mr. Pussy Willow stayed in my mind. I drew his picture.

Dennis left the stick lying on the table. I picked it up and put it in a vase. Then I got out my pellon cloth and painted it gray. I proceeded to sew Mr. Pussy Willow in three dimensions. His ears were painted pink and green leaves, his body gray cloth sticks dressed in a green silk suit and his tail a little gray catkin bud. Dennis laughed, "Oh that's what you saw in the swamp."

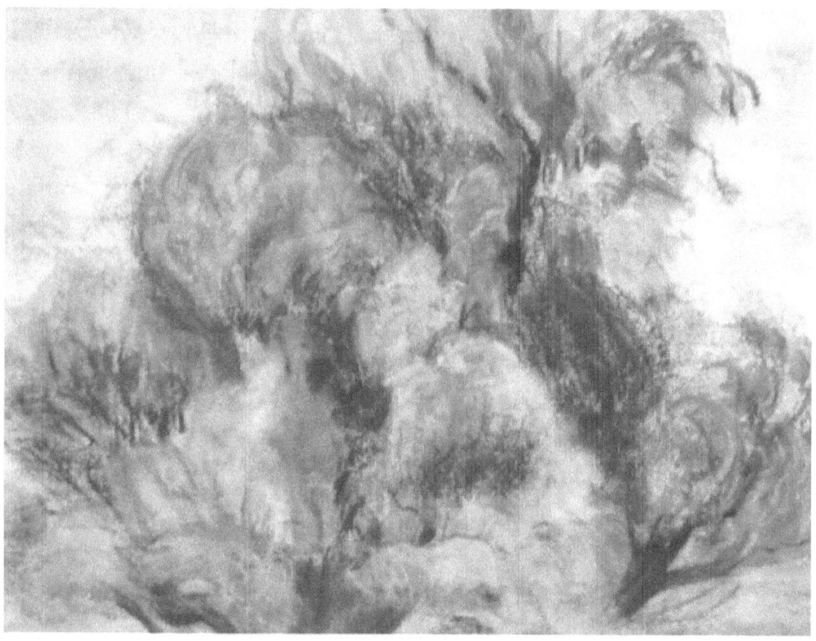

"Willows" pastel 1950s by Sheila Buchanan Buell. To see painting visit blog: Visionsfromtwocontinents.blog

I went back to painting the beauty around me. It was spring, and I made a pastel painting of a willow tree, its leaves turning the lovely spring green that I saw in the field outside my studio window. I pushed the pastel chalk across the paper, and then spread the colors with my fingers. The smell of chalk dust mingled with the fresh spring air coming in my studio window. The wind blew that yellow green back and forth across my mind. The black branches swayed with power, and I was one with nature.

I brought the Willow painting to the house to show it to Dexter. Horace Field came over while it was there. "Oh," said Horace, leaning over for a closer look. "Why, that's just beautiful. I guess I've never looked at the willows before." Then he laughed, "Well if a farmer spent all his time looking at trees, he'd never get his work done."

My heart swelled when he said that my picture helped him to see the beauty of nature. That was my goal. That meant more to me than the words of a famous art critic.

That summer our farm became a real farm. We had grade B dairy cows that we milked every morning, chickens in the chicken coop and hay in the hayloft. Dennis helped, riding in the wagon with Sandy the fox terrier right beside him, putting the silage into the silo.

New neighbors, Edith Erskine, a junior college English teacher, and her four children, moved into a farm just down the road across the creek. The two younger children were perfect playmates for Patsy and Dennis. Johnny was Patsy's age, and Walter was the same age as Dennis. Edith believed children should play, and play they did. The first part of our long circle driveway was their sandbox. They spent hours building castles, roads and rivers. Dexter let them run the hose as much as they wanted. Their biggest triumph was when Dennis and Walter used the posthole digger and struck water about four feet down. They were so proud of their well.

One day Patsy came in crying, with Johnny running behind her, "Mommy, we can't find Dennis and Walter anywhere."

Dennis and Sandy helping with the silage

"Where did you see them last?"

"We were in the hay loft and then they disappeared."

I hung up my dishtowel. "Okay let's go find them." My mind worried that they were suffocating under piles of hay. We climbed the steep staircase above Dexter's shop. Looking over the hay bales I noticed they had been moved around.

"Dennis, where are you?" Silence was my answer. Then I heard a scuttling in the hay, like there were huge mice under there. "Dennis, Walter, come out here and tell me what is going on."

Dennis came crawling out from under the hay, with a sheepish grin on his face.

"Dennis, you could suffocate under there if the bales collapsed," I said, worry elevating my voice.

"No, Mom, we used boards for extra support so it is totally safe, see." He proudly showed me the boards they had put under the hay bales.

I was amazed by their engineering skills. They had constructed tunnels throughout the hayloft, and also installed a telephone so they could warn each other if Patsy or Johnny were trying to find the entrance.

I told Patsy and Johnny, "Just let them be, you two can play in the sandbox."

"But, but I want to go in the fort!" Patsy protested.

"Just let them be. They'll soon be bored."

Dexter helped Dennis and Walter install a rope swing in the hayloft. They threw a rope over the rafters and all the kids took turns climbing up on the hay bales, swinging over an open space and landing on a pile of soft hay. Dexter laughed with joy at their antics.

One day I stepped out the back door to see Dennis sitting on the roof of the curved hayloft, about four stories in the air. I gasped, but tried to stay calm as

I asked Patsy, "How did he get up there?"

"I'll show you," she said. We walked around the back of the barn where there was a ladder reaching up to the roof. Then on the rounded roof there were wooden slats nailed in place, making a ladder to the very top of the hay loft roof. "Can I go up there too?" she asked.

"No, you most certainly cannot. Dennis, Dennis, get down from there right now," I yelled up into the sky. But he was so high up he couldn't hear me. I had to wait, terrified, for him to come down. After a while he came wandering into the house. I opened my mouth to speak but decided to wait till his dad came home.

As soon as Dexter got in the door I said, "Did you leave a ladder against the barn roof?"

"Sure, I was working up there."

"Well Dennis climbed up to the very top of the hay mow roof. I was terrified."

"Oh don't worry, he'll be just fine." I opened my mouth to reply then closed it, *never mind, men will be men,* I thought.

Dennis came in one day and said to his Dad, "Can we build a slide from the top of the hay mow down to the house?"

Dexter agreed. "That sounds like a great idea but I don't have time right now."

I think if he'd had the time he would have built that slide. Dexter was up before dawn, milking the cows. The barn cats would crowd around and he'd laugh and squirt milk into their mouths as he milked. Later, after he installed milking machines, he'd often take time to squirt some milk to the cats before he attached a cow to the machine. He loved to ride the tractor out in the fields and he invented a huge disk machine to plow under the weeds in the fields. This was an organic farm, so while other farmers were using chemicals he was inventing things to help nature out. He seemed to enjoy every minute of the work, but then his mother would call and he would race off to the city to do her bidding.

Sometimes Dexter just exasperated me. One time I saw a tornado in the sky. I took the kids down into the well room in the basement, but Dexter stayed up on the couch, laughing at the storm. He seemed invincible. A friend that he had taken up in his single engine plane told of the day the engine stopped.

He said, "I asked Dexter, 'What's going on, has the engine stopped?'"

"Dexter answered as calmly as could be, 'Ya, and we're going to land right down there.' He glided the plane in, safely landing in a shallow swamp." He always had a sense of humor, and loved to tease the neighbors, flying low over Horace Field as he worked out in his pasture. When we were supposed to be helping Lucille and Henry build their house, we ended up flying low over the building site while the rest of the family worked. I heard about that from the family for years afterwards.

I worked in the gardens. We had a huge strawberry patch, and I picked strawberry after strawberry. I didn't know what I was going to do with all those berries. Then I remembered how the children loved popsicles. I put the berries in a large cheesecloth bag and hung them up to get the juice out of them. I froze the juice in ice cube trays. The children came from miles around to have one of those popsicles. The freezer was full of them, and they could eat all they wanted.

One day Dexter showed up with a dog in the back seat of the car. "Where did that come from?" I asked.

"Poor thing, I found him wandering at the end of the driveway, lost I guess."

It was about a six-month-old puppy. He looked just like a collie, but he had a short nose. The kids crowded around, "Can we keep him?"

"We already have a dog. Sandy might not like him," I said. "If he is lost, his owner might be looking for him."

"He can be an outside dog. I'll build him a dog house," said Dexter. "Of course if his owner shows up we will have to give him back." Dexter and Dennis built him a house of straw bales, followed by an insulated house with a picture window and real siding for the winter. We named him Laddie, the male version of Lassie in the TV show that the children all loved.

Laddie loved the farm and everything and everyone on it. In the swamp he'd catch frogs and carefully let them go. He even became friends with a skunk. I watched him go out at night and play with a young skunk. Sandy, a city dog, thought he'd take care of this thing. Sandy snuck up behind the skunk, and opened his mouth to bite. At precisely that moment the skunk let him have it. Sandy got sprayed right in the mouth. He yowled and ate dirt and rolled in the dirt. Despite being the indoor dog we did not let him in the house for a few weeks.

Patsy sat for hours with Laddie on top of his hay bale house. If I'd let her I think she would have slept out there with him. One day she came in the house and asked, "Mommy can I marry Laddie when I grow up?"

"Oh no dear. Laddie is a dog and you are a little girl, so you can't possibly marry him. Just love him every day."

Patsy looked at me and walked away. She didn't argue, but the corners of her mouth turned down in a pout.

I grew cucumbers in the corn, and decided to paint them. The mosquitoes had a feast, munching on me, while I captured the twisting green vines with bright yellow flowers clinging to the

"Peace" pastel Sheila Buchanan Buell 1953

stately corn stalks, with my pastels. I entered that painting into the rural art show at the University of Minnesota. It was given an award and the University asked to purchase the painting. I wasn't sure, I didn't want to part with it, but I thought *it will be preserved in a museum,* so I let it go.[203]

One morning I woke up with my stomach churning. I went to the bathroom and vomited. I didn't have a headache; I didn't have a fever. Was it true? Was it possible? I was almost forty years old, too old to be having babies I thought, but I was pregnant

203. *The St. Paul Pioneer Press* published a photograph of Sheila standing in front of the painting. The painting was supposed to be in the collection managed by the University of Minnesota Libraries on the St. Paul Campus. When I contacted them in 2010 the painting was listed as missing.

with Dexter's third child. We were both excited about this unexpected happening. Except for that little bit of nausea I was healthy throughout the pregnancy, gardening, painting, cooking, freezing and painting some more. I worked in pastels that winter, creating an image that reflected the peace I felt, and wished for the world.

I was still working on that pastel when my body said it was time. Dexter rushed me to the hospital, a full hour drive from the farm. There, a beautiful little boy that we named Eugene Charles Buell struggled his way out. He wasn't a large baby, but they cut me to get him out. I wasn't doing very well, and I was in the hospital over a week. I was very embarrassed when Dexter brought the painting and my pastels to the hospital.[204] *What will people think if they see this nude painting.* But I forgot my pain. I forgot even that I was in the hospital as I worked on that picture.

I finished it in the hospital. I was totally at peace, nursing my little boy. My mother stood beside me in the hollow. I was one with the flora and the fauna. The birds were not afraid, resting on my fingers, as the tiger lay down beside us.

I could not imagine a happier life than the life I was living at this moment.

---

204. Sheila tells this story in her video, Arty Pink Toes.

"Peace" pastel Sheila Buchanan Buell 1953. To see painting visit blog: Visionsfromtwocontinents.blog

CHAPTER 26

EVERYTHING CHANGES

When I finally left the hospital I wasn't ready. Dexter helped me walk into the house carrying the baby. He placed the donut pillow the hospital had sent home with me on a chair. As I slowly placed my tender bottom on the chair Patsy cautiously approached me, "Mommy, are you all right?" she asked, her forehead wrinkled with worry.

"I'll be all right. I'm just a little sore," I said, as I smiled through gritted teeth.

Dennis asked, "Can I get you anything, Mom?" I smiled at him, thinking how blessed I was to have had Dennis ten years ago, and now his little brother.

Then I remembered the Ginny doll I'd fixed for Patsy while I was pregnant. She was six inches tall and I'd had so much fun staying up at night sewing tiny clothes for her, tiny skirts and dresses and even a hula skirt made with thick white thread that hung down to the Ginny doll's bare little feet. Dennis had watched me sew after Patsy was in bed, so I said, "Dennis, go and get the box in my bedroom, you know the one."

Dennis smiled, or maybe smirked, proud that he knew something that Patsy did not. He ran into my bedroom and came back with a shoebox that he presented to Patsy.

Patsy wasn't sure what to do with the box. It wasn't Christmas or her birthday so she wasn't expecting a present.

"Go ahead open it. It's for you," I said, encouraging her.

Slowly she opened the box. "Oh, my," she said, her blue eyes sparking as she carefully picked up the little doll. Then she held up a tiny pleated skirt. "Oh, my," she repeated. Then she picked up a tiny blouse, a little dress, tiny shoes and the white hula skirt. "Oh thank you, thank you so much Mommy," she said, with tears in her eyes.

Dexter carefully helped me get to bed and laid Eugene down next to me. I smiled as I nursed Eugene and thought *it was worth every minute I spent creating those tiny clothes.*

As soon as I felt better I got out my pastels and made a quick sketch of baby Eugene. He stayed totally still, stopping his constant movement, his blue eyes blazing into mine. My hand moved the pastel without my looking down at the page, just into those blue pools. When I finally glanced down at the paper I was amazed to see a completed picture.

By summer I was as active as ever. I planted a huge organic garden following all the tricks I'd read about in Rodale's *Organic*

Farming and Gardening Magazine.[205] The children helped plant a hill of pumpkin seeds at the back of the garden. I showed them how to make manure tea by taking dried manure and covering it with water in a watering can. Since the manure had been dried this did not stink. Every week we lugged a big pitcher of manure tea up the hill and fed the pumpkin. It flowered and grew and grew. I created a Pumpkin Fairy story, which I told Patsy:

> Once upon a time there was a family like ours. They grew a huge pumpkin, and in the fall when they carved it to make a Jack-O-Lantern, instead of little seeds inside they found one gigantic seed. The next year they planted that unusual seed. They took special care of it, for it seemed magical. It grew and grew into a pumpkin the size of a small house. At harvest time they didn't try to carve a Jack-O-Lantern, instead they carved a door on the side of the pumpkin. As soon as they opened the door the Pumpkin Fairy stepped out. "Hello, thanks for taking such good care of my house," she said.
>
> "Who are you?" the children asked.
>
> "I'm the Pumpkin Fairy. I must take care of the forest, and all the animals and plants in it. She stayed just for Halloween, then waved her magic wand and flew away into the woods. But she came back every Fall.

As Halloween approached I asked Patsy, "What do you want to be for Halloween?"

"I want to be the Pumpkin Fairy," she said, her eyes shining with anticipation.

So I made her a Pumpkin Fairy costume. It had a shiny orange flowing skirt and a black puffy-sleeved blouse with orange pumpkins on the sleeves. When Patsy tried it on she twirled around

205. *Organic Farming and Gardening* was first published in 1942. When Dexter and Sheila bought the farm in Anoka County they followed the ideals put forth by Rodale. There was no market for organic products at the time.

making the orange fabric stick straight out so her underwear showed. Then I made a black lace slip with orange trim and black panties to wear under the orange skirt so it would look proper when she twirled around. I made a magic wand for her to carry and a huge pumpkin seed purse with a zipper for candy corn.

At her school in Anoka all the children got out of classes to march through town in the annual Halloween Parade. Patsy won a little fuzzy pin of a poodle dog as a prize for the most creative costume in the 1953 Anoka Halloween Parade. She wore it proudly all year.

The year 1953 was not a good one for farmers. The price of milk fell 30 cents per 100 pounds. "I don't know how they expect us to sell them milk when we're not making enough to buy feed for the cows," Dexter said. Luckily we raised most of our own feed, but we were not making enough to pay for the farm and the farm machinery. Dexter had tears in his eyes when he had to return his beloved tractor to the dealer, but we just couldn't make the payments.

Dexter said, "We've got to do something different. This just isn't working. I need to get out on my own and pay Mother off. Do you think you could handle things here if I went to work in Greenland for a year? Some guys I worked with at the Ford Plant are looking for an ace mechanic to keep things running on a project in Greenland. They are paying really well. I could make enough, and we could buy an airport. I could fix airplanes. Maybe Mother could do the books."

I took a deep breath. I knew things weren't going well but I loved the farm and I knew Dexter did too. "Greenland? Isn't that awfully far away? Can't you find something around here?"

"Not that pays like that. I can make enough money in six months to pay for everything," Dexter replied, convinced that this would straighten things out.

"Okay, I can handle the kids just fine, but we don't need your Mother doing the books. I can help, or we can hire someone. You said you were going to try to get away from her," I said, with a sigh.

"I know I can get the job. They were really interested when I talked to them. But first I have to pass a physical. I should be fine, although I didn't pass the physical for the Army. They said I had a bad back."

It sounded risky, but I knew I couldn't talk him out of it, nor would I want to stand in the way if that was what he wanted. I knew I could deal with the kids and the farm. We were a team, and we'd make it through if we worked together.

The next morning I went into the bathroom that Dexter had installed in the house. He'd forgotten to flush the toilet and there was blood in the toilet bowl. "Dexter are you feeling all right?" I asked, concerned.

"Oh sure, I'm just fine. Just a little constipation, maybe I strained too hard," he said.

He never went to the doctor, but he went to get his physical. They thought they could fix his back with surgery; medicine had advanced a lot since 1943. He'd be laid up for a few months during the winter, but then he would be ready to go to Greenland next summer. I made a nurse's outfit for Patsy so she could help me take care of him during his recuperation. It was a nurse's cape and a little hat with a cross on it.

In early November, I took Dexter to the hospital. He'd never been sick a day in his life, and he hated to sit still for one minute. I just couldn't imagine what kind of patient he would be.

I sat in the waiting room, waiting for the surgery to be over. It was supposed to take a few hours. I had a good book with me, but I just couldn't concentrate on it. After only 30 minutes I looked up and saw the surgeon standing by me.

"Mrs. Buell," he said, pausing as he looked into my eyes. "I'm sorry," he continued.

I jumped up. "Is he dead?" I asked, my voice shaking.

"No," he said, but did not smile. "We cannot operate on his back. He has cancer."

"What?" I shook my head, totally confused.

"He has colon cancer. He will need to see an oncologist for that."

Despite the marvels of 1950s medicine, everyone knew that if you had cancer you were dead. How could this be? It must be a mistake. We had an organic farm, he ate well, he was young, only 40-years-old. But they say he has cancer?

We went to see the oncologist. He wanted to operate and remove his colon.

"There's got to be something else we can do." Dexter said.

His mother did some research and found a cancer clinic in Dallas, Texas, that said they could cure it without surgery. We flew down to Texas to see Dr. Taylor. We took a commercial flight, as Dexter was too ill to fly his own plane. It was the worst flight of my life. My own colon became spastic, forcing me to wait in line for the smelly bathroom in the back of the lurching plane. When we walked into Dr. Taylor's clinic, I could smell rotting flesh. Patients sat waiting in the halls, their faces filled with fear. They pumped chemicals into Dexter's body, making him violently ill, but it did not stop the cancer.

We came home uncured. Dexter decided to go ahead with the colon surgery. After surgery he came home with a bag attached to his side that had to be changed every few hours. He stunk and was totally miserable, yet the cancer continued to grow. Patsy used her nurse's costume, but he was too ill to stay at home. He moaned and groaned all night long. His mother's place was close to the hospital, so he stayed there and then went back into the hospital. I came home when the kids came back from school and left very early in the morning. Janice Field came over every morning and braided Patsy's hair before she went to school. The baby and I stayed with Dexter as much as we could.

Baby Eugene grew quickly, and moved fast. He started to walk without bothering to crawl. He climbed up on the stove and turned on the burner. Luckily, it was a slow heating electric stove and I caught him before it got hot.

It was the first of May, May Day, when I went to the hospital and Dexter lay there unconscious. I had to reach him. No one was in the room—so I danced for him. I danced a dance of life. He opened his eyes and smiled.

But the next day, May 2, 1955, at 3:00, he died. As I sat beside him, I felt a cold chill.

CHAPTER 27

AFTERMATH

I felt numb. All emotion drained out of me. I did not cry, my eyes were dull and my heart ached. In my grief the children seemed far away, as if in another world.

Irene took over. She made the funeral arrangements. I did not care anymore what she did. I arranged for Janice to watch Patsy, Eugene and Dennis. I would not have their last memory of their father be his funeral. The vivid image of my father, lying in a coffin when I was eight years old, blazed in my mind's eye. Why, oh why, did history have to repeat itself? Was I cursed?

I went through the motions of getting dressed and going to the funeral. Irene and Dexter's sister, Laura, cried their eyes out, but I just sat, stone faced, on the hard wooden pew. I heard them whisper, "She's just a cold bitch who doesn't even cry when her husband has died." I was too broken to cry, or even to respond to their whispers.

My doctor gave me a prescription for antidepressants. They made me lethargic. I went through the motions of my day like a zombie. I got Patsy and Dennis up and out the door. I watched them walk down the long driveway to catch the school bus. Then I changed Eugene's diapers and fed him, and put him down for a nap. I sat and stared out the window. It had been raining for days and the driveway was wet squishy sand. A car pulled in the driveway, but I didn't get up. Laddie barked, and then there was a knock at the door. Startled out of my zombie state I forced myself to get up. I wasn't expecting anyone.

"Hello, Sheila," said a tall, somewhat handsome man, smartly dressed in a suit and tie with his hair parted on the side. "I've come to see how you are doing," he said, with a concerned look in his eyes.

I stepped back, holding the screen door closed, trying to place who this man was. Then it dawned on me. It was Mr. Gates, the Principal at Johnsville Elementary School, where Patsy was in second grade and Dennis in sixth grade. "Are the children doing O.K. at school?" I asked, opening the door.

"Oh, they're doing fine. They are really holding up well. I just came by to see how you were doing," he repeated.

"Would you like a cup of coffee?" I politely inquired, surprised that he'd drive all the way out here just to see me.

"Yes, please," he said, seating himself in Dexter's steel padded chair.

When I turned back from the stove I saw his eyes staring at my legs. I placed a cup of coffee in front of him and sat down across the table, carefully crossing my legs. He stared at me and moistened his lips.

"Are you hungry?" I asked, starting to get up again. "I've got some fresh rolls I baked yesterday."

"No, not at all. Please sit down and take it easy. I can see you've been working too hard."

Feeling uneasy, I pulled my chair back just a little, and crossed my legs tighter, at the same time trying to relax. *This is the School Principal, surely he has good intentions* I thought. As soon as I reached for my cup of coffee he placed his hand on mine, patting it. "I'm so sorry for your loss my dear," he said, as the pat turned into a caress up my arm.

I recoiled in horror. He stood up, engulfing me in his arms, patting my back and pulling my body into his. "Oh my lovely dear," he said, as I pushed him away, stamping on his foot.

"Get out! Get out of my house right now," I yelled.

"I was just trying to help you feel better," he mumbled as he reluctantly left.

I collapsed in my chair, shaking and sobbing. How could he, the Principal? How could he come out here like this? I longed to have Dexter back, for somebody to help me.

Eugene had slept through all of this. I quietly peeked in his room and walked out the back door, hoping the spring air would calm me down. Usually spring made me happy but now I only felt sad and alone. I could not feel the fresh plants pushing up from the damp earth. Suddenly I was not alone. I felt him, Dexter, standing right behind me, like he was trying to tell me something. He'd never believed; never went to church, he didn't believe in life after death or that he'd ever die. "No, no," I said to the air. "You, you shouldn't be here." He had died, so therefore he should not still be on this earthly plane.

Suddenly I remembered eighteen-month-old Eugene was in the house alone. I wasn't sure how long I'd been outside. Eugene knew how to crawl out of his crib. I raced back into the house as fast as I could go. As I stepped in the door I sensed something was wrong. It was quiet, much too quiet. I started towards the bedroom when I heard a thunk from the bathroom. I ran into the bathroom. There was Eugene, on the floor, with my antidepressant pill bottle open next to him.

I shook him and his eyes opened just a little. I held him in my arms while my heartbeat pounded in my ears. Frantically, I called the pediatrician, the dial on the phone seeming to take forever as it slowly spun the numbers. I don't remember my voice talking, only the directive.

"You must get him to the hospital immediately. And someone needs to keep him awake."

I dialed Horace Field's phone number, my sweaty fingers pushing the phone dial. He came immediately. I yelled at Eugene, I shook him, I slapped him across the face while we drove as fast as possible over the wet dirt road, the car sliding back and forth across the yellow sand. Finally, we were on the blacktop where we went faster than that car had ever gone before. It seemed like an eternity but we finally arrived at the Anoka Hospital. I raced out of the car and into the emergency room, still shaking Eugene's almost limp body. They pumped his stomach and kept him overnight. When we came home I took what was left of those pills and flushed them down the toilet. Eugene was not the same. He was unable to walk for three months. I silently prayed for his recovery, constantly keeping him in my sight. I could not forgive myself for what had happened

While all this was going on, my first born, Ernest's son, Brian, was in the Anoka State Hospital. They said he was a paranoid schizophrenic. I'd known something was wrong since high school, but I never knew what. He was brilliant, but he wouldn't finish high school. He didn't get along with people, and always imaged someone or something was out to get him. I went to see the psychiatrists at the hospital, thinking I'd finally know what was wrong. They told me that he was this way because I had divorced his father. If we had stayed married this never would have happened. I felt guilty at first, my feet so heavy I could hardly walk out the door. Then when I got in my car I slammed the door. *Damned idiots*, I thought. As I drove home the anger rose up like a volcano about to explode. The car flew along the straight highway from Anoka to the farm. Luckily, there was little traffic and no police or I would have gotten a ticket, or worse, in an accident. I was disgusted; I knew I had done everything I could for my children, including Brian. The only mistake was those damn pills, and now some idiot doctors.

After I got home a plan started to form in my head. I was determined to be there for my children. I would not leave them, nor leave them alone, while I went to work. Maybe that was what I'd done wrong with Brian. I had had to leave him when I went to work during the war years.

I knew what it was like to be an orphan. It was bad enough when my father died, but after my mother died I'd felt so alone in the world. Even now I longed to talk with her. My children were not going to be orphans.

I hadn't the slightest idea how I was going to pay the bills or run a business. During the war when I'd had my job, I got paid, cashed my paycheck and paid my bills with cash. I'd never even written a check. Everything, the farm, the apartment buildings were all titled to both Irene and Dexter Buell. Sheila Buell's name was not on anything except for the little lot I'd bought with my inheritance from Aunt Bella. That I'd put in my name and Dexter's name. I remembered Irene had accused me on putting it just in my name, and I'd wondered, why?

After the funeral, Irene said, "Don't worry Sheila, I'll take care of things. Just have a sale and put the money in Dexter's checking account."

This sounded reasonable. I was taking the medication the doctor had prescribed, and my thinking was fuzzy but I didn't think much about it.

I sold the cows and the farm machinery. One nice gentleman bought tons of stuff and wrote me a check. The check bounced. I didn't even know checks could bounce. I put all the money I did get into the checking account like Irene suggested, but I had no checks. I had no way to get access to any of the money that I deposited.

Totally frustrated and worried, I called Irene and said, "I need my own checking account. I need to have my own money."

"Oh, that's not necessary. I'll give you an allowance, and you won't have to worry about a thing. I just need you to sign an agreement that you will take care of me in my old age."

By this time I was off the medication and I remembered what she'd been doing to our family. "I'll be happy to take care of you, but I will not sign anything. I need my own money." My stomach turned and my head ached, as I calmly said those words. I knew from Dexter that an allowance from Irene came with strings and more strings attached. My children and I would be at her beck-and-call forever.

Irene hung up on me. I was desperate. I felt like crying, but I was the mother with young children to protect. I would not let them see me cry. With barely enough money to buy gas, I loaded the children in the car and drove to my sister Lucille's house. I didn't call first or talk on the phone because you never knew who was listening in on the party line.

Lucille ushered us in and sat me down with a cup of coffee. As soon as the children went in the other room to play, I said, "Dexter's mother won't give me any money out of Dexter's account for food for the children or gasoline."

"She what?" Lucille asked. Then she yelled, "Henry get in here you've got to hear this." I waited for Henry to come in the room then I explained.

"I put all the money from the sale of the farm and machinery in that checking account and Irene won't let me have access to it."

Henry said, "What? She won't give the money to her own grandchildren? You need a lawyer. I know just the one. Do you remember Roger Rutchick?"

I never paid much attention to politics or lawyers, but I did remember that name. "Wasn't he the lawyer that was the Secretary for Elmer Benson?"

"Yes, he's brilliant. He was the first Jewish lawyer to serve as Assistant Attorney General in the history of Minnesota. I remember, he was just 35-years-old at the time, way back in 1933.[206]Later, when Benson was Governor of Minnesota, he was his Personal Secretary. But remember in the 1938 election Benson lost due to a smear campaign that asked voters to "block the efforts of the present Governor and his Communist Jewish advisor to perpetuate themselves in power."[207]

---

206. http://www.jta.org/1933/01/19/archive/roger-s-rutchick-named-assistant
-attorney-general.
207. http://karmak.org/archive/2004/06/fla3hist.htm.

"Why would he be interested in helping a poor widow?" Lucille asked.

"I don't think Sheila is poor, and besides I know Roger. He did help the Communist Party, even though he never joined. He's had a hard time, just like the rest of us, getting work. During the McCarthy accusations he was constantly being called before the House UnAmerican Activities Committee."

We called Roger and he met with me the very next day. He got me enough money to start my own checking account. He showed me how to write checks and balance the account. Irene hired him too, since she also knew and trusted him. I wasn't sure we should both have the same lawyer, but I didn't know anyone else. Besides, he was so calm and helpful.

Without a will everything went to Probate Court, and we had to wait for a settlement. Irene had spent the money I'd put into the checking account on improvements for the apartment building on Western and Selby Avenues. When I found that out, I was so glad I had refused to sign the agreement and hired Roger. Roger found what Irene had done with the money. He also discovered that building was in Dexter's name, as well as his mother's name, as was our home on the farm. Roger made Irene sell that building and give me half the profit, and she was to receive half the profit on the farm, since it was in her name, not mine. Then there was the question of inheritance tax, which at the time was substantial. Roger successfully argued before the State Inheritance Tax Department that I was a co-tenant, not a joint tenant, and therefore not subject to inheritance taxes.

In the meantime, we were stuck on the farm and winter was coming again. I was terrified. I just didn't know how we'd get out when the snow started. The first snowfall came in early November. Large flakes glided down from the sky and piled up, covering the long circular driveway. I went to sleep thinking I'd have to see if there was any way Horace Field could help, but he and Janice had done so much already when Dexter was sick, that I was reluctant to ask. I woke up to the sound of a loud motor coming up the driveway. Looking out the window I saw the county snowplow plowing our driveway. I went to the door and opened it, staring out amazed. "I hope you don't mind Ma'am, but we always plow for widows."

"Oh, thank you. Thank you so much," I said, yelling out the door. The joy I felt was so overwhelming and tears welled up in my eyes. What a pleasant surprise to find out the county highway crew knew I was a widow and that they were allowed to plow driveways.

That first snow melted. Shortly after Thanksgiving there was a huge thunderstorm. Lightning flashed and the lights went out. We got out the candles and huddled together in the living room.

"Sandy needs to go out," Dennis said.

Sandy stood at the kitchen door whining. I looked at the dog and said, "You don't want to go out there in that storm."

He stared back at me, his old eyes insisting. He wagged his tail, while his back legs shook, and he barked, "Yes I do, right now."

Reluctantly I opened the back door. The freezing rain pelted me in the face as Sandy raced out into the storm. I quickly pulled the door shut. A few minutes later I opened the door and called, "Sandy, Sandy," but he didn't come back. I waited fifteen minutes and called again, still no Sandy. Every hour throughout the evening the children and I took turns yelling out into the storm, "Sandy come here, Sandy come back now." He always came when he was called, but not that night. In the morning we found his stiff body lying flat under the car. He was old and it was his time, and now Sandy was gone. At least we still had Laddie. Laddie stayed back by his dog house, his tail wagging slowly. He did not run up to greet us. It seemed Laddie knew Sandy was gone too.

Soon it was December and Christmas was fast approaching. Just after the children got out of school for Christmas vacation, Roger Rutchick came out to the farm. He had some papers for me to sign, but he also brought presents for the children. They were excited to open these unexpected gifts. They enjoyed playing with the large wooden cards with notches cut in the corners. By notching the cards together they built tall buildings.

It was our first Christmas without Dexter. Quietly, but sadly, we opened presents that Christmas Eve on the farm. Dennis and Patsy knew there wasn't a Santa and Eugene was too little to care, but they all loved Christmas. Christmas Day we spent at Lucille's new house. My sisters Marge and Lucille stepped up to create a lovely Christmas dinner for the family.

Finally in January the sale was pending on the buildings. The apartment building at Western & Selby sold for $25,419.96 and the farm for $13,617.69.[208] Out of that total came the expenses, including my expenses living on the farm since last May. Roger Rutchick charged $2,500 for his services.[209] After expenses I was to receive $17,360[210] and Irene the same amount. I was also left with the medical bills. Roger arranged for me to get a lease from the buyer so we could stay on the farm until spring.

In March, Brian was released from the hospital and stayed in my studio on the farm. He seemed a lot better, and he was very happy to be out of that mental hospital.

I thought if I was careful and bought a rooming house near the St Paul Campus of the University of Minnesota, I could rent out rooms to help pay the mortgage and have an apartment for the children and myself. Then I would not have to leave them and go to work like I had had to do with Brian. I looked and looked, but there simply was nothing for sale in St. Paul. So I looked in Minneapolis, and found one building. Mrs. Burks was selling her rooming house at 510 12th Avenue S.E. It had an apartment on the first floor, four rental rooms on the second floor plus an apartment and one additional room on the third floor. I

---

208. Letter dated January 4, 1956, from the Law Offices of Roger S. Rutchick. In 2016 dollars Western and Selby sold for   and 600 acre farm for
209. In 2016 dollars $22, 274.00.
210. In 2016 dollars $154, 673.00.

made a substantial down payment and on April 2, 1956, signed a mortgage for $5500.00 with the Twin City Federal Savings and Loan Association.[211] I agreed to pay $59.69 per month with 5.5% interest on the principal until it was paid off.

I was very relieved to have found a way to stay home with my children. By renting out the rooms, and working at home on my paintings, I should have enough to get by. It was very hard to leave the farm, but at least I had some land next to Lucille's house where I could still have a vegetable garden.

Brian had learned to be a cook when he was with his Dad so he got a job as a cook and an apartment of his own. I hoped it would last, and he could succeed on his own.

---

211. Mortgage note on file with author.

CHAPTER 28

TWO YEARS LATER

The big Buick lumbered along Highway 36. Eugene jumped up and down in the back seat then crawled over the seat to sit briefly next to me. I had my arm ready to hold him back in case of a sudden stop.[212] I had to tell my sisters but my stomach clenched at the thought. Would they think I was making a mistake?

It was early June. My plan was to talk to Lucille first, after working in my garden. I'd made this trip at least twice a week since Dexter died, driving out of Minneapolis, to this quiet lot that I had purchased with my inheritance from Aunt Bella. In this little lot I'd grown almost all the vegetables we'd needed for the last two summers, with help from Henry and Lucille. My car almost parked itself and I hurried past Lucille's house to my garden. I wasn't ready to talk to her yet. The wonderful smell of hay filled my lungs as I spread it around the tomato plants that I had planted two weeks earlier. The soil felt warm, and the hay would make a blanket around the tomatoes, keeping them warm and preventing weeds from growing.

Lucille called out, "Sheila, come in. It's time for coffee. I've got fresh pie and milk for Eugene too."

---

212. Baby and child car seats and seat belts were not installed in cars at this time. Seat belts were made mandatory in the USA on January 1, 1968. Infant seats are governed by state laws. Minnesota first required them for children under age seven as of August 1, 1986.

I laid down my rake, and slowly walked through the gate, and down the path. Eugene raced ahead of me. My thoughts wandered back in time to when Charlie had invited me to go to Australia, so many years ago, and I'd said I'd never leave my sisters, but now. . . .

I sat down and added some milk to my coffee, slowly stirring it with a spoon, as I chewed on my lower lip, trying to figure out where to start. "I'm selling the house," I finally blurted out.

"You're what?" Lucille asked. She raised her voice and her eyes widened, then shrunk to slits.

"I'm selling 510, the rooming house. I've got our passports, and we're going to Australia."

"Who is going to Australia?" she asked, finally beginning to understand.

"The children and I, as soon as the house is sold."

"What about your garden?" Lucille asked.

"I'm not sure when. I don't know when I'll get the house sold," I answered. "I'll probably be here all this summer."

"Oh," she said. But I thought I saw tears forming in the corners of her wrinkled up eyes. "Australia is a long ways away."

"Charlie thinks he can find work for me there. I think it would be good for the children. Things are just not going that well running the rooming house," I said, trying to explain, without telling everything. I couldn't tell her about the heavy weight on my chest that only lifted at the thought of being in the Australian Bush. I couldn't tell her about the grief that had not gone away until I got to know Ali. But now Ali was gone too and the grief was all back. I felt as if I'd been knocked to the ground. I dreamed of a trip to Australia via the Suez Canal. I'd be independent and I could see Ali Marie in Cairo. He'd wanted me to go off to Egypt with him. He even said he'd care for the children, but I knew that would never work. And yet I wanted to see for myself.

Lucille just stared off into space. She looked so sad, that I decided not to say any more about it.

"Anyway, I'm sure I'll be here this summer yet. See you next week." I finished my coffee, grabbed Eugene's hand and we hurried out the door. I wanted to catch my sister Marjorie right after she got home from work. Marjorie worked at the library. Alfred finally had work in St. Paul, in construction, but Marjorie continued to work.

It would be easier to talk to Marjorie. She was always so practical. I drove in the driveway, and parked under a big oak tree. The bees were humming out back. Marjorie's husband Alfred kept beehives, and they were feasting on the spring flowers that filled Marjorie's gardens.

"What a pleasant surprise," Marjorie said, as she opened the door when I knocked. "Come on in and have some coffee."

Eugene and I sat down at the large kitchen table. Marjorie had just gotten home from work and was bustling around the kitchen making dinner. She always had a meal ready for Alfred when he got home.

"There's something important I need to talk to you about," I said.

"What's that?" Marjorie asked, her eyebrows rising.

She probably thinks I'm going to get married again, or maybe she thinks I'm pregnant. Just like that terrible day twelve years ago when I was pregnant with Dennis.

"I'm going to Australia." I said it quickly, just to get it out of my mouth, past the lump in my throat.

"Are you sure about this?" she asked, her controlled voice not revealing any feelings. It reminded me of a courtroom drama saying, *just the facts please.*

"Yes, I've written to Charlie, and he thinks he can get me a job, plus I will still have my Social Security for the children. The exchange rate is pretty good. I've even got our passports."

"You have been busy," Marjorie said, without smiling. She rarely smiled ever since Mother died.

"I have to sell the house first."

"You will need some references to find work, and for the immigration authorities."

"I hadn't thought about that. It's been so long since I've had a job."

"Maybe you could write to Arthur Foote at Unity Church and get a character reference from him. He's known you for a long time now."

I thought about how Marjorie had taken me to the church when I was pregnant, and what a big help the minister had been.

"I think Dr. Foote is on vacation now."

Marjorie took out a pen and paper. "Here's his address. I'm sure he'll write a letter for you."

We finished our coffee and Marjorie tucked the paper into my hand.

"Thanks, thanks so much. Patsy and Dennis are coming home from school to an empty house." I said, as I quickly left.

That evening, after the children went to bed, I sat down and wrote to Dr. Foote, describing how I was going to Australia to be with my brother. This time the tears flowed as I wrote, *I really don't understand why this happened to Dexter, he was so young.*

Dr. Foote was at his summer home in Maine so I didn't expect to get a reply for some time.

Hardly a week had passed when Patsy brought in a letter addressed to me from Maine. It was in a Unity Church (Unitarian) envelope, but the postmark was from Maine. I thanked Patsy for it, but I didn't open it then. I did not want her asking what it was about. Children did not need to be burdened by adult worries and concerns.

Later, after the children were in bed, I carefully opened the letter. It was all written by hand, dated June 28, 1958. The reference was on top:

Unity Church — Unitarian
PORTLAND AND GROTTO
ST. PAUL 4E, MINN.

CAPITAL 6-3489

ARTHUR FOOTE, Minister
RONALD J. WALRATH, Minister
ELIZABETH M. WHITMAN,
    Director of Religious Education

June 28, 1958

To whom it may concern:

Mrs. Shiela Viola Buell has been personally known to me for more than five years, through her participation in the life of Unity Church. I believe her to be a woman of excellent character, dependable, law-abiding and stable.

Arthur Foote

This was followed by a long letter. As I read the letter tears welled up in my eyes and thoughts jumped into my head.

Dear Sheila Buell

I am happy, of course, to write the enclosed reference, and I trust that this is the sort of statement the immigration authorities want. Sorry to be without typewriter, but I don't suppose that makes any difference.

Oh no, I bothered him during his vacation, so of course he didn't have a typewriter. But I don't suppose it makes any difference either. I thought.

Your plan to return to Australia is a complete surprise, naturally, but it sounds rather inviting. Leastwise, I've always wanted to visit "down under."

I'm so glad Brian is well again, and his illness only a memory. This must be a real comfort to you. Will he stay here, or go with you?

Brian, Brian, I sure hope he is well. He wouldn't be coming right away, but maybe he will want to come on his own later. He's not very happy about this idea, and neither is Dennis, but he is too young to know.

Here in the beauty of this fair isle[213] I find myself often asking the question you raise in your letter. From the window just now, as I have been writing, a fish-hawk has been soaring over the cove, a vision of grace. Then he plummeted, with a sharp cry, into the water, emerging with his strong talons sunk into his prey, a small fish. The beauty and cruelty of the world seem forever inextricably intertwined; and if there is a true and satisfying answer, I fear our finite minds cannot encompass it.

---

213. An island in Maine where the Foote Family spent their summers.

But then, the problem of good seems to me as deeply mysterious as the problem of evil. And perhaps it is the part of wisdom to have faith that behind the veil of mystery large and good purposes are moving toward consummation. Indeed, to abandon such faith is to take the road to the madhouse. It may be scant consolation when tragedy strikes, and what is dearest is cruelly snatched away; but often I grow aware that if the growth of souls is the business of this planet, and so I do believe, there must be problems, crises, hard-knocks. In a conventional paradise, all growth would cease. Temptation brings one man to a tragic end; another to a noble victory.

I have had my fill of hard knocks. I have faith, but that faith has been sorely tested. What more can possibly be asked of me?

If we cannot answer "why," we can accept a philosophy which counsels us to be healthy-mindedness, an acceptance of life as it is, strangely sweet and devastatingly bitter; and which teaches us to respond to it as a challenge, to play our part as well and as bravely as we know how, to seek for all the beauty and joy and goodness we can find, and to avoid the tragic moral mistakes that tempt us, and whatever happens to eschew self-pity.[214]

Yes, Life is strangely sweet and devastatingly bitter. The sweetness of love, the bitterness of loss, I've been through it all. I want to paint to seek the beauty, the beauty of Australia that I know so well. I must be brave. I have hope.

He ended his lovely letter with a request to see my paintings. I clutched the letter to my heart; more determined than ever to go home to Australia.

---

214. Letter written by Author Foote, Minister for 25 years at the Unity Church – Unitarian, Portland and Grotto. St. Paul Minnesota. Printed with permission from the family.

I had everything ready. The letter of recommendation from Dr. Foote, and the passports for the children. They asked for a picture of the family together. I had this picture taken with Eugene in front, me then Patsy and Dennis:

1958 Eugene, Sheila, Patsy and Dennis for Passport

There was a buyer for the house, 510. All we needed to do was finalize the deal, and I could buy our tickets.

AFTERWORD
Her Daughter Patsy's Voice 1998

The sale fell through. It was like the walls caved in, and we stayed where we were. I felt the weight of loss again, especially the loss of joy in my mother's face. She wanted to go home, we were going, and now we weren't.

Mother fell into survival mode and did very little painting. In fact, she almost destroyed her paintings when a renter decided that her nude painting, "Peace", was a sexual invitation. "He chased me around the table, I had to shove the table at him, yell at him to get out of my house." She cried when she finally told me about the incident. "The only reason I didn't burn them all up, was that night I saw an interview with Georgia O'Keefe who said, "If they think a painting is sexual, that's their problem, not mine."

I was relieved that the paintings were saved, yet I don't think she ever completely recovered from that attempted assault. She did very little painting after that, just some flowers and birds, and cartoons, but certainly she never attempted to do another nude. She started a portrait of me a couple of years later but left it unfinished when I wasn't able to sit still.

Mother's survival was linked to nature. Her little city flower garden, a vegetable garden, the birds at the birdfeeder and plants that filled every window in the house, they brought her joy. She taught me, and anyone who would listen, to love gardening and nature.

When she was 70, Eugene had some extra money from his successful business and bought her a ticket to go back to Australia. Her brother Charles wasn't alive anymore, but she got to meet all of his children. She stayed for one month. I sent a video of her paintings, so they'd know she wasn't just an aunt they'd never met, but an artist too. She had a wonderful visit but was not feeling well. A few weeks after she returned home, she collapsed in her kitchen while a friend was visiting. Her dog stood next to her, refusing to let the medics examine her. Sheila's heart was stopping, but a pacemaker gave her 15 more years. She lived with Eugene and his wife, teaching them how to garden.

In the winter, when she was 85, she broke her hip filling the birdfeeder. Her hip seemed to be mending when her back collapsed, due to severe osteoporosis. Before that she'd been active writing letters to her friends, driving her car, taking the dog to be groomed or to the vet. She ended up in bed, writing notes on little sheets of paper. When the pain was too much, she was moved into a Hospice at the University of Minnesota Hospital.

I was at work teaching children with special learning and behavior problems, "Take a deep breath into your stomach and blow out through your mouth. Let all that tension go." I told Jimmy, one of my students, coaching him through the steps to control his emotions. The rest of my small class sat working quietly at their desks. As I spoke those words, I took a deep breath into my stomach. While I exhaled my thoughts went to my mom, in hospice waiting for my visit after school.

My brother had said, "She doesn't have much time left."

"I'll come right after work; I can't get a substitute teacher. My students just don't behave for a sub." My feelings were torn between being with my mother in her last hours and being with my students.

The principal knocked on the door and motioned for me to come out. I wondered, *what did Jimmy do now?* as I stepped in the hall.

"Your mother has died; I'll take over your class." He said in a low calm voice.

Tears welled up in my eyes. "I, I was just going to visit her after school." My mind screamed at me silently, *What was I going to do now. Who would I visit?* Confusion overwhelmed me, I felt like collapsing against the wall, I took a deep breath. I was supposed to leave, to go to the hospital.

First, I went to the office to use the telephone. I called my minister Rev. Jean Parker Vail; she would know what to do. My father had been a staunch atheist, but mother never spoke about her own faith. When she'd stayed at my house before she went into hospice, I'd had Rev. Jean come over and bring her communion. Mother was overjoyed to receive communion. After Rev Jean left, mother turned to me with tears in her eyes, "I thought I wouldn't be allowed."

When mother had been divorced and remarried to my father, her Catholic sister-in-law told her she'd sinned, and she never wanted to see her again. A rejection that mother never forgot.

Feeling numb even in my fingertips, I dialed the church number. Rev Jean answered the phone, I whispered "Mother just died," not wanting the school office staff to hear.

"What?" she asked.

"Mother just died, in hospice, I'm going to see her," I repeated more clearly this time.

"Tell them not to move her. I'm coming. I will give her last rites."

I wasn't sure what last rites were, I had not been raised in the Episcopal tradition, but I wanted someone there who knew something close to the Catholic tradition mother had known as a young child.

I made one more call to hospice, and raced out the door to my car, hoping I'd beat the Rev. Jean to mother's hospice room at the University of Minnesota Hospital.

As I drove on autopilot my mind filled with mother. Mother had stayed alive to be at my daughter's wedding just two months before. She was in pain, yet she beamed through the whole ceremony. Confined to a wheelchair, her long white hair perched in a bun on top of her head reflected the lights of the reception hall as she spoke to everyone at her table.

The Rev. Jean Parker Vail was the celebrant at the wedding; her face was always serious yet kind. She wore her blond hair curled under, just below her ears, above the Episcopal collar that she wore with pride. She was the first woman to preach at our church. My brother-in-law's Catholic wife said, "I wasn't sure about a woman priest, but she did a good job."

I remembered on my last visit to Mother in hospice she'd seemed to be perking up. She looked out the window from her bed and said, "I wonder if I'll ever run again."

Mother loved running. Even when she was 65, she ran around the track on the University campus for exercise. Now even on painkillers, she couldn't walk, or move, it wasn't like my mom. I just could never imagine her as being old. To me she was forever young, exercising, painting, creating - that was Sheila Buchanan Buell, my mom.

Finally, I arrived at the hospital, and raced up to the hospice floor. The Rev. Jean was already there, her presence calmed me as I hurried through the door of the sterile hospital room. I'd never been in the presence of a freshly dead body before. Her long white hair hung in a limp braid, next to a white stone-like face. That face couldn't be her face, it wasn't smiling, the corners of the eyes didn't turn up. Mom wasn't there anymore. Logically I knew it was her time. She'd always been there for us; our father died when we were young, but mother held us together, fed, warmed and loved. Even up to last year we'd gathered at Christmas to be with her.

The Rev. Jean sprinkled the body with holy water and helped me to say a prayer with her. Then the staff took the body away. I went home and even managed to teach the next day, going through the motions, but feeling empty; part of me was missing.

Over the weekend I went to my brother's house where mother had lived before she went into hospice. My brother was a staunch atheist like his father before him. His wife, Kim, was cleaning out mother's room and asked me to help. Kim was an artist too and loved my mother like a daughter. Kim's long blond hair seemed to sweep the floor as she leaned under the bed and picked up a small sheet of paper.

"Here it is again, another one."

"Another what?" I asked, confused.

"I keep finding this poem, written on little pieces of paper, all over the room." "Do you think she wrote it?"

"I don't know. Let me see it."

Hope is the thing with feathers,
That perches in the soul
And sings the tune without words
And never stops at all.

I stared at the tiny scrap of paper, written in mother's almost illegible handwriting:

"She was a painter, not a writer, but this, this is beautiful," I said. "I think we should read it at her memorial service."

Kim said. "She must have written it so many times for a reason."

I left that room where mother had lived until just a month ago. Every step I took felt heavy, the world was empty without her. I went to the funeral home, wrote the obituary, and arranged a memorial service at St. Martin's on the Lake Episcopal Church for the following Saturday with Rev Jean.

During the week I went through the motions of teaching and on Friday I made an appointment with Cynthia, one of the mothers from school, to get a haircut in her home. I'd asked her to trim my hair just once before. She led me through her neat living room to a back room that had a sink and a salon chair. I sat down feeling a heavy weight upon my chest. I took a deep breath and thought, *I might as well tell her why I'm so sad.*

"My mother died; we are having her memorial service tomorrow." I blurted out, almost mechanically so the tears would not start flowing from my eyes. Somehow, I still couldn't believe that mother had died.

Cynthia picked up her scissors to begin cutting my hair and then put them down suddenly. She looked up into space, and walked out of the room saying, "I have something for you."

I sat waiting, wondering. What is this about?

Cynthia returned, carrying an open book. She put it on my lap and trimmed my hair. I picked it up and started to read. My hands trembled as I read:

Hope is the thing with feathers
That perches in the soul,
And sings the tune without the words,
And never stops at all,

And sweetest in the gale is heard,
And sore must be the storm
That could abash the little bird

That kept so many warm.
I've heard it in the chillest land,
And on the strangest sea;
Yet, never, in extremity,
It asked a crumb of me.

My eyes swirled with tears, and I read it again. Finally, I was able to open my mouth. "This is the poem my mother was writing before she died. The first stanza was on little sheets of paper all over her room. Where did you get it? How did you know?"

"I don't know," Cynthia said. "I just got a message to give that to you."

"A message?" I asked, not sure what this meant.

"It was a strong feeling that I needed to give it to you. Sometimes that happens to me," she said, somewhat embarrassed, so I didn't question her further.

I turned the book over. It was a slim thrift edition, Emily Dickinson SELECTED POEMS, it said on the cover. I got ready to leave, saying, "Thanks for showing me the poem."

"No take the book, it's for you." she said.

I walked out carrying the book, still shaking my head in disbelief. What did this mean? Was she saying, "I didn't write that poem, don't forget it was written by Emily Dickinson?" Mother was an artist; she would never want to take credit for another's work. But it was more than that, it seemed like a message from the other side. Mother was telling us, "Yes there is Hope."

BIBLIOGRAPHY

"The American Aerospace Industry During World War II," http://www.centennialofflight.net/essay/Aerospace/WWII_Industry/Aero7.htm.

The Argus (Melbourne Victoria) Saturday September 27, 1919. From online archives. http://nia.gov.au/nla.news-title13.

Australia Central Army Records Office correspondence to Rosalyn Buchanan, 1986.

Baime, A.J. *The Arsenal of Democracy: FDR, Detroit, and an Epic Quest to Arm an America at War.* New York: 1914.

Buchanan, Charles.

Letters:

January 10, 1918

January 18, 1918

October 22, 1918

September 10, 1923

October 6, 1923

December 3, 1923

August 23, 1924

March 7, 1928

August 30, 1937

August 24, 1942

Buchanan, Charles and Peggy. Letter, September 1, 1943.

Buchanan, George Charles. "Against or for Australia," poem written in 1917.

Buchanan, Lucille. Diary of trip to Australia.

Buchanan, Lucille. Unpublished essay on Christmas in Australia (date unknown).

Buchanan, Marjorie. Unpublished essay written in 1936.

Buchanan, Peggy. Letter, February 22, 1928.

Buell, Sheila Buchanan. Letter, April 12, 1928.

Buell, Sheila Buchanan. Description of Australia from High School Journal, 1929.

Encyclopedia Britannica. http://www.britannica.com/biography/William-Z -Foster

http://www.britannica.com/event/United-States-presidential-election -of-1932.

First World War 1914-18/The Australian War Memorial. https://www. awm.gov.au/articles/atwar/first-world-war.

Fischer, Bernice. "Growing Up in St. Paul: Mechanic Arts—An Imposing 'Melting Pot' High School that Drew Minorities Together." *Ramsey County History Magazine*, vol. 39-1, Spring, 2004.

"Franklin D. Roosevelt, State of the Union Address, January 6, 1942," American Presidency Project Website, http://www.presidency.ucsb.edu/ ws/?pid=16253.

Goodwin, Doris Kearns. *No Ordinary Time: Franklin and Eleanor Roosevelt: The Home Front in World War II.* New York: Simon and Schuster, 1994.

Greenberg, Brian, Linda S. Watts and Richard A. Greenwald. *Social History of the United States.* ABC-CLIO, 2008.

Grey, Jeffrey. *A Military History of Australia.* 2nd ed. Melbourne: Cambridge University Press, 2008.

Instruction on how to drive a model T Ford detailed - YouTube. *www .youtube.com/watch?v=n0hQh_Ej_34*

Katznelson, Ira. *Fear Itself: The New Deal and the Origins of Our Time.* Liveright Publishing, 2013.

Keneally, Thomas. *Australians: From Eureka to the Diggers.* Allen & Unwin, 2012.

Keneally, Thomas. *The Daughters of Mars: A Novel.* Atria Books, 2013.

Kennedy, Dave. *Minnesota Goes to War: The Home Front During World War II.* St. Paul: Minnesota Historical Society Press, 2009.

Kennedy, David M. *Freedom from Fear: The American People in Depression and War, 1929-1999.* Oxford University Press, 1999.

Larson, Bruce L. "Lindbergh's Return to Minnesota," 1927. www.mnhs .org/mnhistory 1970.

Launius, Roger D. " Sputnik and the Origins of the Space Age." https:// history.nasa.gov/sputnik/sputorig.html

Lindbergh, Charles A. Of Flight and Life. New York: Charles Scribner's Sons, 1948.

Lindenmeyer, Kriste. *The Greatest Generation Grows Up: American Childhood in the 1930s.* Ivan R. Dee, 2007.

Loukinen, Michael M. "Cultural Tracks: Finnish Americans in Michigan's Upper Peninsula," http://www.folkstreams.net/context%2C127.

Malen, Gordon. "Blackout Called 99% Perfect from Air View." *St. Paul Pioneer Press,* July 17, 1942. Minnesota Historical Society.

Marrin, Albert. FDR and the American Crisis. New York: Knopf, 2015.

McClintick, Lillian. Affidavit written in 1922. On file with author.

Minneapolis Star Journal, December 8, 1941, front page.

Pariseau, Ruth. Letter, March 1, 1947.

PBS Timeline http://www.pbs.org/wgbh/americanexperience/features/ timeline/rails-timeline/

Peachester News. Article, 1921.

Peachchester [sic] Pioneers: The Continuing History, October 1998. Compiled by the History Committee. The Peachester Historical Society, Queensland, Australia, p. 32.

Perkins, Frances. *The Roosevelt I Knew.* Penguin Classics, 1946.

Rockhampton Morning Bulletin, June 8, 1912. Found at the Australian newspaper website. http://trove.nla.gov.au/ndp/del/article/53266462.

Ross, Carl. Transcript of Interview with Wilbur Broms, October 7, 1987. Minnesota Historical Society, 20th Century Radicalism in Minnesota Oral History Project.

St. Martin, Tom. Decade of Disconsolation Minnesota Weather 1930-1039 http://climate.umn.edu/pdf/Decade_of_disconsolation.pdf

The St. Paul Daily News. Microfilm at the Minnesota History Center:

Friday May 20, 1927, front page second section

Sunday May 22, 1927, Front page

October 29, 1929, front page

July 6, 1930, help wanted-female

May 14, 1934, home edition

Sauk Center Herald. January, 1928.

Schlesinger, Jr., Arthur M. *The Crisis of the Old Order 1919-33* (The Age of Roosevelt, Vol. 1). Mariner Edition, 2002.

Social Security Administration, http://www.ssa.gov/history/briefhistory3.html.

Space sounds, http://www.dd1us.de/spacesounds%201.html.

Statistics on the influenza pandemic of 1918-1919. https://virus.stanford.edu/uda.

Stern, Philip Van Doren. *Tin Lizzie: The Story of the Fabulous Model T Ford.* Simon and Schuster, 1955.

Trove: http://trove.nla.gov.au/ndp/del/printArticleJpg/71056389/3?print=y

Voices of Democracy, The U.S. Oratory Project. http://voicesofdemocracy.umd.edu/fdr-the-four-freedoms-speech-text/.